Banquet of the Beasts

To Allison

May the beasts
be with you !

Happy reading

love

Tim Cox

20/6/21 x

Banquet
of the
Beasts

Tim Cowen

Matador
9 Priory Business Park,
Wistow Road, Kibworth Beauchamp,
Leicestershire. LE8 0RX
Tel: 0116 279 2299
Email: books@troubador.co.uk
Web: www.troubador.co.uk/matador
Twitter: @matadorbooks

ISBN 978 1800462 793

British Library Cataloguing in Publication Data.
A catalogue record for this book is available from the British Library.

Printed and bound in the UK by TJ Books Ltd, Padstow, Cornwall
Typeset in 12pt Adobe Garamond Pro by Troubador Publishing Ltd, Leicester, UK

Matador is an imprint of Troubador Publishing Ltd

For

Maggie

the beasts

and the resistance

Part One

——

FIRE

ONE

The beginning
of the end

The starling is a small bird. Many people would consider it a drab bird. But catch their feathers in the right light and you will be surprised. At the greens, the purples and the flashes of mother of pearl. Shining with a luminescence that belies a reputation for being a dull bird.

The starling is a sociable bird. They dance across the sky at dusk. Forming shapes, forming patterns, forming waves. The murmuration, a swirling mass of bodies moving as one.

The starling is a wise bird, a special bird. Their call is like no other. There is a reason for that. They can hear voices. All sorts of voices. Both real and imaginary. Both past and present.

Separate a starling from their roost though, and they become something else. Someone else. Separate a starling from their roost, and a little bit of them dies. Their body and mind wither with loneliness.

However, there are birds that don't fly in formation, that can form different patterns.

Monday, 8th April 2013. The day they told us that Margaret Thatcher had died.

A starling, separated from her roost, hears a voice she had not expected to hear. And the voice said just one word: 'Fire.'

His lips graze her forehead. A gentle kiss. He can smell the coconut from the face cream he had bought her yesterday. Lynton Chilcoat stood. His emotions and thoughts were clattering inside him. Reverberating, echoing, gnawing. He needed to remain calm. Rational. Logical.

Was her skin getting colder? He kissed her again, this time allowing his lips to linger. Imperceptibly at first, but yes, her skin was colder, drier. Her eyes too, had started to shrink further back. Could this be the final day of waiting?

The room was very familiar to him. He had spent many hours here. The Ritz Hotel. Her final resting place. He too lived in the Ritz. Initially on the floor above, but for the last month in a suite in the same corridor, just two doors down. He poured himself another whisky and stood back. Taking it all in. The silver curtains, the maroon ottoman, the blue cushions, the intricately-woven rug. The splashes of colour sporadic and indulgent. His suite was a mirror image, everything identical but on the other side.

Not long now until she could rest properly. Not long before her real hibernation could begin.

His thoughts were interrupted by a noise. A strangled, guttural clicking noise. He returned to the bed and leant over her, seeking out her eyes, her brilliant blue eyes, and then her hair, still holding echoes of the stiff curves that he so much loved.

Another noise. The same deep clicking. Rasping. Puncturing. Releasing.

And then, and then. Silence. Her chest was no longer moving. Her eyes, they held a colour, an opaqueness that seemed different from just a moment ago.

This was it.

Chilcoat grasped her left hand between his outstretched palms. He rubbed, like a father warming his child's hands after a winter's walk. As if waiting for a spark, for something to be lit. Margaret Thatcher's hand held a residue of warmth. A degree of suppleness he was not expecting.

He kissed her palm. This time with more abandon. An almost disdainful relish. And then he let it fall. Lifeless. Awkward. Hanging. A trickle of his saliva forming a tiny pool in the bony cup of her hand. He didn't cry. He wouldn't cry. After all, this was a moment of release, a moment of relief rather than sadness.

She would be freed from the tired shell of her body and rejuvenated. She would be freed from all the baggage that had grown around her and restored. She would be freed from this era of tedium and mundanity. And she would be welcomed back to her rightful glory.

The Iron Lady was for returning and Lynton Chilcoat would be at her side forevermore.

TWO

Cells of resistance

Three years old. Green eyes. White tail. Black-tipped ears. Ginger fur. *Fox 118* the label on the cell said. His cell. Twelve foxtails long. Twelve foxtails wide and although he hadn't measured it, twelve foxtails high. His name was Logan. Logan Fox.

He was watching the badger, *Badger 33*. Watching him pace. Walking in circles around the cell next to his. Clockwise at first and then, after twenty laps, anti-clockwise. He'd lost count of how many times he had been round now.

'Hey,' Logan called.

The glass panel between them was thick, and sound didn't carry well. It was difficult to hear unless you yelped at full volume, with your mouth right up at the glass. And even then, the badger would have to be looking, be lip-reading, to grasp his fox dialect. Logan noticed that although his own food bowl was empty, Badger 33's remained full.

Still walking anti-clockwise. Snout down, but not sniffing. There would have been nothing to smell except for the sickly lavender substance they used for cleaning, and the strange metallic scent of the food. And now the badger changed direction, clockwise again. Giving Logan a better view of his face. This didn't look good. There was something about his demeanour. His eyes.

'Hey,' Logan called again. 'Hey, my badger friend. Are you OK?'

'HEY!' Louder this time, patting at the glass with his front left paw as he called. He jumped back. 'Sweet mother of Reynard.'

Electrified. The wire frame to the glass gave out a shock. He knew that. Of course, he knew that. After all, he had been here for over one hundred moons. Logan retreated to the far side of his cell and licked his paw.

On the other side of the glass Badger 33 continued to circle. A rumbling noise. Getting louder. Logan looked up. A man in a white coat pushing a trolley. On it, cardboard boxes. Seven or eight boxes. Another rumble. A second man. Also in white. Pushing another trolley. This time with fewer, but larger boxes. The two men had stopped pushing. Logan stepped to the front of his cell and tilted his head so he could hear better.

'We need to get it all out before lunch,' said the first man.

'They should've given us more notice. I'm pure building up a sweat with this lot,' replied the second. And then they moved off.

Logan looked at his paw and then scratched at his ear. These last few days he had been hearing more human voices. No, he had always been hearing them. These last few days he felt he had begun to understand.

Three more trolleys, then no more. He glanced at Badger 33. Still he circled.

7

Logan's cell was identical to the badger's. Two walls and the floor were solid, painted white. The ceiling, front wall and panel between cells were mainly glass. Each cell contained a water bowl, a food bowl, a litter tray and a small area of bedding. The bedding, in Logan's case, an old blanket, was at the back of the cell.

Once, sometimes twice a day, a guard would enter the cell either to clean it or top up the food. The Red Cross Moment, Logan called it. For as they came in he would have to sit on a cross painted in the rear left quarter of the cell. If he moved, or didn't sit in the right place, the guard would take out his metallic stick which emitted a poisonous ray. 'Taser.' That's what Logan had heard them call it. Yet today, nobody at all had been in his cell.

Logan was hungry. His neighbour, Badger 33, was still circling, but his bowl was full, so he couldn't have been protesting about the lack of food. Another thing. Where had the humans gone? Normally, there would be men with clipboards, with handheld computers, going from cell to cell, checking on the screens, adjusting the air pressure, taking readings.

Comings and goings. Apart from the men with trolleys there had been nobody and they seemed to be only going in one direction. Away. The humans all seemed to be going away. Badger 33 was still circling. There was an intensity to him that Logan found unsettling.

Logan walked to the front glass. Opposite him was a row of cells, less than a quarter of the size of his. Stacked three high. Within them, smaller mammals – mice, rats, weasels, stoats. 'Hey,' he called.

No movement.

'Hey,' he called again. Louder.

A pair of eyes. *Weasel 27.* A female weasel. Brown eyes. Chestnut fur. White chest. Less than six inches long. Cell 462. Second storey, third from the left. The weasel was in line with Logan's eyes.

She came to the front of her cell and mouthed something. Logan shook his head. He couldn't make out what she was saying. It had been a long time since he had heard weasel tongue.

She spoke more slowly. Exaggerating the sounds. That helped Logan translate her words into fox dialect.

'I'm scared,' she mouthed.

Me too, thought Logan, but said nothing.

A flickering of light. The fluorescent strip in Logan's cell momentarily extinguished before returning to full glare. That hadn't happened before. And again, the same flicker. This time the lights stayed off for a full fox-breath before coming back on.

Logan retreated to the back of his cell. Stood on the red cross. *This must be a warning,* he thought. The men would be angry he had been speaking to the weasel.

He glanced across at Badger 33. He had stopped circling and stood at the front of the cell on his hind legs. Both his front paws stretched out on the glass. His claws scraping, up and down. Shimmers of light coming from the glass. His scraping intensified. Became even more manic.

Again, the lights in Logan's cell flickered, this time staying off for a full three fox-breaths. And it wasn't just his cell, or Badger 33's cell. The weasels, the stoats, the mice, the rats, the rabbits, the hares, the cats, the dogs. All the lights were going off and on.

Badger 33 continued to scrape. His fur standing on edge. Logan could smell the static. As if a lightning storm was coming. He glanced over to the weasel. She was watching the badger. Her eyes transfixed.

Scratching, clawing. Faster and faster. Sparks coming off the glass. Blue and white. The scent of something burning.

And a voice calling. A bird's voice calling. A choke of a scream. The words, indistinguishable at first, and then startlingly clear: 'Get out. We all need to get out. The fire is coming.'

And then a crack. A loud, uneven, echoing sound.

Badger 33 stood in front of Logan's cell. Not adjacent but in front. On the wrong side of the glass. He was out.

The badger held his paw to the glass of Logan's cell and pressed. And before Logan could say anything, a diagonal crack appeared. He was cutting through the glass with the static contained in his paw.

'Stand back,' he said. Logan obeyed, retreating again to the red cross. The glass shattered. 'Come on, we haven't got much time,' the badger called.

And then darkness. The lights stayed off this time.

THREE

Removal

Monday, 8th April 2013. Nine, nearly ten months since my gran died. Four months since probate was granted. I was finally moving in.

The journey to Granny's cottage had taken twice as long as it should. The bypass at Stevenston was closed. Burst water main near the old industrial estate, the van driver told me. It had given me time to think. Firstly, I'd have to stop calling it *Granny's cottage*. Start calling it my own.

Secondly, I'd have to take driving lessons. Relying on my bike and the hourly bus service would be okay in the summer, but come the cold and wet of the autumn, I'd need an alternative.

I had been the sole beneficiary. My parents could add that to their long list of grievances. Put it this way, I doubted they would be coming to the house-warming. Not that I was having one.

I'd added double glazing and a new boiler. Decorated throughout. Well, not me personally. I'd paid someone better at DIY than me to do it all. A small dent in my inheritance. But money well spent.

My phone rang. The piano chord from Japan's single, *Nightporter*. Reached number 29 in 1982, but still my all-time favourite track. It was Mandy. My ex. She lives in Bristol now. A year since we split, but we'd stayed in touch. We were seeing how things worked as "just friends".

'Hey Mandy,' I said, hiding my weariness.

'Have you heard?'

'Heard what?'

'Ding-dong, the witch is dead!'

'Sorry?'

'Thatcher. She's dead. Died eleven thirty this morning. It's all over the news.'

'Oh, I hadn't heard. Not had the radio on today.'

'It's brilliant. We're going to have a party at the weekend.'

We. I noticed the "we". Wondered who the other person was.

'A party?'

'Yes, a great big celebratory Thatcher-has-finally-snuffed-it party. Fancy coming down for it?'

'I'm moving.'

'Moving?' She had forgotten.

'I'm moving house today. Into the cottage. Gran's cottage.'

'Oh, I thought you did that last week.' Mandy's tone remaining upbeat.

'Don't you read your emails? There was a problem with the new boiler and I had to wait on a replacement part.'

There was a brief pause.

'Today's Monday. The party is on Saturday. You've got plenty of time to unpack. You've not got that much stuff.'

Not since you took all the best bits of furniture, I thought.

'Apart from the CDs and books,' I said.

'Which you can alphabetise after you get back.'

'Mandy?' I asked.

'What?' Her tone a little impatient now.

'Have you been drinking?'

'Of course. The witch is finally dead. It's a day for drinking.'

Every day is a day for drinking for you, I thought.

'I've got to go, we're almost at the cottage.'

'But you will come, won't you?' Her voice oozed with fake pleading.

'I'll let you know. I'll see how the unpacking goes.'

Silence.

'Come on, you deserve some fun. All work and no play and all that.'

I wasn't working. Taken a year's sabbatical to sort the cottage out and start writing again. Still eight months left. Maybe she'd forgotten that too.

'Mandy. I'll text you, OK?'

Silence on the other end.

Why didn't I tell her there and then that I wasn't coming? That I couldn't face seeing her drunk, seeing her dance with someone else; to be in the same room without being able to hold her, to kiss her, to be with her?

'You never speak your mind.' She'd told me that many times in the weeks before she'd left. She was right. I didn't.

'This the one, pal?' the driver asked. He'd waited for a pause in my phone conversation to speak. The van had stopped outside the cottage. It stood isolated from other houses. A large rowan tree in the front garden. A new gate. A freshly-painted fence. I gave the driver a thumbs-up and he turned off the ignition.

'Mandy. Got to go. The van's just arrived. I'll text you, OK?'

FOUR

The fire whispers
her name

Her cage was on the second level of the aviary. A cage labelled *Raven 003*. But she wasn't a raven, she was a starling.

Her feathers were an iridescent black, glossy purple and green. Her tail square and her wings pointed and dark. Her narrow bill was yellow with a pink base. Her eyes a pale chestnut and her legs and feet a reddish brown. She was just over eight inches long, about a third of the size of a raven. Maybe they hadn't known the difference. Maybe it was a joke. But that was irrelevant now. Unless she could get out.

She could hear her voice.

Warning her. She could sense it coming. She could feel it about to be lit.

'*Fire.*'

The mesh of the cage was tightly woven. Impossible to penetrate. The cage was locked from the outside. Impossible to open. The service hatch in the ceiling was bolted shut. Impossible to move.

THE FIRE WHISPERS HER NAME

The badger at the door to the aviary. The badger at the door to the aviary was jangling a set of keys. A voice, a nasal tone. 'It has to be one of these.' As key after key was inserted into the lock.

The starling looked at him. At his black snout. His white-tipped ears. His blue-green eyes. His metallic-grey fur that shone with a manic energy. And then the door to her cage flew back. And she watched as the cages next to her also opened.

And she looked around. At the prison cells lying empty. The thrushes, the blackbirds, the crows. Flying in circles. The sparrows, the goldfinches, the wrens. Flying back and forth across the room. Stretching their wings for the first time since their imprisonment.

'There is a fire coming,' she called out in starling tongue. A language other birds often struggled to understand. 'There is a fire coming,' she screamed louder. This time in the universal avian dialect.

But the birds weren't listening. A turtle dove had found a sack of grain that had not been locked up. A pigeon and a rook were helping to peck it open.

There was a voice though. Somebody speaking to her in mustelid tongue.

The badger was looking down at her. 'We have to remove these.'

He pointed at the inside of his left paw. A metallic bead. The size of a grain of rice. Behind him stood a fox. A young male fox. And next to the fox was a smaller creature. A weasel. They were copying the badger, holding out their paws. And the starling looked down at her leg. At the silver-grey ring that clung to her every movement.

'We have to remove these. They use them to control us.' The badger's tone was both authoritative and impatient. She hopped nearer to him and closed her eyes. The badger bit carefully, precisely onto the ring. It cracked on the first bite. It split on the second. And fell apart on the third.

And then she pecked at the badger's, then the fox's and then finally, the weasel's. Piercing the skin, picking out the beads, spitting them out.

'Thank you,' said the fox.

'My name is Raven. I am a starling,' she said.

'I'm Logan. Logan Fox.'

'I'm Walinska, Walinska the weasel.'

They spoke rapidly, full of breath and doubt. The badger was examining his paw for remnants of the device. Satisfied there was none left, he looked directly at her before speaking.

'My name is Marek. Marek Dogovsky.'

FIVE

The return of
a Nobler Age

A care home in Twickenham. One of a dozen he had on standby. The only one that timed it just right. An elderly female. Similar build. No relatives. No visitors. Antonia Benjamin was her name.

Antonia did not wake up that morning. She was discovered just after breakfast. Her family, what little there was left, had long since emigrated. Paid the fees by direct debit, never came to see her, not even at Christmas. She would be the body. In the coffin, at the state funeral in just over a week's time.

Antonia's coffin would be weighted by bags of sand. A funeral without mourners.

Chilcoat was back in his own suite. Two doors down from the Great Lady's. He would visit her tomorrow. Help her settle in, reassure her, make sure she did not feel alone.

What to wear? He paused in front of his wardrobe.

Lynton Chilcoat was slim, skinny almost. Everything about him was slender. His jet-black hair clipped short, his lips thin, his eyes narrow, his nose long. Put an expensive suit on him though, and you didn't notice. He filled it so nicely. Seemed stockier than he actually was. You could still see it in his fingers mind, if you looked very closely. The bones and tight flesh.

Because of his skinniness he'd always felt the cold. He would have to wrap up warm. The morgue man had warned him about the temperature. A dry and sapping chill. He also advised about the need for cleanliness. Even in their frozen state, bodies could pick up infections, run the risk of contact sores.

Chilcoat was making a list, a mental list of what to bring with him. Latex gloves. Antibacterial hand-wash. Dustpan and brush. He would choose them all himself. Get the right colour. The perfect shade of blue. Bin liners too. They would have them at the warehouse. He could pick some up on his way there.

He slid the wardrobe door shut. No time for such pondering. There was so much to do. Chilcoat opened up his laptop. Tapped in the security code and waited for the retina detection to click in.

Scrolling through the images. He found the final one, the design he had chosen yesterday. Given himself a day's grace before signing off. No need to change his mind though. It was a good choice.

Understated. Simple. Uncluttered.

Over the next month they would be seen at just about every bus stop, every roundabout, every advertising hoarding – the length and breadth of the country.

Two slogans:

The Return of a Nobler Age and **Nobler Age Foods. There is no such thing as food poverty**.

It had to be right. It was right. A balance between old and new. A balance between clarity and confusion.

Nobler Age Foods. A new nationwide chain of food banks. Serving traditional British dishes with added spirit of Thatcher, or more accurately, added gene of Thatcher.

Tested for five years in the laboratory on animals of every shape and size. Refined, modified and retested. And now ready to be fed to the human population.

Exposing the poor and unwashed to Thatcher's cleansing power. Creating a popular uprising in support of her values, her philosophy, her way of being. Laying the foundations for her return.

No changes needed to the artwork. He would proceed as planned.

Pouring himself a whisky. A double. Bell's. Something else he shared with the Great Lady. The love of a good Scotch. 'The only good thing to come out of Scotland is their whisky.' He'd lost count of the number of times he had told her this. It had always made her smile.

Chilcoat closed the laptop. The lab, that was in Scotland. A disused industrial estate on the outskirts of Stevenston, North Ayrshire. He would have preferred something closer to London, but Ayrshire property prices were so damn cheap, he couldn't resist.

He glanced at his phone. 1400 hours precisely.

Ignition time.

The fire would be started by sixteen detonators. Four on each floor.

Thirty-nine minutes to burn down. That's what the computer modelling said it would take. A decade's work, gone up in smoke in less than forty minutes. He could watch it on live-stream. The drones would record everything. But he had calls to make.

Starting with Farringdon Crull. Environment secretary. The last Thatcherite left in the Cabinet.

SIX

Skylight

Logan held the weasel in his mouth. Badger 33, Marek, was calling something, but he couldn't make it out. Logan tilted his head to the left.

'Don't look back.' The words recognisable this time.

His body seethed with heat. He put the weasel on the floor and rubbed at his snout. Panting to try and cool down. He looked behind him.

There were a dozen of them left. The ones who the bird had pecked out the beads from. Everyone else had gone down the stairs, not up. He still did not understand the badger's logic. Heat travelled upward. The exits were on the ground, not the top floor.

And yet the bird had agreed with the badger straight away. What did they know that he didn't? The air felt as if it was shrinking. Another glance behind him.

Two otters, a young badger, four foxes and a toad. Add on the bird, the weasel, Logan and Marek – that made twelve. Just twelve. He didn't know the foxes. Didn't recognise their scents or their clan. They had exchanged glances, but not words.

'Don't look back. Keep going,' Marek growled as the group paused.

'But…' one of otters started to speak.

'To look back will slow you down. If you want to die; look back, hesitate, burn. Watch others burn. If you want to live, do as I say.'

Logan found the badger's confidence irritating rather than reassuring. And now another dead end. The door in front of them locked shut.

'Up, up.' The bird was hovering near the ceiling. A faint glow of light. Logan could hear coughing. A rasping, wheeze of a cough. A female fox cough.

He turned. The vixen, half a dozen paces back. The youngest of the group. She was lying down. Her body began convulsing. The other three stood over her.

Logan rushed over. The other foxes, young males, made room for him. *Their eyes are full of fear*, Logan thought.

'Your sister?'

The fox on the left nodded. The vixen's eyes were half-shut now. A blackness was closing in on her. Logan stretched out his paw and whispered to the vixen, 'Be brave, you are not alone.'

The black smoke was circling, almost reaching her. It wouldn't be long now. Logan could see another shape. The young badger was on her side. Her breathing uneven, her mouth gaping open and shut.

'Marek – badger down,' Logan called out ahead of him. No response. Marek was pushing at something. A metallic, grey filing cabinet.

'For fox sake, help me with this, will you?'

'What?' Logan asked.

'There's a window in the ceiling. Help me push this under it.'

Logan looked up. He could see a small swirl of light. Natural light. Daylight. What time of day was it now? Was it still daytime?

The bird was circling. Logan left the vixen and scampered to help Marek. He felt a warm paw on his shoulder. An otter was also pushing.

'Stop. That's enough. Now someone give me a paw up, will you.' Marek issuing orders again. Logan watched as the otter supported the badger's weight and Marek scrambled on top of the filing cabinet. Standing upright on his back paws, he pushed at the glass.

'Help me.'

'Will someone help me?' A different voice. A male voice. One of the foxes. Circling manically around his fallen sister. Logan went over to him.

'What is it?'

'I'm scared. I am finding it difficult to breathe.'

All the while, the sound of scratching and scraping. Marek had been unable to find a way through the glass. And then. A crashing. A loud and persistent crackling sound.

'The flames are coming.'

It was the otter who spoke. The one at the base of the cabinet. The bird too, was circling. 'Please just let us live. I'm not ready to die.'

Her voice sounded strange. Human almost. The light was disappearing. The whole room was descending into grey. Logan sprang up over the otter and onto the filing cabinet. Marek was panting. 'I can feel it moving. But it won't give.'

Logan looked above him. At the thin sliver of daylight.

'I'll count to three. On three, we both leap up at it, OK?'

Marek nodded and Logan began his count.

SEVEN

The others

Everything happened so quickly. The sound of the glass breaking. Then the fox and badger disappearing. The flames. Yellow flames. Funnelled into a column. And the heat. An intense and agonising heat. The smashed skylight acting as a chimney.

The fire being sucked out by the blast of air above. Everything was burning.

She could see the foxes. She could see the otters. She could see the young badger. And hear his guttural, wrenching cry as the fire engulfed him.

They didn't stand a chance.

A shrill high-pitched scream. The weasel lying at the base of the filing cabinet. Raven hovered to the left of the flames and looked upward. There was no gap between the flames and the edges of the broken glass. The black smoke swirling higher now. Halfway up to the ceiling.

Don't look back, Marek had warned them. But she did look back. And she saw two eyes. Two brown eyes. The weasel standing on her hind legs. A small speck of life amid a tsunami of flames.

'*Now or never. It's now or never.*'

23

That's when she heard it. Her mother's voice. The same one that had warned her the fire was coming. '*Be yourself. Don't be afraid. Don't be alone.*'

And swooping down, she clutched the weasel in her beak. Eyes closed. Flying upward. Going faster. Pushed along by the hot air.

'*Come to me.*'

Her mother beckoning, calling her from above. The currents. Floating up on the currents. Ignoring the heat. Ignoring the flames. Focussing on the air. The scent of fresh air.

And then, and then. She is outside. Above the building. Except it is not a building. It's a bonfire. A huge, raging bonfire. The shape of the building is invisible. The scale of the fire overwhelming. A cloud of black smoke hits her.

She has to fly higher to escape the darkness. All the time holding the weasel in her beak, not thinking about the extra strain on her body its weight is causing.

And then, and then. She is above the cloud. Clear air. Daylight. The heat merely intense rather than overwhelming.

Where are they? The fox, Logan – and the badger, Marek. They had escaped through the broken glass, twenty, maybe thirty breaths before her. Where are they?

A new sound. A tree. A tree screaming. A rowan tree next to the building is ablaze. Her leaves burning red. A sense of autumn berries even though it is only spring. And beneath the tree. Movement. She sees movement.

Two silhouettes. Two shapes. Running. Zigzagging away from the fire. Away from the flames. And towards. Towards. A fence. The fence. Almost as high as the trees. She could fly over it, but how would they get out? Had they come this far only to remain imprisoned?

A wriggle and a moan. The weasel in her beak is uncomfortable. A surge of fatigue. She must get to the ground. Put her down. Rejoin the others.

EIGHT

Fenced in

Logan lay on his front, panting for breath. A fence, a great big wire fence.

He strained his neck, tilted his head up, but couldn't see where it ended.

Don't look back.

That's what Marek had said. Logan had looked back. More than once. At the tower of flame. The huge red, orange and yellow tower that had once been a building. And surrounding it all, framing the whole glowing canvas was a thick black smoke.

There was very little wind and the smoke was hovering near the ground. They were perhaps one hundred foxtails from the edge of what had been the building. Small pockets of burning debris littered the route they had come.

Logan forced himself up into a standing position. His tail was horizontal, tense. His nostrils filled with the smell. A scent. The scent of death. Covering his eyes with his right paw, he slumped back down.

There was a darkness descending. He could feel it, sense it. Not just the cloud of smoke, but something more menacing, something more disturbing. He hadn't felt this way since. Since the day the men in black came. Six of them with dogs. And guns. The day they shot Rosa.

And now he was going to be with her again.

They were trapped by the fence. Still prisoners. If he walked back into the fire. Then he could end it all. Burn himself free.

Would he see her again? Would he?

All these thoughts going around in his head. In a few seconds. Memories and fears bombarding, colliding, confusing. Then he heard him. Badger 33. Marek Dogovsky. Standing in front of him. His mouth opening. A sound coming out that was not badger tongue. A sound that wasn't Marek's voice. Logan's eyes darted sideways. There was nobody else. A trick of the air perhaps. Smoke and mirrors.

For Marek's voice wasn't badger. It was human. A dialect not familiar to him. Not Scottish, not from these parts. Not English either. But definitely human. Logan sat up on his haunches.

'Sorry,' he murmured anxiously.

'We have to dig our way out. We have to dig.'

Logan stared. He could see Marek's mouth moving. But the sound still wasn't badger tongue. And then he was gone. Back to the perimeter fence. A ripple of muscle across the back of his neck and the sound of claw on mud.

Logan turned to look at the building. The flames. Red, orange and yellow. And again, he thought about walking back into them. To burn away his fear. To find a way back to being with Rosa. And then he looked again at Marek. By the fence, digging.

Of course, he's digging an escape tunnel. Logan should have thought of that. Logan was a great digger. The fastest in his den.

Should he join him? He should join him. He really should. Unless he gave up now. Just gave in to the darkness.

Logan panted. He was struggling to breathe, to stay in focus. He glanced back, and forwards. Trapped. Trapped in his indecision. And that's when it landed.

The weasel dropped inches from his left paw with a tiny thud. And next to the weasel was the bird. The one from the cage. The one who had pecked away the beads.

The starling whose name he couldn't remember.

'Is there anybody else?'

'Is there anybody else?'

'Is there anybody else?'

A female voice. Repeated three times. And Logan glanced over again at Marek. Looked at him all alone. Digging. And ran over to be by his side.

NINE

Modern life
is rubbish

I am in the cottage surrounded by boxes.

Everything looked smaller now.

My furniture. That looked out of place. Old, marked by years of cat-clawing and tatty in comparison to the cleanliness of the freshly-painted walls. Not that I have a cat anymore. Siouxsie had died last winter. A 17-year-old tabby.

'Never recovered from me leaving,' Mandy would say.

'A stroke caused by old age.' My standard retort.

I'd buried Siouxsie in the back garden of the cottage. Even though I hadn't moved in then.

Unpacking. Where to begin? The kitchen. I'd start with the kitchen. At least that way I could eat.

Cookbooks. The first box was full of cookbooks.

The Great Potato Cookbook. The Enchanted Broccoli Forest. Rose Elliot's The Complete Vegetarian Cookbook.

I'd been vegetarian for six years. Just after I met Mandy, in fact. An alternative cinema night in Glasgow. She was collecting tickets. Invited me back to the after-party. The party where she shouted at me for eating meat. The party where she challenged me to be vegan for a month, and we settled for simply meat-free.

She was younger than me. Three years younger. But had done more. Travelled, organised, agitated, experimented. Drifted from job to job, city to city before settling in with an artsy crowd in Glasgow.

She was twenty-five, I was twenty-eight. A fortnight later. My 29th birthday party. That's when we got together.

Mandy was five foot eight with long hair, forever changing in colour. I was two inches shorter, with chestnut brown hair always cut short. She dressed in loud hippy frocks and tie-dye leggings; I always wore some combination of black and purple. She would love to be the centre of attention, to perform and show off her latest half-baked attempts at comedy or political satire. I was much more insular. Always with my head in a book or scribbling down some unfinishable verses of polemical poetry.

We argued a lot, about my unwillingness to share what I was writing and my lack of confidence in my creative abilities. I was too risk-adverse she kept telling me, not wanting to expose my work to criticism or even constructive feedback from friends. And the more she told me this, the more withdrawn I would become. By the time we split, I had turned in on myself, stopped writing altogether, fully pulled up my creative drawbridge.

For at least six months Mandy had been going out without me most weekends. Meeting people I didn't know, staying overnight after parties and coming back smelling of cannabis and aftershave.

I never confronted her about her behaviour. Just sponged it all up. Turned my attention to cooking to cope with the stress of it all. Hoped I could win her back through making her lovely meals. She ate it all, but rarely complemented me on my culinary creations. Instead, she told me I was boring. Middle-aged. Mediocre. Her cynicism and verbal abuse became part of who we were. Until last Easter she finally snapped. Told me she had enough and that she was off to live in Bristol.

We were a couple for just over six years, lived together for two of them, been split up for over twelve months. I'm past my 35th birthday now. Didn't have a party this year. Hired a cottage out in Argyll for a week, went there on my own. Went walking and cooked myself a cauliflower curry on the day of my actual birthday.

I'm in the kitchen, looking at the books. Mandy let me keep the cookbooks. Said she looked up everything online now. All the recipes she could ever need were "a few clicks away". I guess I was more old-fashioned than her. I just loved books. The feel of them. The look of them. The touch of them. Had never tried a Kindle, still didn't have a Facebook account. Let alone Twitter or Instagram.

Half of the boxes I had loaded into the van had been books. A big chunk of the rest my vinyl and CDs.

Sitting cross-legged on the kitchen floor. The maroon vinyl floor. Flicking through the soups, the salads, the cakes. The stains marked the pages I had cooked from the most. The memories and tastes.

I held my hand across my mouth. My left thumb turned upward towards my eye. I could feel something wet.

I was crying. Tears. Running down the back of my thumb. Onto the back of my wrist, and onto the neck of my T-shirt. My red *Modern Life is Rubbish* organic cotton T-shirt that my friend Mike had bought me for Christmas.

Only from one eye. I could only feel tears from one eye. Was it normal to do that? To cry one-sided?

I hadn't cried, since...?

Not at my grandmother's funeral. Not when I buried Siouxsie under the rowan tree. Not even when Mandy finally packed her bags and moved down to Bristol.

And yet now. At 2.38pm on Monday 8th April 2013, I was crying. The day Margaret Thatcher died. The day I started to cry.

TEN

Ravenous

Hatherington's. The most upmarket restaurant in Grantham. The two of them sat furthest away from the window, in a small alcove. A space usually reserved for businessmen entertaining their mistresses.

Farringdon Crull was immaculately dressed. There was something of the dusk about his appearance. His grey-blue eyes, his silver hair, his black tie with subtle tones of blue and mauve. He spoke with a Home Counties accent and a sense of entitlement. His tendency to say 'f' instead of 'th' suggesting his upbringing may not have been quite as straightforward as he would have people believe.

Crull had finished his starter, but Chilcoat was still sipping at his soup. 'So, have they set a date for Fatcher's funeral?' he asked.

'The 17th. A week on Wednesday.'

'Eight days' time, there will be a lot to organise.'

'Thankfully not my responsibility, but they would have had a template to follow,' Chilcoat said, putting down his spoon.

'How was the soup?' Crull asked.

'Too much salt. They could do with going back to basics here. I heard the chef is European and they simply do not know how to cook British food.'

Their conversation paused as the waiter cleared their plates.

'Another bottle of Château Haut-Brion, sir?'

Chilcoat nodded.

'Everything go according to plan in Scotland?' Crull asked, once the waiter was out of earshot.

'Perfect. Thirty-seven minutes. Two minutes faster than the computer modelling.'

'And what happens next?'

Farringdon Crull had leant back in his chair, undoing the top button of his waistcoat.

'As I told you last week, the warehouse is ready. The stocks will arrive on Monday.'

'I saw the posters. Very effective. I approve.'

Chilcoat smiled a half-smile. He didn't need Crull's approval. That's not what he was there for.

'And when do we go live, as they say,' Crull asked.

'Wednesday 17th April.'

'Same day as the funeral?'

'The whole world will be watching events in London. It seemed…' Chilcoat paused. 'Appropriate.'

'And six months you reckon?' Crull leant forward, speaking in a virtual whisper.

'Indeed. Of course, we will be monitoring before then. Monthly at least. By six months, there will be sufficient data to know if our little experiment has worked.'

The two men paused. A waitress had returned with the wine. She was in her early twenties, a long blonde ponytail. She poured a quarter of a glass for Crull to taste. Crull swirled the wine, once, twice around his mouth. Putting the glass down, he nodded. The waitress filled both their glasses and glided away.

Chilcoat watched her closely, his eyes drawn to the tight curves of her behind, the faint line of knicker visible through the blackness of her trousers.

'By six months there should be sufficient exposure for us to see marked changes.'

'And do you foresee any challenges?' Crull asked.

'Nothing which can't be overcome.'

Chilcoat's face hid the slightest of grins. The biggest challenge he faced was not being able to share his real mission. Not being able to boast about how in six months' time he was going to bring Margaret Thatcher back from the dead.

He would regenerate her using genome implants collected from the frozen bodies of dozens of young people. People who would have mysteriously disappeared after visiting one of his Nobler Age food banks. The food banks that would also prepare the way for the resurrected Thatcher being accepted as the rightful heir to the Tory crown. The GM food served at the food banks would cause a return to a Nobler Age, an upsurge in appreciation for Thatcher's values by exposing masses of the population to food which had been impregnated with her genes.

People would fall in love with Thatcher again. Through the food banks he was changing attitudes. Restoring morals. Creating a new generation of Thatcher disciples. Ensuring the right conditions for when he could bring her out of hibernation and back to life. Paving the way for her return to power.

And at the same time he was carefully monitoring whoever came to the food bank, so that he could select the right genetic samples for the organ transplants, the multiple skin, body and tissue parts that he would assemble in his new Grantham laboratory. He would store their body parts in state-of-the-art freezers and if his computer modelling was correct, in six months' time he would be ready to regenerate the love of his life.

The years of experimenting on beasts of all shapes and sizes had tested his theories, helped him refine his technique. He was excited about what would be coming next.

Yet Crull knew nothing of this. For him the project was about the undeserving poor becoming worthy again. For Chilcoat had told him that Nobler Age Foods would be giving the poor genetically modified food that would cause in them an emotional compulsion to accept lower wages, worse conditions, longer hours. It's longer-term aim? Nothing as fanciful as bringing Thatcher back from the dead. Simply a way of creating more Tory voters by getting the working classes to ingest the Tory gene.

Oh yes, they had talked about Thatcher. And Tebbit. Reminisced about his wondrous on-your-bike speech. But Farringdon Crull, the ambitious environment secretary, knew nothing of the real plan. There were lots of people Chilcoat had given a jigsaw piece to, but nobody had seen the full picture of what he was assembling.

His accomplice at the morgue. The one who had released the body for a five-figure sum. He was convinced that Chilcoat was merely a collector of the great and the good, who wanted her for his own private mausoleum. The nurse, the nurse who collected the blood samples. Well, that was a different story. One he shouldn't be thinking about now.

For Lynton Chilcoat was a master at telling stories. A master of remembering who he had told what. Though there were times, were moments – like this one right now – where he would quite enjoy just telling the truth.

Crull was still talking. Chilcoat only half-listening, lost for a moment in the magnificent enormity of what he was doing. 'You can rely on my discretion, Lynton. Nobody else in the Cabinet even knows we are meeting.'

'Thank you, Farringdon.' Chilcoat was holding up his knife, polishing it with his napkin. Looking, just for a second at his reflection in its silver blade. He was content. Enjoying himself. The Great Lady would be proud. 'This has to be on a strictly nobody-else-needs-to-know basis. If the great unwashed find out what they are eating, or the press get a whiff of this, then the data will be useless – the experiment will take so much longer to come to fruition.'

'The *placebo complex* you called it last time we met. I remember.' Crull took another mouthful of wine. His glass almost empty now.

'Indeed, if people believe that eating something will make them fart, they fart. If people think that eating something will make them want to work harder for less money, they won't eat it. The placebo complex. PC. We must be PC at all times, Mr Crull.'

'Very good, Lynton.' Crull smiled. Chilcoat looked ahead. The blonde waitress was returning. Carrying two plates. The air filled with the scent of crisped lamb and mint.

'Oh good, our food at last. Don't know about you, Environment Secretary, but I am absolutely ravenous.'

ELEVEN

Voices from
the other side

She is restless. Unable to settle. Since the fire she had remained silent. The smoke that day had been so thick, so choking, that it was as if she was still holding her beak closed. Too scared to speak in case that meant ingesting more of the acrid fumes.

The colours of the fireball that had swept through the aviary were seared into everything she saw. Even when she closed her eyes the bold, dancing flames were still there.

She didn't understand how she had made it out alive. It was a little less fragmented now though. She could recall the sound of glass smashing and being sucked out into the daylight. Flying up the chimney. That's what it felt like. With something or someone in her beak.

She remembered finding herself next to a perimeter fence in total blackness. The sun unable to penetrate the dense clouds of smoke. There were three others beside her that had made it out.

'Can you fly? Can you fly? Can you get over the fence and tell us if it is safe?'

It was the fox who had spoken. A male fox; young, his white chest stained with either soot or soil. His words still itched away at her even though it was now four moons later.

So too, that sound. The scraping sound. The frantic clawing of the earth. The badger digging with a manic determination, for his, for their lives.

The third one, the weasel, lay motionless just to her right, her body lurching with deep, awkward breaths. Raven could remember now how her fur had seemed charcoal rather than chestnut. And the weasel's mouth opening. She was trying to speak. Raven had hopped closer still, tipping her head to one side to hear.

She was so close that she could scent her fear. How familiar that now tasted. She was so close that she could see the faint lights that glimmered in her eyes, her brown eyes. Raven had seen this gaze before but could not place where she first came across its patterns and echoes.

She took a deep in-breath, holding her throat closed, quietening the sound of her own breathing to try and make out what the weasel was trying to say. The phrase the weasel repeated three times in a tongue that also seemed somehow familiar.

'Is there anybody else? Is there anybody else? Is there anybody else?'

Now a beakful of days on, these words were everywhere. In the rustling of the trees. In the streams of traffic. In the mumbles of human conversation from the shops and parks.

'Is there anybody else? Is there anybody else? Is there anybody else?'

The weasel's words filling her head every second of every day. Stifling her. Suffocating her. Swallowing her.

Not one bar, one verse or a solitary alarm call had she

muttered since that moment. As if her beak had become glued shut with sadness. The pain. The guilt.

It was not just the weasel who taunted her. Every time she stopped to peck at the earth, in search of a worm or a beetle that may temporarily satisfy her pangs of hunger, she heard Marek. The bravest of all of them that day.

'Logan, just help me dig!' And she would stop pecking. The earth would be left undisturbed. Her hunger unabated. A passing car. The humming of an engine. The sound of a train passing on the hills. These mechanical noises brought new terrors.

'Look up there! Get in the tunnel now.' The desperate shriek of the fox. Still calling to her to hide.

Every human-made thing she saw, from the lights on the street to the reflection of something grey and metallic in a car's wing mirror. She would crouch down, waiting for another machine of death to hover in the sky and shoot arrows of fire down at her.

She would hear his warning and stumble forward. A few breaths later she would compose herself and take a look at what was causing the alarm. There were no flying machines of death where she was now, no metallic discs in the sky flashing, whirring and beeping within a menacing cloak of destruction. Only animal voices taunting her, punishing her, reminding her of her cowardice and duplicity. Badger, fox and weasel.

Is there anybody else? Is there anybody else? Is there anybody else?

That's when the final scene would replay and replay and replay. Stuck in an endless loop. The view she had as she flew up, and over.

'Can you fly? Can you fly? Can you get over the fence and tell us if it is safe?'

The badger scooping up the weasel with his front right paw and pushing her into the freshly-dug hole, the fox diving in after her. The badger shielding them, his dark fur melting into the shadows of smoke and soil. The explosive bang, bang, bang of the disc as it fired down at their movement. The dull thud of the mud wrenched from the ground with the force of its impact.

Is there anybody else? Is there anybody else? Is there anybody else?

The final scene. Four moons ago. Yet she could still taste the soil. She still sensed their fear. She could still hear the fire approaching.

She could not escape the guilt of abandoning them.

She had flown over the fence and kept flying. Not looking back once. She left them behind. She does not know if they are alive or dead.

Is there anybody else?

She had journeyed in fits and starts. Never going to the same place twice. Avoiding any of her old haunts.

Is there anybody else?

Not mixing with any other starlings, not exchanging glances, let alone greetings with any other birds.

Is there anybody else?

Snacking solely in the wild – earwigs, woodlice, earthworms, ants and beetles. Never a full meal. Always on the move. Too afraid to risk the bounty that human gardens offered. Resisting the lure of fat ball and peanut feeders, despite the clamour of their smells.

The night-time terrors were the worst though. Without a roost she feels naked, as if all feathers had been plucked from her back. Without a roost there is nothing to hide her from her guilt and shame.

Today, she awakes at first light after another night of disturbed sleep. So alien, not to have a roost or companions to guide her morning journey. No morning chatter about feeding grounds and places to bathe. This morning, there is no cloud. The sky is blue and the air still. She spots a rowan tree. Its bark seems welcoming. Its leaves are calling to her of spring.

She hears for the first time since the fire another voice. Not the fox. Not the badger. Not the weasel. But a starling. Her mother. Singing to her a rhyme she has not heard since she was a fledgling. An old, soothing rhyme handed down from starling to starling since the age of the Avian.

TWELVE

Mutation

Logan licked at his right paw. His tongue was dry, and his red fur matted with mud. He would need to find fresh water to wash himself clean. He stared at Marek who lay in the shadow of the oak tree. Logan closed his eyes. Opened them again, looked away and then back.

Still no badger.

No claws, no grey fur, no white stripe, no black snout, no short tail. Just… just a horrible peachy-pink colour all over, save for a small crown of black hair.

It was hard to believe how this could be the same beast. The one who that night had dug, had clawed, had tunnelled them to safety. It made no sense. Marek sleeping there all relaxed as if he had been in human form all his life. What was it? Five, maybe six moons since the fire, half that time since… since… Marek changed.

'Oh Rosa, what is happening to us all?' Logan whimpered. His jumpiness as they had journeyed through the forest had heightened tenfold since Marek had changed. The scent of burning still trapped in his nostrils, the colours of the flames bouncing off every leaf in the moonlight.

Would it be any wonder if he was struggling to stay sane? There had been just four survivors that night.

4 out of 937.

The sky darkened. The moon fully submerged behind a cloak of grey. That is when it began. A pain that he knew straight away wasn't imaginary. A sharp and incisive tugging. A stretching, pulling sensation. At everything. In everything. He had watched Marek mutate. Seen him lie down in a ball and convulse. Now it was his turn.

Logan let out another whimper. And then a higher-pitched yelp. A cry that jolted Marek awake. The badger-human rose slowly to his feet and stood upright. *He's so tall,* thought Logan. *I don't want to be that shape.*

And now as the tugging receded, a new sensation. Pins and needles having a disco in his hind legs. Clusters of them dancing in ever bigger groups until he could no longer feel the base of his tail. And that's when the nausea began. Retch after retch. Logan's windpipe almost bruising with the force of the spasms.

'Oh Rosa,' Logan called out during a moment of respite. 'Did you suffer this much too?'

'Stay calm, Logan. Don't fight it.'

Marek stroked gently at the fur above Logan's snout, but his words bore him little comfort.

'Oh God. That hurts.'

A kick in his skull. A huntsman with size-eleven Doc Martens. Again and again.

'Don't worry, it won't last much longer.'

Logan was winded. Struggling to breathe.

'Just count to ten, keep counting. Don't focus on the pain.' Marek had moved position. He grasped Logan's front paw and squeezed.

'One, two. Jesus. Oh sweet mother of Reynard when will this stop?' A giant crab claw running up and down his spine.

'Keep counting. It will help. Honest.' Logan was shaking. A loud cracking noise in his neck, his front legs.

'Three, four.' Logan spat out the numbers. His gums dripping with blood.

'Five.'

'Six.'

Logan paused. He was burning. Every inch of fur was covered in sweat. A black tar-like sweat. Oozing, stinging, itching. Marek had said they were the worst. The sweats and the nausea. Retch after retch of nausea.

'Fuck no, I don't want to do this.' His colour was changing. As tight as he scrunched his eyes shut, he knew his fur was fading.

'Keep counting. Don't fight it.' Marek sounded anxious for the first time.

'Seven.'

'Eight.'

His stomach, an elastic band about to snap. Knotted and tearing. His throat swallowing fragments of wire with every laboured breath. His windpipe bruised with endless spasms.

'Nine.'

Marek was rocking him in his arms, speaking to him gently but Logan could hear nothing. A blade running fast over his body. Cutting into him. A lawnmower shaving fur like wet grass, coming off in sticky clumps. Cold and shivering taking a hold. 'T-t-t…' Stuttering, his teeth chattering, cracking.

'Ten.'

THIRTEEN

The crossing

Walinska knew that she did not have long left. Her mouth was gaping open, her tongue drooping. Each breath a spasm of panic as she gulped for air. Her eyes though, retained a flicker of colour. A thin sliver of brown.

She was less than a year old. The fifth born of a litter of six weasels. All six of them were taken. The crisp bright light, the chilled edge to the breeze, the lengthening shadows of the trees in the late afternoon sun. Taken to the white building that autumn day.

She tried to conjure up a different image, a different memory. She thought of her brothers. Four of them. Their chattering and unfettered playfulness. Thought of them as they used to be in the forest – not in the white-walled room. But her mind couldn't keep still, couldn't hold tight on their faces. Her mind thinking only of the silence and passivity of their imprisonment.

And then she was back thinking about the flames, the fire that engulfed them. Their tiny voices, screaming. Her gulps for air more laboured now. Blinking fast, she saw her face. The rounded features, the scar on the left of her nose, her bright brown eyes. Her sister Rowan had been the last to burn. She had reached the landing but headed down rather than up.

Maybe. Maybe. There was no use. She couldn't have survived. The collapsing of the ceiling. The flames too high, too fierce.

Free from the whiteness of her cell for the first time in countless moons. Her first time truly on her own in her short weasel-life. At least now she could die next to the earth in the warmth of daylight, and not in the human-made lights and cold surfaces of the white room.

Her breathing slowed slightly as she enjoyed for a moment the scents of the grasses. How long was it since she had said goodbye to the fox and badger? Told them to go, to leave without her? That she was too weak to travel with them, would only hold them back. How long was it?

She had lost count of the moons since that night. Forgotten if it was five, six or even seven. Time was slowing down. Nothing seemed real anymore. Was this how it was to die? Did time slow down to a standstill? Did reality fade into nothingness? Would she simply pass from this world to the next without noticing?

Dusk. A stillness was descending. The moments in between where everything became clear. She had travelled less than 100 weasel-lengths since daybreak. The grass verge was thinning out. Replaced by a dark grey surface. Cold and hard. Her nose twitched. She could sense its vibrations.

A crossing path. For a moment she was back in her den, her nanna warning her. Her words warm, but full of authority and wisdom. The six of them gathered round her in silence. 'Take care on the crossings. That is where the humans come with their monsters. They will crush your dreams in an instant. Take care on the crossings. That is where the humans will flatten your body and destroy your soul. Take care on the crossings. That is where the humans travel faster than the raindrops. They will kill you in an instant and no weasel will be able to bury you as your body will have melted into their deadly pathways.'

She saw a light approaching. A flickering white light. And a sound. The sound of heavy breathing. A mechanical whirring and the scent of oil on metal. The light was getting closer. Behind it another flickering red beam. The contraption was heading straight for her.

Twenty lengths, ten, five and then… and then…

A fury of noise, a human voice screaming, swearing.

'Fucking pothole. Fucking pothole!'

Upended, the two-wheeled contraption lay on its side, its chain spinning. The human lay on the crossing-path inspecting his outer skin that was grazed red by his fall. She watched this for an instant and then drawing a deep breath, she leapt upward and landed just inches from where the human sat. And it was only then that she could smell it. The sweet, sweet scent of blood.

'Rowan, I love you,' she whispered. Then she took a step forward. Knowing that this was her moment, her final moment. And opening her mouth, she sank her teeth as hard as she could, biting down with all her remaining energy. And the human screamed out. The last sound she was to hear, for in the following instant, she was breathing no more.

FOURTEEN

Arrival

Logan stretched out his right hand. Turned his wrist round anti-clockwise and looked at Marek.

'I think it's stopped raining. I can't feel anything. I mean I can't feel any rain.'

His limbs felt so bare, exposed. No fur, just a tiny layer of ginger hairs. 'How do humans keep warm without their coats on? How do they keep dry with such pathetic little bits of fluff? I am always...' He paused. 'So cold... and wet.'

Marek was walking on, a good twenty badger-lengths ahead and perhaps no longer in earshot. 'You ignoring me? Hey! Hold up, will you?'

Logan tried to quicken his pace, but the aching in his calves had returned.

'Four legs good, two legs bad. It's just fucking cumbersome.'

He smiled, not sure where that word had come from. His human vocabulary was expanding rapidly. His walking though, was still awkward. His stride uneven and he was struggling to keep up with Marek. 'Hey, slow down, badger-man. You've had more time to get used to this upright perambulation malarkey.'

Logan stared ahead at Marek, now twenty-five lengths in

front. Marek's body was tall yet sturdy, both muscular and curved. His flesh was pink, a pale candyfloss pink; a luminescent shapeless grey shivered around his frame.

Marek had finally slowed down, allowing Logan to close the gap. He could see the stripe now, a pale stripe, off-white in colour, down the middle of his back, just to the left of his spine. As Logan reached his side, Marek started to walk again. His pace a little slower than before.

The two of them continued in silence. Their strides now even in length, but their gaits very different. Whereas Marek's arms rested in a static position, Logan's flapped.

'I still don't know what I should do with these. With these. With these front limbs.'

'Arms, Logan, they are called arms.'

Marek sounded tired, his nasal tone pronounced. Logan waved his arms in a broad windmill arc, then stopped walking. He was staring at his hands, more specifically his two thumbs.

'Are you not worried about your two of these as well, Marek? I mean they are at such a strange angle, I'm sure that can't be right.'

Marek though, wasn't listening, and had quickened his pace once more.

'Hey, badger-man. Your tight pink arse is receding. Let me catch up again, will you. I don't like the view from this angle. I'm going to be dreaming about your butt all night if you don't let me walk alongside you for more than five badger-breaths. I've been staring at your arse for...' Logan paused.

How long had it been? He had lost all track of time. Lost count of the number of moons since their escape.

'And it don't look right without a tail on it,' Logan shouted.

Maybe he shouldn't have said that. Marek had stopped.

Had held up his right hand. In that gesture which meant only one thing. 'Shut up, fox.'

Logan drew level and whispered, 'What's up?'

Marek pointed.

'Oh.'

They had reached the edge of the trees. Ahead of them the path turned from mud to tarmac, sloping upwards towards a gate. Beyond that a sliver of artificial yellow.

Logan sniffed. 'Humans?'

'Yep,' Marek replied. He was rubbing the side of his nose. 'I can hardly smell anything with this tiny snout.'

Logan licked and held his finger to the air. 'It's an easterly wind, blowing from in behind us towards the house. Maybe that's why you're not picking up their scent.' Marek continued to rub at his nose.

'There's a house over the hill,' Marek said. 'Looks small but might be part of a bigger farm. There's only a handful of street lights so I don't think we are in the city yet.'

Logan whined. It was the way that Marek had emphasised the word *yet*, that set off the rhyming in him.

They walked naked down the hill,
The farmer realised they were ill.
He gave them tea and crumpet
And a blast of his trumpet
And the village came out to see
The fox and badger being set free.

The poems had started on the second day of his mutation. The more stressed he was, the hungrier or more tired, then the words just spilled out in a Tourettic poetic tirade.

The wind it blows from the east,
From the land of the magical feast.
Come to me, you beastly sinner,
I've made you a beautiful dinner:
Food from every nation,
To give you eternal salvation.

A high proportion of his 'poems' centred around food. They had eaten nothing for the last two days except ramsons: wild garlic. The forest floor had been coated in them.

Logan sniffed. Staring up the path where the lights were coming from. 'Wind's changing. The branches are blowing the other way.' He turned to look at Marek. Except he wasn't there.

'Marek?' Logan called out.

'Marek?'

A snuffling noise.

'I'm up here, you idiot. Ahead of you.'

Logan stared at where the nasal twang was coming from. But he couldn't see him. A nip on his ankle. 'For fox sake!'

Marek was badger again.

FIFTEEN

At the platform's edge

The station was empty. Sparse and desolate, though the sickly-sweet smell of discarded Buckfast and fading echoes of diesel still lingered. Raven clung uneasily. The fourth night she'd spent here. Roosting – if you could call it that – underneath the footbridge. The torn netting giving her a foothold – the extent of the rust on the bridge even more apparent from her being so close.

She needed sleep – but without the comfort of her old roost she couldn't relax, couldn't drift off. At least here she was hidden from view – not going to be disturbed until the early morning trains started trundling past. She knew the timetable well now from the automated announcements that greeted every train. The woman's voice making them rippling with false sincerity.

Next to the station was a car park, empty by night – not exactly full by day. The night-time trade was young and carless. Tracksuited, often drunk and loud. Occasionally, a teenage couple would sit on the platform snogging and groping. The station had too many security cameras along the platform for them to get too carried away. They would 'go somewhere else to fuck,' she said out loud to herself on her second night. It worried her how often she was thinking distinctly human thoughts, beginning to express herself in *their* crude language.

She was tired. Exhausted. Was the bridge her waiting place? A metaphor perhaps? For her crossing. From starling to…? She still didn't know what she was turning into.

She had found it difficult to get used to the bright artificial lights that rested underneath the footbridge – but after the second night the warmth they emitted offered her a modicum of comfort. Without the company of the roost, she still failed to sleep a proper sleep. Hunger pangs gnawed at her every time she closed her eyes – but it was the loneliness that disturbed her the most.

She had flown here after hearing her mother recite the old rhyme. *West is Best.* She hadn't heard that since, well, since she first fledged. So she had flown west for half a day, until this particular section of railway track had caught her attention. A familiar track, and a familiar station: Saltcoats. Although it was many, many moons since they had harvested salt from the sea here, it still had a scent that spoke to her.

And at the station, that old roost she had experienced that night as a juvenile. Her first roost away from the home. Her and her sisters. For one night only. The scolding they got on their return. She recalls it with ease and embarrassment. And now she was back. And her sisters? Well, none of them could have survived the fire. She would have sensed it if they had.

Is there anybody else? Is there anybody else? Is there anybody else?

Her sleep was fitful. She dreamed solely in monochrome. Her senses too, were misted. Lacking in energy, she flew a circuit that kept herself close to the station. West to the beach whose tranquillity was disturbed by the construction of a new sea wall being built next to the railway. East to the small park where dog walkers gathered in the morning and teatime but was empty the rest of the day. South to a derelict council office, whose rear yard was overgrown with brambles and nettles. And north to a solitary rowan tree standing in a driveway in the backyard of a house which was silent and unlit.

She avoided the church and its grounds for that is where the local starlings roosted. Until now she had succeeded in preventing any encounters with them. The roost, though small in number, was loud in chatter. A chatter that contrasted starkly to her silence.

She was waiting. Listening for further messages. But all she could hear was becoming muffled. The fox, badger and weasel no longer taunted her for abandoning them. Though this made her guilt worse, not better.

She wished that she had died in that fire. She wished she had been burnt alive with the rest of the birds – the mistle thrushes, the song thrushes, the crows, the jackdaws, the blackbirds, the robins, the wrens, the collared doves, the turtle doves, the magpies, the ravens, the pigeons, the house sparrows, the tree sparrows, the greenfinches, the chaffinches. And the starlings. The starlings from her family, from her roost.

Instead, she was alone. And it was so alien for her, a starling, to be alone for so long.

The only words that she could make out in her head were part human now. She was watching people as they came and went – wanting to reach out and touch them, talk to them. She noticed men, women, children – she saw faces, she saw people talking and heard what they said – she began to understand their words, their expressions – could tell their emotions from the way they walked.

She noticed less the other birds – she still heard their calls – but easily blocked them out without listening. She had a ringing, a constant ringing, a tinnitus inside her head which was beginning to hurt. She didn't know what to do, to feel, to think.

'Is there anybody else?' she called out in starling tongue.

Silence.

'Is there anybody else?' she shouted.

Silence.

'Is there anybody else?' she screamed.

Silence.

First light. Maybe five moons since she had headed west. The sensations she felt were strange; distant, removed. The food she ate at the lab had tasted metallic, adulterated – unnatural. What was in it? What were they trying to achieve? She was tearing herself apart with such unanswerable questions, such circular torment. She longed to be normal again.

This was unbearable – perhaps she could just sit on the track and let the train finish what the fire had started. She knew the timetable now. The first train to Glasgow had passed fifteen minutes earlier at 6.40am, the first from her platform would be the 7.01am.

She hopped down from the tangled wire of the footbridge.

Five to seven. Six minutes. Too soon; she jumped back onto the platform and stood at the edge, just behind the yellow line.

A small smattering of people waited with her. Four people: A man in a suit looking at his phone; a woman dressed in black, smoking a cigarette; a man pacing anxiously, looking at his watch and the train departure screen whose messages scrolled across in a fluorescent yellow; a woman with large earrings and a big flat case propped up against the side of the bench.

Many more people were heading into Glasgow from the other platform – most enclosed in the confines of the ticket hall's small waiting area. She looked up at the display and then down at the track. 6.58. Three minutes. The anxious man sat on the bench, rubbing his eyes. He took his phone from his pocket and started tapping out a text message.

'Morning, starling. You catching the train too?' It was the woman with the earrings who spoke to her.

The woman in black flicked her cigarette onto the track.

'That starling was here yesterday, too. On her own. Funny, I always thought they went around in wee gangs.'

6.59. Two minutes.

'Are you sure it's the same one?' asked Earrings.

'Pretty much. She's got the most beautiful feathers, if the sun catches them. I've always had a good eye for birds. My mum used to feed them when I was wee.'

'She's a beautiful little thing. I would love to paint her, but she would never stay still and besides, I've got a breakfast meeting at the Barony I've got to get to.'

The woman's voice. Unmuffled. Clear. Warm. Honest. Kind. Then an interruption, ScotRail's computer announcement.

'I am sorry to announce that the – 7.01 – train to – Largs – has been delayed by approximately – 9 minutes – we apologise for any inconvenience this may cause.'

'Fuck. Could've had another ten minutes in bed.' It was the man on the bench speaking.

'I could do a quick sketch, maybe?' The woman was opening up her big case, taking out a drawing pad. 'Finish it off at college tomorrow.'

7.01am.

The starling stood on the platform's edge, not moving. A train pulled into the opposite platform. Around fifteen people got on, just two got off.

She was uncertain what to do.

7.03am.

Quietness again. Distracted. No longer sure if this was the right time for things to end. And then a voice. Her mother's, telling her, 'Be careful. Look. Look now.'

The station clock read 7.04am. A van had pulled in next to the station ticket hall on the opposite side. A large white van emblazoned in a pattern. A familiar-looking pattern. Oh my. That couldn't be right.

7.05am.

A man got out. Opening the back doors to his van, he took out stepladders and a large rolled-up tube.

7.06am.

The man was opening up a display case on Platform One. Taking down an old poster advertising Two Together railcards.

7.07am.

'The next train to arrive at Platform Two will be the delayed 7.01 departure to Largs. This train will call at Ardrossan South Beach, West Kilbride, Fairlie and Largs.'

Raven had barely moved. Unaware of the woman drawing her.

7.08am.

Unrolling the new poster. Standing on the second rung of the stepladder to smooth down the top corners.

7.09am.

'The next train at Platform Two is the delayed 7.01 departure to Largs. This train will call at Ardrossan South Beach, West Kilbride, Fairlie and Largs.'

7.10am.

The train pulls in. She does not jump onto the track but takes a single hop back from the platform edge and flies back to her footbridge roost. The four passengers climb on. The woman with the earrings peers out of the window and smiles.

7.11am.

The man is back in his van. The train pulls away from the platform. She can see the display cabinet now. The poster with its black font on a pale blue background:

Nobler Age Foods

Landing next to the poster, she examines it more closely. Underneath the writing is a wavy line of triangle and squares. The same squiggle that she had stared at every day for six months in the laboratory. The same marks at the back of her cage. The same emblem on the lab men's uniforms. And on the wall opposite her cage. And on the boxes she had seen them carrying out on that final day.

SIXTEEN

Lullabies and hullabaloo

I was in the kitchen, reinspecting the cut on my finger. Working out if it needed a new plaster. The wound was itchy rather than stinging. It looked clean still, but probably best to cover it up again. I smeared a little more tea-tree cream on before wrapping a fresh plaster around it.

A weasel bite. What were the chances of that happening? A dead weasel bite. How could I explain that? For its body was stone cold by the time I had unlocked its jaw from my finger.

At the time the cut was deep, the bleeding profuse. I staunched the flow with a sock I'd found in the bottom of my pannier. I'm not sure what the sock was doing there or if it was hygienic, but needs must. I'd felt a little faint, so I called Ayrshire Cabs, asking them to run me home. Asking for a five-seater so they could fit my bashed-up bike in too.

I looked up stoats and weasels in my gran's copy of *Thorburn's Mammals* when I got home to work out exactly what it was that

60

bit me. Weasels are smaller. No black tip on their tail. The pure white of their chest more clearly delineated.

That was Monday. Now it was Wednesday.

I wasn't expecting to see the weasel still there, in the bottom of the pannier. Just lying there. Well, I guess that's what dead weasels do. Blake Hardie, hoarder of dead carnivores. What would my gran think? I had a flashback of her coming into my bedroom with a glass of orange squash and a plate of Jaffa cakes. Cheering me up after my ant box disaster. I'd built an ant castle out of cardboard boxes, collecting the ants from the garden, but I'd woken up to find them all gone. There was no roof. They'd simply climbed out whilst I'd slept.

Yes, right then I could remember the ants. But I had no memory of bringing the weasel back with me. Maybe my tumble from the bike had given me a spot of concussion as well as the grazes and bruises. After picking the dead weasel out of the pannier, I bathed her chest clean with damp cotton wool and groomed her tenderly with an old toothbrush.

I don't know what compelled me do it. I guess it just seemed the right thing to do. Nor was I sure why I felt so much compulsion to give her a *funeral*. After all, this wasn't a pet, nor a friendly wild animal I had met before. Our only encounter had been brief and painful. I'm saying *her*, just because she didn't look like a male, not that I was much of an expert on weasel anatomy.

I could have simply dumped the body next to the trees at the back of the garden. Or thrown it in the bramble bush next to the compost. I could have covered her body with some old leaves or just put her in the brown wheely bin for garden waste. Maybe it was the date. Wednesday 17th April, Margaret Thatcher's fucking funeral. If she could get such pomp and ceremony, why not a small dead weasel who had ripped a hole in my finger?

I had carefully wrapped her body in a paper handkerchief and placed it in a small box. I even coloured in the box with a black marker pen to cover up the writing. Carrying the box carefully so it would stay the right way up, I made my way to the back garden. And to the largest of the three rowan trees.

The garden had been my gran's pride and joy. The place to come when memories got too raw, or the loneliness of being a widow became too great.

It was over nine months since she died: 11.49pm on June 21st 2012. Summer solstice. The longest day. Knocked from her bike, on a country lane, by a car that didn't stop. At the age of 78. My grandmother, Charlotte-Ann.

It was over twenty years since her husband Karl had died. 27th April 1992 to be precise. More than two decades as a widow. Karl's death was sudden too, a brain haemorrhage whilst out walking with Charlotte-Ann on Arran. Sitting down with a flask of tea, before the descent down Goat Fell. He just slumped over. And that was that.

They'd been the perfect couple. Charlotte-Ann and Karl. Always dancing, always laughing, always so kind to me. Unlike my parents. The artist mum and the accountant father. Always arguing. Always absent. They couldn't agree about anything. Not even how I got my name. My mum said I was named after Blake the poet and printer, my dad insisted it was Blake from *Blake's 7*.

Granny's cottage. My home now. Ten days after I moved in, but still I thought of it as Granny's cottage. I guess it wasn't that long since I'd unpacked the last of my cardboard boxes.

Maybe it was the residual tiredness from the move. Maybe it was being back here, all the memories that made me sing that song as I buried the dead weasel. Charlotte-Ann's lullaby. The one she sang when my parents' arguing had stopped me from sleeping.

Scattering the soil. Throwing on some petals.

Be quiet my love.

Be hushed my sweet.

The trees are asleep.

Wiping away a tear. Covering back the soil into the hole I'd just dug. Standing for a few moments.

Be quiet my love.

Be hushed my sweet.

The trees will protect you

And will bring you peace.

With the words of the lullaby repeating. In my mind and out loud. Coming back into the house as the light was fading.

Stay strong, stay brave, don't be afraid.

Listen to the words the trees gently sing.

Washing. Dressing my cut. Looking out from the kitchen window, through the dusky light. Looking at the shape in the garden and realising what it was. A fox.

Wave away your fears.

Wipe away your tears.

Close your eyes.

Opening the back door. Worried that I had failed to dig the grave deep enough. Thinking how much I wanted the fox to go. How quickly it had been attracted by the scent of freshly-dug soil.

Open your heart

To the sounds of love.

To the sounds of laughter.

To the scent of flowers

And the wonder of the trees.

Half slipping on my shoes. Not stopping to undo my laces. My heels squashed uncomfortably as I tiptoe back onto the lawn.

There was something not right. There was no fox. But there was a badger. Black and white, not red. And the badger was holding something in his front paw. And there was something else in the garden too. On the lawn, just lying there – sprawling as if a small puddle struggling to break free from its surroundings. Something unrecognisable. A shape I couldn't piece together.

You'll be safe here tonight.

Safe here tonight.

Tonight.

I stopped. Wondering if I could find the number for Hessilhead Wildlife Rescue.

The trees are cradling you

In their arms.

The trees are whispering their love.

So hush my darling,

My beautiful darling.

You are safe here tonight.

The lullaby finished. Silence. The only noise, the wind in the trees. The shape to the badger's right. Not a fox, but a human. A naked, red-haired human. Lying face down on the lawn. This was getting more than a bit weird.

'Hello?' I called out, not knowing what to expect.

'Hello.' A nasal twang to the reply.

I froze.

The badger sat up on his haunches and held out his paw in greeting.

SEVENTEEN

Camouflage

Logan had tried to hide. Tried to make it to the rowan tree. But his human limbs were clumsy and unresponsive. Collapsing beneath him in his hour of need. And that's when the rhyming started again. In his head. Silent verse.

Unseen by human eye,
Don't discover us.
Unseen by human eye.
On the invisible grass
I will lie today
And the badger will slip
Safely away.

But the idiot badger was talking. Holding his paw out in greeting to the human. The small and skinny human. With the crooked nose. With short brown hair and big brown eyes. And huge eyebrows perching like two hairy caterpillars above them. The man didn't smell like a farmer. Though he smelt of soil. And weasel, there was a faint scent of weasel.

And still Marek was talking to him.

Logan stretched himself out, prostrate on the grass. It felt

65

wet and damp. It felt cold. Without fur, everything felt this way. Everything felt – exposed. And now Marek was pointing at him. And the human was stepping towards him. And Marek was saying something about not being well, about needing to be safe. And the human was looking at both of them. His eyes darting. His big brown eyes wide open. And Logan heard Marek say, 'Sit up.' So he sat up. And the human had gone into the house. And Logan started to rhyme again. In his head, that is.

Let me into your paradisal home
With warm fire
And tasty bone.
Let me into your human abode.
I'm tired
From my days
On the forest road.

And the human was back. With a cloth. A large red cloth. And he placed it in front of Logan. On the grass. And stepped back.

'The blanket is for you, Logan. To get warm,' said Marek.

'Blanket?' asked Logan.

'The red thing, it's called a blanket.' The human spoke. His words surprisingly free of menace.

Logan went to grab it with his mouth. 'Use your hands, Logan. Use your hands,' urged Marek.

And Logan was wrapping the blanket around himself. It felt soft, reassuring. A portable coat. Not as soft as fur, but definitely better than being naked. The human had his back to him now. Was walking into the house. And Marek was following on all fours. He stopped at the entrance and called out, 'Don't just sit there, Logan. Come on in. The human is going to cook us some dinner.'

And Logan struggled himself upright and followed them both in.

EIGHTEEN

Patterns and clusters

'Fucking idiots.'

His visit to the burnt-out lab had revealed nothing new. He had hoped that seeing in person the perimeter fence where the bastards escaped would have offered some fresh insight. It was the failure to preserve the scene that had upset him the most.

He snorted. 'More fucking footprints than Glastonbury.'

And now with all department drivers sequestered to *funeral* duties he was forced to take the train back to London.

'Fucking idiots.'

The other passengers in the first-class carriage, a tweed-clad couple in their late sixties, exchanged nervous glances. Lynton Chilcoat had one of those faces you did not want to engage with. Today he was angrier than usual. Spitting out his words as if chewing a wasp.

An almost 800-mile round trip and he'd found out fuck all. The CCTV cameras detected four life forms circling the perimeter fence some twenty minutes after the fire ignited. The cameras were not the model he had asked for. Not sufficiently robust in a fire. A short circuit meaning no footage was gathered after 2.27pm.

'Fucking idiots.'

The tweed couple were standing in the aisle now. Peering into the next carriage. Considering their options. Then returning to their original seats.

Chilcoat took his iPad from its Union Jack sleeve and tapped the 13-digit access code before holding the screen up to his face to enable the retina detection to kick in. He knew he shouldn't do this in a public space, but with every driver, every fucking driver – fannying about after the VIP funeral guests, what choice did he have? Plugging in his headphones he watched again the familiar footage. Ten days and this was still the best they could come up with. Smudges of shadow within a fog of grey and black.

'Fucking idiots.'

A decent drone would have detected any movement above them and not just below. '360 degrees you fucking idiots. I asked for 360 degrees.'

Decent infrared cameras and they wouldn't have had the short circuit due to the heat. And there would have been footage from underground, within the tunnel that the fucking mutants fucking dug right under their fucking noses. He should never have trusted the Scots with the finer details. 'Fucking idiots,' he said out loud again.

An almost 800-mile round trip, a night in a basic-as-fuck hotel as his usual suite in the Hilton wasn't available, and he had learnt absolutely fuck all. Chilcoat resisted the urge to punch someone or something. This wasn't the time. He should refocus his anger on something more constructive. Revisit the data once more.

What did he know? Four body-forms, two large, two small. None with any microsensor readings. Microsensors that would have been picked up automatically by both the drones. Why and how had the four survivors all removed their tracker beads before the fire?

'I just don't fucking get it.'

The train had stopped. Carlisle. Taking a sip of his whisky, Chilcoat sighed. He tapped angrily on his iPad. *Urgent. MBT records from 1-8 April. Email me raw data. Highlight any static ratings. NOW!* And then he sat back in his chair. If he couldn't trust the department to get the security details right, how could he trust them with the data analysis? He would do it himself.

An instant reply: *Onto it.*

Fifty-two minutes later two spreadsheets arrived in his inbox. The MicroBead Tracker data already partially grouped. By the time the train arrived in Preston he had narrowed down the potential field of survivors more fully than the department had done in the last ten days.

This is how he started. Number crunching. Though it was commodities, hedge funds and the stock market rather than *livestock* he was used to studying. He still loved the thrill of getting numbers right. But there were bigger targets, grander schemes he was calculating everything on these days. The genomes. The sequence of life itself. A handful of data from a burnt-out animal laboratory was like doing the two-times table compared to what he had been working on.

His mood was calming. Amongst these numbers, there would be anomalies. Patterns and clusters. Patterns and clusters. That is what he was looking for. The data was indexed according to identification number, date of detention, species, cell number, experimental category, diet, medication and the final columns of data, genetic recoding level and MicroBead tracker movement patterns.

Obvious really. But clever. Thirteen of them in total. The final column that revealed identical positions. Twelve static devices, not moving. Then sixty seconds later, just one tracking device starts to move. Cross reference with GPS and you could work it out. Twelve micro beads had been removed, and then given to another bird to swallow, less than ten minutes before the fire started.

'Fed to a fucking pigeon.' It took him just a quarter of an hour to work that out. Pigeon number P45.

Pigeons. Rats with wings. They would swallow any old shit. He should have told the department to include that possibility in their methodology. But they should have had the fucking brains to work that out themselves.

He needed some pattern, some way of narrowing things down still further. But the whisky on the train tasted like toilet water and he wasn't at his best without a Bell's in his hand. Something he and the Great Lady had in common. He would wait until he had the Spectrum report from Moscow. After a week of waiting that was due tonight.

The train had stopped. Looking up, he noticed for the first time the tweed couple who were disembarking. Peterborough, last stop before London. At least there would be a car waiting for him at Euston.

The Wi-Fi signal at the station was better than on the train. If he was quick, he'd be able to email the data with full encryption. Giving Harry time to run a more detailed analysis before his call tonight.

Forty minutes later on the platform at Euston. Stretching his neck from side to side and rolling back his shoulders as he walked along the platform. Reaching the navy-blue Rover Saloon, he nodded silently in acknowledgement to the driver. He grunted the name of his hotel and slumped down into the comfort of the leather seats. It felt good to be back in London.

A slight raise of his left hand to Mustapha on the reception desk. One of the longest-serving of the Ritz's employees. Throwing down his hand luggage, picking up the phone next to the bed and calling down to order dinner. Oxtail soup, lamb cutlets with extra mint sauce and spotted dick pudding with custard. He would have time to shower before it arrived. Rinse away the last of the dirt from his train journey. Like a Virgin train fucked for the very last time. An old joke. He couldn't remember the punchline though. He smiled as the hot jets of water bounced off him.

Changed into beige chinos and a grey-and-white-striped polo shirt, he walked over to the drinks cabinet, pouring himself a generous whisky. Tonight, he would be staying in, seeing no one, so no need for the suit.

His dinner arrived, left outside the door with the porter tapping three times followed by two louder knocks. The agreed protocol. Settling himself down at the table next to the window, he ate at a steady pace. The food was inconsequential to his mood, though the more he ate the clearer his thinking became.

There seemed to be no discernible patterns for those who had removed their tracking devices in advance of the fire. No clear patterns relating to experimental types, species or even where in the lab they were caged. The first removals had occurred twelve minutes before the fire started.

Fucking typical that Moscow had sat on the files for over a week. Yet they were the ones with the expertise to make black scenes look white, to shine a light where the department's cameras were just too damned grey. If they weren't too pissed on vodka and cabbage, then he would have had the results back days ago.

He had a call scheduled with Harry at 10.30pm for an update. Looking at his watch, he saw that it was almost ten already. Leaving his dirty plates on the trolley outside in the hallway, he pulled the door shut, locking it as well as putting it on the chain. Opening up the drinks cabinet again, he opted for port rather than another whisky. Walking a few paces to the coffee table, he picked up the TV remote. Flicking the buttons, he called up the BBC News channel. The ten o'clock news was just starting. A special bulletin repeating the main moments from the morning's funeral.

He had an invite, of course, but he had paid his respects to her already on the morning of her passing. Part of him wanted to have been there in the cathedral with the rest of the great and good. To take part in the pomp and ceremony, enjoy the spectacle – but he would have had to be polite to so many people he could not stand. And besides, funerals only really matter when someone has actually died.

NINETEEN

Un-natural

The human seemed friendly, welcoming, but Logan did not feel relaxed, could not sit still. It was his skin. Or rather the clothes the human had given him. They pressed against him in strange ways. Both loose and tight at the same time.

Un-natural, that was the word for it. Un-natural. Sure, they made him feel warmer, but he also felt soiled, trapped inside a layer of something man-made. He wouldn't complain though. Not yet. It was still his first day here. To complain now would be rude, ungrateful. Give it more time, maybe he'd get used to it after a few more fox-moons had passed. Maybe it wouldn't be too difficult to adapt to.

The human was in the kitchen. There was a smell of metal and potato. As a fox he had eaten everything raw, fresh. But he had heard tales of ancestors who roasted things on flames, who used the sun's rays to turn stale meat fresh. Logan rubbed at his stomach. His hand moving clockwise across his torso. His gut cramped and gurgled.

Vegetarian. The human had said he was vegetarian. Had apologised for having no meat in the house. Marek had to explain to him what that meant. Eating no flesh. No dead animal. But Logan didn't mind. He didn't fancy eating meat now, not with his gut the way it was. And besides, how could he chew it without his proper fox teeth?

He would eat what the human gave him. If he liked it, he would ask for the recipe and offer to cook it again the next day. That would be the polite thing to do. That would help persuade the human to allow him to stay another night.

Logan burped once, twice, and then a third time. He felt a lump of vomit in his throat and swallowed hard to send it back down. Since he had arrived at the cottage, he had not felt right. Had felt uneasy; a dark and unsettling sense of foreboding.

The human.
His name is Blake.
Can I trust him?
Or is he a fake?
The badger has gone all quiet,
He hardly says a thing.
I feel that I am all alone
And really struggling.
I am a failure of a mutant,
Stuck as homo sapiens.
Marek changes back and forth
But for me this is the end.
I'm a fox trapped in a human shell.
I'm a fox trapped in a living hell.

'Did you say something, Logan?'

Marek was back in the room, in his human form, wrapped in a blue-and-grey tartan gown.

'Nothing. I said nothing.'

A shout from the kitchen. 'Dinner is ready. Do you want to sit at the table?'

'The table, Logan. It's that rectangular, wooden thing with legs.' Marek pointed behind him as he spoke.

'How come you know so much and I know so little?'

Marek shrugged, said nothing. He took his seat at the table. Logan watched carefully how he did it. Watched where he put his legs, his arms. And followed him over.

TWENTY

Heat disturbance

Chilcoat switched the TV off after less than twenty minutes of *funeral* coverage. He had seen enough. So many faces. So many hypocrites. She would have hated it. Besides, they had told less than half of her story. The best was yet to come.

Tomorrow he would return to Grantham to see her in person. He should be excited, but his mind kept drifting back to the other unfinished business. The escapees from the fire. An irritation. That's for sure, but he chided himself for his lack of focus on the real work. Preparing the way for her return. The launch of Nobler Age food banks.

The visual identity was complete. The marketing materials already being distributed. Colossal in scale. A logistics operation she would be proud of. Yet irritants could turn septic if you scratched them too much. He would have to be careful not to overthink them. Take decisive steps to eliminate them. He would be seeing Crull at Sunday's hunt. If it wasn't resolved by then, he could initiate a contingency operation.

Chilcoat moved over to the chaise longue. He stretched out his legs, kicked off his shoes. Saturday was his sixty-fourth birthday. April 20th. So far, he hadn't made any plans. He worked through the possibilities in his mind. A double session with Suzanne perhaps, if she wasn't already booked. If he asked her to be gentle he could probably still cope with riding the next day.

No, let's wait until he knew what the Russians had come up with. Didn't want events to get in the way. It was 10.31pm. Harry was late. He picked up his phone to check the volume was turned up. He was just sitting back down when it rang. Rod Stewart singing *Maggie May.* He had downloaded the song's opening line as a ringtone the day that she had *passed.* It still brought a smile to his face every time it rang.

'Harry, what have you got for me?' Harry Turner. Chilcoat's Head of Logistics. Thirty-nine years old. Six foot two, shaved head, blond and blue-eyed. A rugby-playing Londoner, from north of the river. Bright, ambitious and energetic. Though tonight he sounded a little weary.

'We've revisited all the data in light of the updated MBT findings.'

My updated findings, thought Chilcoat, *not* the *findings.* He let Harry continue.

'The Spectrum report came in just after 21.00 hours. Good stuff. Worth the wait. We've done initial cross-tabulation. Bit of a slow process due to some software compatibility issues, but the boys in the lab have just sorted that. They will be doing an all-nighter to get a full scripted analysis.'

'I don't need all the details, Harry. You will be telling me what you had for your dinner next. Just cut to the chase. Do we know who the little fuckers who survived the fire are yet?'

Chilcoat was back on his feet. His phone propped under his neck. Pouring a large whisky.

'I haven't actually had dinner yet, boss. It's mixed news really. Positive IDs on Alphas 1 and 2, but less clarity on Beta 3 and Charlie 4. Who do you want to know about first?'

'Give me the uncertainties first, Harry.'

'The Spectrum team took the footage to maximum resolution. Clever stuff. But the smoke interfered with visibility something chronic, so visuals are still a little patchy in places.'

'Patchy? I've waited ten days for *patchy* data to come back?' Chilcoat's tone was more exasperated than angry.

'The Spectrum boys helped pinpoint movements rather than statics. To cut a long story short, it meant we could do instant analysis on body temperature data on Charlie 4. Conclusion: probably reptile or amphibian.'

'Probably?' Chilcoat had put down his glass and picked up a pen but had yet to write anything.

'Too cold for a mammal or bird,' Harry continued, 'unless it was moments from death, so Charlie 4 is either cold-blooded or cold toast. The only cold-blooded sample on your MicroBead Tracker longlist was a category GH toad, female, security risk negligible.'

'I don't see how something in that category could've made it out of the fire. Seems impossible to me. What about the mammalian Charlies? How many are we talking about in that size range?'

'Half a dozen, boss, from your list, that is. But I'm just off the phone to the mammal boys. They agree that if it was a mammal its body temperature was so low its chances of survival were minimal – unless it crawled back into the fire to warm up. Given the background heat from the fire you would expect mammal temperatures to be above, not below, normal. They are as certain as certain can be that Charlie 4 is not mammalian.'

'So I am right in concluding that Charlie 4 is not the biggest of our problems, what about Beta 3?'

'Yes, boss. Charlie 4 isn't our main concern. As for Beta 3, bit of a blank I am afraid. This is the one we know least about still. I've got a team arranged to start again tomorrow. Resources were a bit stretched today, what with the funeral and everything.'

'The Russians never came up with anything positive?' Chilcoat's mood was darkening.

'Afraid not. Basically, it's a shadow of a shadow smothered in a silhouette of black smoke. Small, static and not responding to any of the data runs for a positive ID.'

'Great.'

'I've seen the Spectrum footage, boss. Maximum magnification. Full pixel resolution, much better than ours. I'm coming to the same conclusion that our senior lab guys did on day one. They think it's a phantom, an illusion caused by the smoke – and that Beta 3 is just some heat disturbance from the fire that's making our life sensors oversensitive.'

'And does Spectrum concur with this phantom theory?'

'Not sure yet, boss. Got a Skype call scheduled with Ivan at 06.00 hours tomorrow, UK time.'

'And this is meant to cheer me up? I've been on a West Coast Virgin train for five hours and my happy gene has receded so far into the rectum that they call *first class*, that I'm worried it may never come out again. You aren't helping with its extraction.'

Harry laughed. Unlike just about everyone else in the department, Chilcoat had a good working relationship with

Harry Turner. He respected his work ethic. Appreciated how he shared his devotion to the Great Lady.

'Well, hopefully I can help there, boss. Two definites. One fox, one badger. Our top mammal guys have taken a look at the new footage and agreed with the Spectrum analysis. Alpha 1 is a male fox, young adult, physically strong – seemingly uninjured too. Alpha 2, a male badger, also fully-grown, considered to be an older specimen, but still in good physical shape.'

'Retina scans to confirm ID?'

'First thing we tried, boss. Too far away for positive ID. However, the updated MBT list included five foxes and two badgers. But if you rule out the females and juveniles then that only leaves one fox and one badger who match both Spectrums and the mammologists' conclusions.'

'At last, I can feel my happy gene emerging from that dark passage.'

'The thing is, boss…' Harry paused.

'Yes?'

'Both Alpha 1 and Alpha 2 come from Category WW.'

'Harry – I am hoping I'm not hearing you. Both Willie Whitelaws?'

'Afraid so, boss.'

'Fuck.'

A moment's silence.

'Boss – I can get full security profiles sent over to you tonight. Won't take long to pull together.'

'It's been a long day, Harry. Meet me for breakfast tomorrow. 7.30 in the lobby. Bring me a printout of the profiles then.'

Chilcoat stood by the window. A tiredness was beginning to seep through him. 'And Harry, keep this on a strictly no-other-fucker-needs-to-know basis? This could be complicated.'

'Yes, boss. You know you can rely on me. Anything else I can do for you tonight?'

'Have a drink, son. Raise a glass to the Great Lady. She'll be watching over us now, waiting for us to get things back on track. I'll see you tomorrow, son.'

'Ok. Good night, boss.'

'Good night, Harry.'

TWENTY-ONE

Low tide

Low tide. A dozen seals balanced upon rocks in small clusters. Raven watches them from the uppermost branch of a bent tree at the top of the terrace. She flies down to the grass. The lawn is uncomfortable. She can smell the chemicals. If she stayed motionless she would know its toxicity levels, her feet would sense how much it had been sprayed. But no need for her to stand still, the sickly metallic scent told her there would be no worms, no insects. She looked up at the tables. Empty. The wind was cold and there was rain in the air. There would be few diners outside today.

She takes off and lands on the beach. The sand is damp from the earlier shower and as a result it sticks to her beak as she pecks in search of food. She flies further out and comes down next to the tideline. For the first time, there is near silence in her head. The voices have faded to a mere jumble of echoes.

By the water's edge. A clump of brown seaweed twists around the base of a rock. She pecks at it. A new noise emerges. In the twists of salt. A man's voice. An English accent. Not somebody she recognises. An echo of darkness. A menace without a shadow. She hops along the tideline to escape him. The spray of water cleanses away her unease.

She is no longer by herself. A woman is sitting on a small stool. Sheltered by a large turquoise umbrella. Raven looks at her, her head turned ninety degrees to the left to get a better view.

The woman is drawing. She follows her eyeline and sees that it is the seals that have brought her out here.

The woman's hair blows in the wind, it ripples with green and blue.

The voices have all faded now. Then. Recognition. She is the one from the platform. She hops nearer. The woman has not seen her. Raven calls out to her.

'Is there anybody else?' She speaks in human tongue. It comes out all of a bluster.

The woman stops her drawing. She looks to her left. Then to her right. Raven calls out again in human tongue.

'Is there anybody else?'

The woman is standing up. Her face is troubled. The bird tries to speak, but nothing comes out this time. She hops closer. Opens her beak and again, human noises come out. 'I am alone. Please help.'

The words are condensed, cluttered. The woman has turned her back on her. She is packing up her things. Her drawing pad, her pencils, her eraser and sharpener. She is folding up the umbrella and stool. Stuffing things into a large backpack. She is rushing, uneasy.

Raven speaks again. This time as a starling. She is cawing random words. Strings of syllables. Incoherent. Incompatible. The woman is bending over, pulling on a white wire. Headphones. They are tangled around her pencil case.

'Come on,' she urges, 'I haven't got time for this.'

As she tugs at the wire, the contents of the case spill over the sand. 'Fuck's sake.'

Raven calls out, trying to reassure the woman. But her tongue is still starling and the woman pays her no attention. The air is colder. Rain is beginning to fall. An adolescent seagull is hovering over the two of them. His call is shrill and wearing.

Raven is distracted, watching the gull. She readies herself for a quick take off in case it attacks.

The woman is walking away from the shoreline. Her pace is quickening. She is heading towards the hotel. The gull hasn't followed and is flying away from the land. Sensing the change in weather, the seals are one by one, slipping off the rocks and into the water.

Raven hops slowly to where the woman had been sitting. Something has been left on the sand. A small plastic card. Dark green with two white strips, and above them a barcode. A name and a signature, but the ink is faded and the writing isn't legible. She flips it over with her beak. The writing on the other side is clearer. Green ink in a white box on blue background. *Library Card.* And the woman's name. *Amy Carson.*

The rain has started. She picks up the card in her beak and flies towards the hotel.

TWENTY-TWO

Happy birthday

It was just the two of them. On his birthday. A private dinner. Time to talk things through. It was cold here. He knew that, of course. Had come prepared. Plenty of layers to keep warm.

He told her everything. About the funeral. The crocodile tears of the prime minister. The outpouring of love and grief on the streets outside the cathedral. And he told her about the fire, how beautiful it was. And how bright, powerful and destructive. And after but a flicker of hesitation he told her about the escapees, Alpha 1 and Alpha 2. Still on the run. 'It's good news, really. They were both category WW. Top of the scale, the most important specimens.'

She lay in silence, not responding.

He'd forgotten, he hadn't explained it to her yet. So he told her about the scale. The classification index he had invented. It had ten points. At the bottom were GH (Geoffrey Howe) and MH (Michael Heseltine) the least genetically altered and interesting, going up to an NT (Norman Tebbit) and WW (Willie Whitelaw) at the top. Only a handful of specimens had been classified WW. The most experimented upon, the most valuable specimens. The most impregnated with her genes. He sensed her smiling, even though her flesh didn't move.

'Not literally Willie Whitelaw, of course. It's just a name. But it shows their potential, our potential. That those most loyal to you are the bravest, the most resilient.'

He knew that she was approving, contented. He was hungry. It was time to eat.

She never touched her food. He didn't mind that at all. Just being with her was enough. He was clearer now. Knew what he was going to do.

'I have a plan, of course. To take back control, to maximise their impact. But I need a little help. I want you to help choose them. The children. The victims. I have some photos to show you.'

He held them in front of her, one after another. Watching for a reaction.

And so she guided him. He was sure of that. She had selected the right ones. The most photogenic. The most appealing. She had chosen wisely; he had no doubts at all.

He could work on their backstories, the finer details, when he was at the Ritz. He would choose the names for them then, too. He knew what he would tell Crull tomorrow, at the hunt. Knew how much not to tell him, too.

It was late. Almost midnight. Time to be going. He was finding it hard to leave. But knew that he could come back at any time. Only he knew this place existed. Only he knew where she was.

He picked up the plates, the glasses, the cutlery and dropped them into a black bin liner. He picked up a small dustpan and brush from the corner opposite. Kneeling down, he swept up crumbs and any other small bits of food that had fallen from the table. Being careful not to miss anything. He had to keep this place spotless.

It was only then that he felt how cold it was. Time to be going. He tied up the bin liner and returned the brush to its corner.

Now to say goodbye. He leant over her, looking at her for a while. Kissing her gently. Once on each cheek. Cold. He would get used to it soon.

'Farewell, my love,' he said. 'I'll be back soon. Thank you for a lovely birthday.'

TWENTY-THREE

Regeneration

It was raining. A dreich, grey mist snuggled at the base of the hills. But my mood didn't match the weather. I felt happy, joyous almost. For the first time since Charlotte-Ann had died. Or perhaps even the first time since Mandy had left me. I was no longer lonely. I was beginning to enjoy life again.

I'd spent the afternoon showing Marek and Logan some Doctor Who DVDs. The ones where my favourite Doctors regenerated. Pertwee to Baker; Baker to Davison; Eccleston to Tennant and Tennant to Smith. I am not sure it was a wise idea.

I had been struggling to find another way of explaining who or what they were. How they had become human forms of their animal selves. Regeneration. They'd regenerated. That's how I'd started to describe it. They'd been with me over a week now. Eight days since I'd buried the weasel and then encountered a talking badger and naked, red-haired man in my back garden.

A talking badger who became human in the day but reverted to his badger self at night. And a fox whose transition to human form seemed more permanent. 'We come in peace and search of food,' the badger had said when I failed to reply to his initial greeting.

I was dreaming. That's what I thought then. The most logical explanation. The only possible explanation. But somehow this dream seemed too real. Had been going on for too long. Maybe I was hallucinating? An infection from the dead weasel bite? Yet the wound had healed nicely and I felt no fever. If anything, I felt more relaxed than I had for some time. So it must really have happened. And not long after I ushered them in through the back door, I was at my kitchen table serving egg, chips and peas to a badger called Marek and a red-haired fox-man called Logan.

Just before dinner, Marek had gone to the bathroom a badger and came back a human. He warned me in advance what he was doing. 'Don't get freaked, Mr Blake, but I'm just popping up to get changed, so the three of us can sit down at the table and eat together.' And then five minutes later, he returned – in human form – wearing my dressing gown. Complaining about cramp in his calves.

They told me random snippets of their story as we ate. Escape from a laboratory, a fire, drugs, injections. Logan, the fox-man, was initially less forthcoming. It was clear he was still very much shaken up and despite a thousand and one questions running through my mind, I didn't want to push them for too many details. Deciding that I should let them tell their story in their own time.

I watched Logan that night struggling with holding a knife and fork, a small pile of peas tumbling to the floor. Marek seemed quicker to adapt to his new human hands. A week later and they were both equally adept with cutlery. A week later and the roles had reversed. Of the two, Logan had become the louder, more expressive. He spoke almost incessantly, having an air of restlessness about him that only red wine seemed to smooth the rough edges from.

Logan was undeniably good-looking, striking, in fact. His hair was fox-red, his eyes a shining green and his body slender and lithe. He meandered from topic to topic and paced around the cottage as if it were a cage. Speaking less in rhyming couplets than when he first arrived and more in proper sentences now.

Marek, by contrast had become quieter. On the second day he'd asked for a notebook and pen, and often I'd find him in his human form, sitting at the dining table. Writing. Scribbling. Drawing in an intense fashion. Giving off a clear signal: do not disturb.

He had a mysterious, almost malevolent air to him, and yet a calmness and stillness too. Heavyset, his hair in his human form was that of a faded punk – short, spikey with specks of grey and white emerging from his jet-black roots. His human face was unusually long and his eyebrows a vivid grey. Not what you could call classically good-looking, but certainly distinguished.

At night, Marek would retreat to the garden shed where I'd made a bed from an old duvet, sprinkled with some dried rosemary. He had explained that he could change at will by rubbing his nose/snout in a certain way, but that when he did so it was 'excruciatingly itchy' and 'energy-sapping'. So he'd developed a routine. Going to bed a human, sleeping as a badger and changing back to human in time for breakfast.

The last DVD had finished. The rain outside hadn't. 'We are not really the same as the Doctors. I haven't died and come back as a different Time Lord. I've just sort of evolved somewhat rapidly.' Logan was pacing round the room looking for something.

'There was less dramatic background music when it happened too,' Marek mumbled.

'And I am not being played by a hammy actor. This is still me.' Logan waved his arms in a camp fashion before slumping back into the armchair. 'Underneath this human skin is one hundred per cent pure unadulterated fox. My wine glass is empty. Get me a refill, will you?' Logan said, turning to me and staring expectantly.

Duly topped up, he was on his feet again, his glass tilting precariously as he thumbed his way clumsily through my CD collection. The IKEA CD rack rocked under his heavy-handed attention.

'Neil Young, Steeleye Span, Joni Mitchell, Bob Dylan, Simon and Garfunkel. Serious hippy music going down here.' Logan chortled. 'But then I see Dead Can Dance, Cranes, Bauhaus, lots of Cure and Nick Cave, some classic Siouxsie and I think, hang on, this guy is more of a goth. Are you some kind of mutant musical hybrid?' He grinned a huge grin, exposing his brilliant white canine teeth.

Marek sighed. 'Sit down, Logan and leave the man's music alone. And quieten down, will you? You're tiring us both out.' Logan grudgingly retreated into the armchair, crossing his legs repeatedly, muttering 'do as you are told, fox' just loud enough to ensure we could hear him. He stood back up and stared at the armchair's cushion with menace.

He sat back down. Tall and slender, his body wiry and twisting, he filled the armchair with ease. He continued to wriggle uncomfortably, occasionally patting his hand on each of his buttocks or shuffling the cushion slightly over to one side and shaking his head unhappily.

He was dressed in bright-red skinny drainpipe jeans and an orange-and-white tie-dyed sweatshirt. Marek was more muted, all in black, save for a white T-shirt that poked out from the neck of his jumper like a reluctant vicar's collar. They had chosen the clothes forty-eight hours earlier after I had finally persuaded them that if they wanted to leave the confines of *Granny's cottage*, they would have to get some clothes of their own.

Hearing an engine outside, I glanced through the window as the Yodel van pulled up. Jumping up to get the door, I mouthed an urgent 'stay put', hoping that they both felt too self-conscious in their new outfits to risk an encounter with the delivery man. I signed for the parcel and pulled the front door closed behind me. 'I think it's your yoga mat and trousers, Marek.' I dropped the two boxes at his feet.

'Brilliant. Thanks, Mr Blake.' He leant forward and closely examined the address labels. 'Just what the doctor ordered.'

'Now, careful with the packaging. If you don't like it, you can send it back,' I said, remembering the frenzy with which he and Logan had ripped through yesterday's boxes. Marek looked up, a pair of red-rimmed scissors in his hand, ready to attack the brown masking tape.

'Logan, what's up? You haven't sat still for more than two seconds.'

'It's my damned arse,' he said, patting himself down. 'It just doesn't feel right with these pants on. It just doesn't feel right without, you know, my beautiful brush. It's like my bum's feeling lonely and squashed all at the same time.'

I'm suffering without my tail.
I feel like my arse is bound to fail.
I do not feel fully complete

With two arms rather than four feet.
I am a fox in human form
And it cannae be the norm
To sit on the sofa.

His rhyme ran out of steam. He couldn't think of anything to rhyme with sofa.

To sit on the settee
Feeling this shitty.

The rhyme complete, he stood up, headed back to the CD rack and picked out Simon and Garfunkel's Sounds of Silence. Chucking it over to me, he said, 'Put the fox song on again, will you?'

I sighed. 'It's called *I Am a Rock*, Logan. Rock, not fox.'

'You hear what you want to hear, and I'll just appreciate some fine lyrics with my badger friend here.' He slapped Marek firmly on the back. 'Time for a wee refill methinks? Red or white? Gotta be red, of course. Always has to be red. Where's the corkscrew?'

TWENTY-FOUR

And in the forest
he will fall

She is in a forest. The sky is grey, clouded. The summer sun hidden, its warmth absent. A dark green carpet of moss envelops the earth. A single charcoal-coloured rock stands proud and upright in the small clearing. Ahead of her, a stream, behind her, thick brambles. The breeze is from the east. Cold. Persistent. Branches sway unevenly, occasionally a leaf falls under the force of their movement. There is a continual whisper coming from the bark, but the words are too faint to hear.

She is hungry. Needing food before continuing her journey. Too weak to hunt, she must forage to rebalance her fast-moving metabolism. She must find time to snack on insects and fallen berries. Another day alone. Without her siblings, she is smothered in her isolation, unable to recall how she felt before the fire.

Vibrations. The forest floor churning with excitement. Distant noises. Human sounds, travelling fast towards her. Looking around for shelter, a hiding place. The rock summons her over, calling out her name three times:

'Walinksa,
Walinska,
Walkinska.'

She leaps up and bounds towards the base of the rock. It is too exposed. She circles it clockwise, before stopping at its easternmost edge. With her back pressed against the rock she can see a hollow. An old tunnel. Hidden in the roots of the wild service tree. An abandoned badger sett. The familiar musky scent, but no scats, no footprints, no recent sandy deposits. The sett has been empty for some time. She dives in, twisting her body round in a tiny circle several times to get her bearings. Finding an angle at which she can see out, without being seen.

The vibrations are louder now and getting closer. Horses, at least two of them, moving fast. She edges further back into the hollow. She will listen, but not watch. She cannot be seen. She cannot be caught, cannot go back. A clattering now, hooves breaking up the earth. A trail of equine energy reverberating. So loud these vibrations, that she cannot distinguish what the humans are saying. Men's voices. English accents.

A few gaps now. The horses' pace slowing. The noise disturbance receding to a manageable level. The horses are trotting rather than galloping. The ground is too uneven, the trees too close together. She can make some words out now. Spoken by a familiar voice. Dangerous, violent.

He is speaking of death. He is speaking of fire. He is speaking of plague.

Her tail stiffens, fur bristling. She feels dizzy. Faint. Taking deep breaths to try and slow her heartbeat. She is getting cold. The earth feels damp and is reflecting the fear within her body back at her.

Danger! Danger! Danger!

The alarm call of a blackbird fills the clearing. She shrinks downwards, but the tunnel is blocked by the roots of the tree and she can go no further. She must stay still, stay silent. She knows that death is approaching. The vibrations carry it in their path. The whispering trees talk of nothing else.

She will be its witness. She will be its guide. She will be its catalyst.

A sudden cloud of musk jolts her senses. She is not alone. She scrunches closed her eyes in anticipation of a thunderous blow as a heavy paw cleaves at her shoulder. When no pain materialises, she turns to see his face, less than half a weasel-length from hers. The badger has returned.

TWENTY-FIVE

Scarred

Monday morning. Logan is up late. Another troubled night's sleep. He sees Marek is in his badger form, hunched at the kitchen table. 'Good morning.' Marek didn't look up and continued his intense scribbling. Logan yawned.

'You still badger this morning then?' Logan asked. Marek grunted.

'You been doing that more these last few days. Not regenerating much at all.'

Marek sighed. Closed his notebook. Revealing the cover which had drawings of trees in red ink. He neatly placed his pen perpendicular to it.

'What you writing?' Logan asked.

'Notes.' Marek's one-word reply.

'Notes?' Logan was by the kettle, leaning on the counter, waiting for it to boil.

'Yeah, notes.'

'About what?' The kettle clicked off.

'Stuff. You know. Stuff that happened.'

'Cool. Can I read it?' Logan was pouring the hot water into

a yellow teapot, adding a heaped teaspoon of loose-leaf Earl Grey.

'When I've finished maybe.'

'When will that be?'

Marek shrugged, pawing the notebook closer to him.

Logan was sitting down now. 'Where's our human?'

'Supermarket. Said he'd be back around ten.' Marek looked up.

'You'll need a strainer with that.'

Logan leant back and picked it off the work surface. He poured out two cups.

A short silence. 'Did you know that it was me and Rosa's feast day on Saturday?' Logan asked quietly.

'Was it?' Marek mumbled.

'Can you believe I missed it? Forgot it completely. I didn't even know what the moon was. Kind of lost track of time, since being here...' Logan paused.

'This is our thirteenth human-day here.' Marek replied.

'27th moon in the fourth month. That was Saturday. Two days ago. The day we took our vows. I can't believe I forgot.' Logan had begun pacing the room. Marek was blowing on his tea to cool it. He didn't say anything to acknowledge Logan's apparent distress.

'You know what I miss the most?' Logan sat back down, his eyes filling with tears. Marek shook his head.

'It's her scent. The way she smells.'

Logan was rocking in his chair.

'Oak trees and moss, you know. With a wee bit of the exotic wild service tree when it was sunny. I just love the way she smells.'

Marek sat motionless, listening to Logan speaking in the present.

'She is such a wise fox. So, so clever.' Logan paused. Exhaling a deep breath.

'She was.' He corrected himself.

'She walked with a slight limp, you know, her back left paw. Had a near miss with a car when she was a cub. Her fur was the brightest red you'd ever seen. Like a glorious midsummer sunset. And her eyes. Oh god, her eyes, you could simply dive in and swim in them. And her voice, she was so sexy and joyous. Every time she spoke, I'd feel it here.' Logan clenched his fist and thumped it against his heart, twice.

Marek leant forward. His eyes locked on Logan. Paws still wrapped round his cup from which he had barely sipped.

'I should have fought harder, Marek. I should have tried harder. But I couldn't get my legs to work. I couldn't stand. I could not stand up. There were eight of them, eight men and four dogs. They had guns. This was not like the old paintings or stories. This was a different type of hunt. They were all in black. Not red. No ceremony, no drama. Just pure evil. I was on my knees, crawling, watching. Just pathetic I was. When she needed me the most I let her down. I was trying to work out what was going on, but my brain wasn't fast enough. I just froze. Not like her – she knew, she realised straight away.'

Logan was back on his feet. Marek's gaze followed him as he paced.

'It's still inside of me. Every time I close my eyes I see her. See her being ripped apart by the dogs. Every time I close my eyes, I hear her screaming. I see her dying. But at least she fought, at least she tried. And all the time, one of the men was just laughing. And I did nothing. I let them kill Rosa.'

'They'd drugged you, Logan, tranquillised you. The same happened to me. That's why you couldn't stand. It's not you being weak, its them having the ammunition to do us harm.' Marek spoke quietly, confidently.

'It's still inside me.' Logan wept. 'Still inside of me.'

He looked up. His eyes wearied with tears. He looked older. Exhausted. Marek was upright now, on his back paws. He leant forward to touch Logan's shoulder. Logan clasped onto him, gripping Marek in a powerful embrace. Logan began sobbing, and as he sobbed a strange guttural noise came from his throat. And then he howled. A wolf-like howl. Marek said nothing, did nothing except hold him there, letting him grieve.

'It's her scream. Her scream, it's still there. It won't go away. It won't go away. That's the worst of all this. The worst of anything.'

After a few moments, Logan stood back and wiped away a mixture of snot and tears with his sleeve. The air in the room hung still, as if frozen in sadness. 'And now look at me – I am a fucking freak. Not fox anymore, a pretend human. I just want to be me again. To be with Rosa. To be real. I don't know what they wanted to make, but I am a freak. I hate everything about me and I wish it would all stop and go away.'

He was pacing around now, getting louder, angrier. 'The things they did to us, Marek. What were they wanting? Why did they make us suffer like we did? What were they trying to achieve? And why then just burn down everything? That fire was no accident. The bird had warned us that it was coming. She knew it was coming. That's the only reason we are not dead like the rest. But I don't know if it was worth it. If we had not been better off dying. At least then I could be with Rosa.'

Marek waited till Logan finally came to a stop. He pointed at a scar on his paw. A scar shaped like a horseshoe. And clawing at Logan's sleeve, he revealed a similar scar. 'She knew the fire was coming. The starling warned us. That's why we removed the beads. That's why they couldn't find us, how we got away.' He paused.

'Don't you see, Logan. This was meant to be. This is our destiny, our fate. You are important, you are more important than you realise. More important than Rosa could ever have imagined. You can make her proud again. You can make yourself believe again. But to do so, you have to start fighting back.'

'That's what my notes are about. Finding a way we can restore things to the way they should be. It's not easy, but you are going to have to be brave, you are going to have to stop crying and start fighting. For Rosa, you can be brave for Rosa, Logan.'

Logan was back at the table. His body scrunched into a curved ball of tension, his hands clasped over his nose in a prayer-like pose.

'The badger and the fox
Escaped from the lab.
They are on the run
From something really bad.
They... they... they.'

Logan paused. Marek was no longer listening. He was back with his notebook. Scribbling. Writing fast. An intense, but troubled air surrounding him.

TWENTY-SIX

Rough ride

Three weeks. Not a single sighting. Chilcoat had been wrong to wait. He shouldn't have listened to them. Should have followed his instincts.

Cautious, they were all too fucking cautious. Pathetic. Not like her. She never hesitated. Never compromised. Knew what she wanted and just achieved it. At least now Crull had finally agreed. Smoothed the way through Cabinet. The cull plans could kick in properly at last. The problem was the trail was ice-cold. In desperate need of some heat.

Chilcoat's body ached and he winced as he bent down to undo his shoelaces. The ride yesterday was longer, faster than he had been used to. A *hack*, that's what Crull called it. Not the type of hack Chilcoat was used to. He was back in his hotel suite. Waiting for his lunchtime date with Suzanne. Glancing at his watch. Still ten minutes until she arrived. Time to slip into something more comfortable.

Harry had booked him onto Tuesday's sleeper train. He would get to Glasgow at 7am on Wednesday, giving him plenty of time to prepare for the press conference. First though, a little celebration. Toasting the good news that the path had finally been cleared. The home secretary, the PM and of course, the environment secretary all on board with his fox-plague plans.

After Suzanne, a free evening at last. He had the children's photos ready. To show her. Check again with her which ones to use. Chilcoat folded his shirt neatly before placing it in the laundry basket. He changed into his favourite bathrobe. Closing the door to the bedroom quarters, he fiddled momentarily with the dimmer switch to get the right level of light. Time to turn off the phone. He did not want to be disturbed.

He was checking that all he needed was in place. Whisky. Glasses. Ice. A Bloody Mary for Suzanne. The remote control for the screen was next to the bed. He wouldn't lower it yet. Wait until she was here.

Last time it was Rejoice. 'Just rejoice at that news.' 25th April 1982. Today it was St Francis of Assisi. May 4th 1979. How remarkable that it was now almost thirty-four years since that wonderful day. He'd watched it a dozen times this week already. Today's viewing would be special though. A real treat. Already cued up. No need to check the audio levels again.

A knock at the door. Suzanne was early. Great.

TWENTY-SEVEN

The truth
is out there

The broadband in the library wasn't the fastest, but as she was the only one using a computer, it wasn't as bad as it could've been. It was 5am, not long before the cleaner would be in. Her eyes were tired, she wasn't used to reading so many words. Her beak ached from the tap, tap, tapping on the touchscreen.

Largs library wasn't quite where you'd expect to find a library. Tucked down a dead-end side street, next to a garage. But the lack of passers-by had made it easier for her observations to go unnoticed.

She returned to Saltcoats each night to roost. The wire meshing under the footbridge the closest she had to a home, at least for now. But the last three days she'd been outside the library during the day, preparing for this night's work.

The library closed at 7pm on Tuesdays. She could have ten to twelve hours uninterrupted access before the cleaner came in the next morning. Getting into the library undetected was the easy part. She was, after all, very familiar by now with the librarian's routine for locking up.

Each night, the same twenty-five-second delay between the alarm code being entered and the warning beeps coming to an end. Each night the same code: 73209c. Entered on the panel to the right of the ladies' toilet. Each night the women double-locked the front door and lowered the roller shutter whilst chatting about the meals they would cook that night, the TV programmes they would watch.

She had chanted the alarm code so many times, there was no chance she would forget it. She'd practised the tapping pattern she would need to use on a nearby rowan tree. Yesterday, she had risen at first light to be in place ready to watch the cleaner opening up, reassuring herself that the alarm code was the same for turning off as it was for on.

Darting in just as the last customer left through the automatic doors, she had hidden herself behind the taller of the two leaflet racks. The librarians locking up were on automatic pilot, not expecting anyone to be hiding overnight, least of all a starling. They had already checked the toilets, community room and computer suite for any stragglers. They locked up and locked her in exactly as she planned. By the time she had counted to 333 they would be well on their way home to their respective husbands, children and cats.

Although she had held her breath as she tapped in the alarm code to turn it off, her preparation had worked. She had the library, and more importantly, the computers, to herself.

Her first task, turning the computer on, was easy. Pressing the on-switch with her beak. She'd chosen the one with the touchscreen but would use the keyboard if her neck muscles ached from stretching up to the screen. Next, the password.

Four digits. Easy. The numbers came to her in an instant. The last four from the library card she had found on the beach: 0804. Now the altogether harder challenge, trying to piece together some of the jigsaw, the links between the Nobler Age Food poster she saw at Saltcoats station and the laboratory that burnt down.

She had surmised that the lab was probably within a one or two-day flight radius of Saltcoats. Before she arrived in Saltcoats, she had flown little more than a handful of starling territories each day. And that wasn't always in the same direction. She couldn't have travelled that far from the scene of the fire.

So to the internet. First up, searching Google Maps and Google Earth for any clues as to the lab's location. It did not show up on any map. She tried different websites and search engines but drew blank after blank. According to the public face of the internet, the laboratory did not exist.

She tried approaching things from another angle, looking instead at animal rights activity in the area. There had always been strong rumours in the aviary that someone would come and rescue them. She searched more than two dozen Scottish animal rights sites, reading their Facebooks, press releases, blog posts and discussion forums. Not a single mention.

She was tired. In need of a break. One last search. A Facebook page. A directory of community campaigns. Nothing under animal rights she hadn't already looked up. There was however, one picture which caught her eye. An environmental awards ceremony. October 2012. Two people collecting the award. The photo. Her hair. Long, straight. Black, but speckled with green. She looked familiar. The woman on the platform. The one on the beach. The artist. Could it be her?

After searching for what seemed an age, she found a memory stick behind the reception counter and at the fifth attempt managed to insert it into the USB port. She downloaded the woman's photo, saving it both as a JPEG and PDF. It was gone midnight. She took a break, flying twice around the library to stretch her wings.

The next task: researching news items around the date of the fire. Monday 8th April. There was only one story in town that week: the death of Margaret Thatcher. She found herself absorbed in the coverage and the polarised views. The sheer volume of newsprint. How could the death of one old woman provoke so much coverage, but the murder of hundreds of animals go unreported? Another fly round the library, this time anti-clockwise. She snacked on half a digestive biscuit she found in one of the bins. It was gone 3am. She was running out of time.

Her last search. Tapping in carefully: n-o-b-l-e-r-a-g-e-f-o-o-d-s.

The company had a website that consisted of a single holding page. Containing no information other than:

Nobler Age Foods – there is no such thing as food poverty.

No contact number, no email, no mission statement or description of what the company was about. Nothing.

Next, she tried Twitter. Using variations of the hashtag *#nobleragefoods* – all produced the same results. Nothing official from the company. Just thousands upon thousands of people speculating and guessing what this new advertising gimmick was all about. She was getting anxious. The muscles around her beak were beginning to spasm from the endless tapping of the screen. She couldn't face having to do all this again, but still she was drawing blank after blank.

She tried a different search term. Tapping in carefully to get the spelling right first time:

w-h-a-t-i-s-t-h-e-l-i-n-k-b-e-t-w-e-e-n-n-o-b-l-e-r-a-g-e-f-o-o-d-s-a-n-d-m-a-r-g-a-r-e-t-t-h-a-t-c-h-e-r?

She followed a link to Modern Marketing Mayhem that appeared first in the Google list. It was a site analysing trends in social media and advertising, going under the strapline *MMM interesting*. A blog entry published two days ago documented the sudden and unexplained arrival of Nobler Age Foods and had already attracted just under 1400 comments, many of which mentioned first seeing the adverts on the day of Thatcher's funeral.

Skimming as fast as she could through these comments, she grew weary of the lame attempts at humour. A minority were serious, drawing parallels with past viral campaigns and analysing the psychological impacts of repeated exposure to subliminal messaging. It was well past 4am when she reached comment number 1263 – posted under the username *thetruthisoutthere* from Bristol: 'Glad to see MMM finally shining a light on NAF. If you want to know more about them look up their recently-formed parent company MTL Ltd. Dangerous times ahead. Be careful what you eat.'

She took a screenshot of the post and saved it onto her memory stick. She read a dozen or more comments that immediately followed, but nobody had responded directly to *thetruthisoutthere*, carrying on instead a previous discussion about how viral campaigns often end up being an anticlimax when the product was actually revealed.

Opening up a new tab she looked up *thetruthisoutthere* but found nothing related to Bristol. Just a lot of blogs about aliens and UFOs, most of which seemed to be based in South Carolina or Dakota.

Returning to MMM's website, she scrolled back to comment 1263 and squawked angrily. The post had been removed, replaced with *Inappropriate Comment – removed due to breach of posting guidelines.* She opened up the file on her USB stick.

'Sweet feather of starling.' She swore. The file had been locked for editing and wouldn't open. Her whole screen froze. She pecked anxiously at the keyboard. Holding her claw and beak down together she pressed CTRL ALT DEL and managed to reboot, but when she returned to her USB stick there was no trace of the file from *thetruthisoutthere.* She cawed again in frustration, flapping angrily at the screen as it froze.

Your session has timed out – please talk to a member of staff scrolled slowly from right to left across her display.

After more fruitless tapping, she abandoned her machine and booted up the computer next to hers. This one wasn't touchscreen, and much slower. Impatiently pecking at the keyboard, she entered the login details incorrectly four times before finally getting back online. She had less than half an hour left.

She went straight to the MMM website, or she tried. It had gone. Not appearing in Google nor when she entered the domain name. It just came up with a DNS server error. But she remembered the company name that *thetruthisoutthere* had referenced, so she went to the Companies House website. Nine companies had registered with some variation of MTL Ltd in the last year:

Michael Thomas Linklater
Modern Technology Limited
Macdonald Temple Lustgarden

Making Time Last
Mary Thompson Lord
MT London
MT Liverpool
Max Tech Live
Margaret Thatcher Lives.

It was the ninth one which grabbed her attention. Maybe, at last, she had found something. Without a credit card to pay the admin fee, the information she could get was basic:

Company Registration date: 9.4.2013

Company Directors: no annual statement yet submitted

Registered Address: 2-6 North Parade Grantham

Company Description: Not available.

She found MTL's website. Again, a simple holding page. The graphic MTL in large block capitals, underlined, with a smaller font message: *website under construction, check back soon.* She looked again. The underline, this wasn't a straight line. Tapping on *zoom*, she went to magnification of 300. 'Sweet feather of starling!'

Opening another tab, she clicked again on Nobler Age Foods. The same underline.

The two lines were identical. She traced the shape with her beak.

Shaking her head, she squawked out words that at first she didn't recognise. Human words. In human tongue.

'Is there anybody else? Is there anybody else?'

She would look up one more thing – train times to Grantham – before deleting her search history and logging out.

TWENTY-EIGHT

Mutant soup

I was feeling relaxed. I'd gotten used to their company. I say *their*, but it was mainly Logan. We were in the kitchen, working our way through recipes. 'I'm surprised, that, you know, a former fox would like vegetables so much.' I spoke loudly over the whirr of the handheld blender.

'I'm still a fox. Underneath this pinky human skin it's still me. Logan Fox. It's just whilst I'm like this I don't fancy eating meat anymore.'

'And Marek?'

Logan shrugged.

'Is he happy as a vegetarian?' The mixer had finished and we spoke now at normal volume.

'I guess so,' Logan replied, adding a teaspoon of mustard to the leek and potato soup.

'Really? All he seems to do is scribble in that notebook of his. He's asked me to buy him another one as he's running out of pages.'

'Well, it's not easy adjusting to things.'

'Hashtag *mutantbadgerblues*,' I said, trying to lighten the mood.

Logan didn't respond.

'Soup looks great. You having a bowl now?'

'I'm not hungry,' Logan muttered.

'Are you sure?'

'I'm not hungry.' He headed into the living room and slumped onto the sofa.

I watched as he picked a magazine off the coffee table, put it down and then picked it back up again. I sat down next to him. 'I'm sorry. Bad joke. Shouldn't have said it.'

Silence. Logan continued to stare at the magazine.

'What you reading?'

He turned it over so I could see the cover. BBC Wildlife Magazine. An old edition, an article with a large picture of a badger. And a headline that read, '*Meles meles* – national treasure or farmer's nightmare? Your questions answered on the badger cull.'

'You sure you don't want some soup?'

Logan shook his head.

'I've got a headache. Going to lie down. Will eat something later. You have some if you want.'

TWENTY-NINE

Press conference

Chilcoat sat at the back, close to the exit. The press conference was about to start. Farringdon Crull MP, the main attraction, rose to his feet.

Fifty-nine years old. Made his fortune in the City, before turning late to politics. Elected in 2010, for the last six months Crull had served as environment secretary in the coalition government. Already gotten himself a reputation as a political bruiser. A hard man of the right, with little time for his Liberal Democrat coalition partners. Less time still for anything to do with the environment.

Let's see what you are made of, Mr Crull, thought Chilcoat, leaning back with an insouciant grin.

As always Crull was dressed immaculately. A navy-blue suit, a white-and-grey pin-striped shirt and dark maroon tie. He stood behind a lectern, in front of a blue screen. As he prepared to speak, the screen was filled with a single close-up image of a fox's face. Drawing a deep breath, he began. 'Ladies and gentlemen, thank you for coming here today at such short notice.'

Chilcoat half-listened to the preamble, instead scanning the room to see which journalists were here. A good turnout. Crull was done with the niceties. Here we go. The meat on the bones.

'In the last two weeks, eight children across the UK have been attacked by *Vulpes vulpes*, the red fox, the red menace.'

Chilcoat leant forward. That phrase had been his final addition to the speech. *The red menace.* He liked it.

'Six children remain in hospital, four of them critical. A seventh was discharged yesterday after surgery to amputate free fingers.' Chilcoat nodded in approval. Crull was speaking slowly, sticking to the script. No emotion, letting the words do the talking, even though he still couldn't pronounce 'th' properly.

'I am very sad to have to report the death of a two-year-old girl from this fine city of Glasgow. Rhianna died at just after 23.00 hours last night. She had been attacked by free foxes on Monday 28th April at 13.15 hours, whilst playing on the patio of her grandparents' house. Despite the best and most determined medical care, she was just too badly injured, too small, to pull frough.'

The image on the screen behind Crull had changed to the face of a beaming girl. Freckled skin, strawberry-blonde hair, with two pink ribbons struggling to contain a mass of curly ringlets. She was such a beautiful girl, enough to suck the air out of the whole auditorium. The Great Lady had chosen well, picked out the best ones from the photos he had shown her. Crull continued. He seemed to be enjoying himself.

'I know that people will be surprised to learn at this late stage of this sequence of events, but after the first attack in Bristol, the family requested total privacy. This understandable desire to be left alone was shared by the families in Manchester, Liverpool, London and the four families from the Glasgow and Clyde Valley area. That was until last night, when brave Rhianna lost her battle for life.' The screen was changing again. The left-hand side filling with photos of young children; smiling, happy faces; the right side showing close ups of bite marks, ripped flesh, bloodstained bandages.

'The families have given their blessing to release the following details of those affected by the red fox attacks. They are Tommy, aged free; Helen, aged four and Alison, aged five, all from Glasgow and Clyde; Theresa, aged free from Liverpool; Courtney, aged free from Bristol; Henry, aged two from London; and Elsa, aged free from Manchester.' Chilcoat was impressed. Crull was effing delivering.

'We are making news of this red menace public today because of updated advice received by our chief veterinary scientist.' The screen had switched back to the close up of *Vulpes vulpes*. 'I will summarise this advice but am pleased that we have with us today the chief scientist himself. He will be happy to take more technical questions at the end of my statement.'

Franklyn Whitlock, a silver-haired man in his late fifties, with a large white moustache and half-moon glasses, rose to his feet to Crull's right, acknowledged his introduction, then sat back down.

'Good old Frank,' whispered Chilcoat. 'Always so amenable in a crisis.'

Crull continued.

'Our scientists have been working round the clock to look into explanations and exploring solutions for such an unprecedented wave of attacks. Doing so, I must say with unlimited resources at their disposal. Thanks to their hard work, professionalism and dedication to public safety, they have revealed to us the nature of the freat we now face.'

Crull paused. Chilcoat counted. *One, two, three, four, five.* Good lad, he was doing exactly what he was told.

'Tests were carried out after each of the attacks, gathering saliva samples from the children's wounds.' Another pause. This time not as long. 'There is an anomaly. A mutation. A pattern to each and every one of these attacks. A deviation in the red fox's chromosome that is changing their behaviour. There is a clear and substantial danger of further fatalities in the days to come.'

A murmur of disquiet. Hands up in front of him. Questions being shouted from the floor. The journos were getting excited. Crull raised his right hand, holding his palm out. Waiting until he had absolute quiet again. 'Sorry, I'll be happy to take questions in a few minutes when I have finished my prepared statement.

I repeat. There is a clear and substantial danger of further fatalities in the days to come. It is also clear that Glasgow and the surrounding Clyde Valley remains the area at highest risk of attack.'

Chilcoat stood up. He had heard and seen enough. The first batch of Nobler Age Foods was due to be delivered that afternoon, and he wanted to greet it in person. He slipped unnoticed out of the room.

THIRTY

What's cooking?

Logan was in the kitchen making breakfast. Marek stood in the doorway in his human form. Notebook in his hand, pen behind his ear.

'What's up?' Logan asked. Marek shrugged.

'You been writing again?' Marek gripped his notepad close to him.

'When you going to let us have a read?' Again, Marek shrugged.

'The badger could be a good writer,
if only his mood got lighter.'

Marek didn't reply. Instead, started to rub at his nose, pinching it with thumb and forefinger.

'Oh no, Marek, don't you change now. Breakfast is nearly ready. You know you're not so good with a knife and fork when you are a badger, and besides, you'll only have to change back to get on the bus to the big city.' Marek stopped rubbing but stayed silent.

'The fox and the badger,
Going on a bus to Glasgow,

Looking for clues, looking for truth,
Looking high, looking low,
And finding things out – somehow.'

Marek sighed.

'Logan.' His voice dripped with weariness.

'What?'

'Do you ever shut up and think?'

'Not often. I'm an action kind of fox. Never really got on with thinking. Although I didn't think Blake would ever agree to us going with him to the May Day protest.'

'And *why* do you think he did that?'

'Cos he could see we've become stir crazy cooped up in here for over fourteen moons.'

'You don't think that it could be a trap and the police will be waiting for us as soon as we arrive in Glasgow?'

'You can't say that, Marek, after all he's done for us. He was all lonesome and lost before we arrived. And we have restored his va-va-voom. He's so much happier now than he was. And besides, he's not sneaky enough to try and trap us like that.'

Marek was no longer listening but wrinkling his nostrils in an exaggerated sniffing motion.

'Toast, Logan. Your toast is burning.'

THIRTY-ONE

May Day, May Day

Logan's breakfast was delicious, the mess in the kitchen less so. He'd used just about every saucepan, and the whole work surface was stained with coffee grounds, crushed garlic peel and cherry tomato juice. I left the two of them in the living room, whilst I pondered what to clean first. Marek called after me, 'We'll miss the bus if you are not quick.'

'We'll get the next one, Marek, don't worry,' I shouted back.

I heard footsteps and the sound of a door slamming. Marek, I was learning, liked to be very punctual, if not somewhat obsessively early. If I said dinner was at 7pm, he would be sat at the table at 6.30. It had been a mistake to say we could catch a specific bus. He'd be sulking now. He'd been quite moody the last few days. I made a start on scrubbing burnt garlic off the hob.

I was having serious doubts about the wisdom of taking the two of them to the May Day rally. The idea had slipped out in conversation the previous night and then, lo and behold, we had a plan for our first trip to the city. Logan had insisted that a big breakfast would set us up nicely. His poached egg with garlic-infused cherry tomatoes on rye toast, followed by grilled mushrooms filled with crispy halloumi chunks in a rosemary drizzle was sublime. But I would have been happier with a bowl of muesli and a tidier kitchen.

I hoped that, on their first outing, being in a large crowd would keep them anonymous. But I had my doubts, my serious doubts about whether I could trust them to behave as humans should behave in public.

I'd take my time cleaning up. If it meant we missed the next bus, then so be it. Logan poked his head through the kitchen door. 'It's part of the creative process, you know, making a mess,' he huffed. 'You don't enjoy a Da Vinci painting, but then complain that his studio isn't immaculate.' Then he disappeared again.

Great. Now the two of them were pissed with me.

I heard the 11.05am bus rumbling past outside, and then the sound of TV channels being hopped in the sitting room. I turned on the radio, flicking from 6 Music to 5 Live. The same voice on the radio as on the TV. It was only when the sink was full and the taps turned off, that I could actually hear what was being said.

A man I soon found out to be Environment Secretary Farringdon Crull speaking in a rather hushed tone. 'The family of Rhianna have asked me to read out this short statement: "Rhianna was our princess, our angel, the magic fairy dust that sprinkled sunshine into our hearts. She made us laugh every time we held her in our arms. We will never hold her again and now our world is full of tears. At this terrible time, we need to be left alone to grieve and to comprehend what has happened."

"We urge everyone to be vigilant, and not to approach any foxes and to leave it to the government experts to bring this freat under control. Rhianna leaves behind a four-month-old baby brother and we will hold him that bit tighter until the freat has been eliminated. We are heartbroken but drawing strength from the love of those around us and we are determined that no other family will have to suffer like we have".'

I heard Logan shout from the hallway. 'Marek, get your badger arse in here and take a look at this!'

Two minutes later. The three of us sat frozen on the sofa, watching in silence. Time going so slowly. The press conference finished, and the programme cut to a studio. Four white men in dark suits, with grave expressions on their faces.

Logan stood up. 'I'm not listening to this a moment longer.' Flailing behind the TV, he started yanking out cables and wires until everything went quiet.

'This is about us, isn't it? This is about us.'

Neither Marek nor I replied. Logan sat back down, his head in his hands. I wasn't sure if he was crying.

It was Marek who spoke next. 'What time is the next bus to Glasgow?'

'The next one is at 12.15. Gets us in for lunchtime,' I said.

'I'll help you finish clearing the kitchen,' Marek replied.

As I put away the last saucepan, Marek stared right at me.

'We both need mobile phones and someone is going to have to show us how to use a computer.'

'My friend Mike. He's good on IT. He'll be there today.'

Logan had wandered in. He leant awkwardly against the back of the door. Marek continued, his voice flat and monotonous.

'We need more than a couple of hours to get to the bottom of this. How about we stop over somewhere in the city? Give us the chance to do more digging. You got any friends we could stay with, Blake?'

'I haven't been out much, since, you know, my gran died, and Mandy left me. It may be a bit short notice to impose ourselves.'

'A hotel then, reliable Wi-Fi. Somewhere central, easy to get about.'

Thirty minutes later, the three of us were stood with a small overnight bag at the bus stop. A booking made for a family suite at the Alexander Thomson Hotel next to Central Station. Logan was chatting away, reciting a shopping list out loud. Marek was more subdued, lost in his own thoughts.

We'd already been at the bus stop for five minutes. Marek had made us come out early and wait. He was reading the timetable, for the third time now.

'You two need a backstory, something we can say to people who ask how we know each other,' I said.

Logan nodded.

'Well, any ideas?'

Logan shrugged. It was Marek who answered first.

'We're second cousins of your ex. You hadn't met us before as we lived a long way away. We've come over to research our family tree and spend some time to get to know the man our cousin loved.'

'Connemara,' blurted Logan. 'I saw a travel programme on it yesterday. Looked nice. Fairly remote though, so that's why we can't use computers. Not got any broadband where we are from.'

I was about to point out that they mostly speak Gaelic there, though, when the bus appeared in the distance. A single decker bus; blue and yellow with a white stripe.

'Here it comes' said Logan.

'The bus is coming. Soon we will embark on the next leg of our journey,' added Marek, in a surprisingly good Irish accent.

And so we boarded the bus to Glasgow. A bus emblazoned on one side with the company's name, logo and messages about free Wi-Fi and comfortable seats. And a large advert on the other side which contained just three words, black font on a pale-blue background:

Nobler Age Foods

The words were underlined with a slightly squiggly line. As we pulled off, a single male blackbird flew onto the top of the bus stop and sounded an alarm call. A call that he would repeat three times.

THIRTY-TWO

There is no museum

Queen Street Station, Glasgow. Not a patch on Central Station, she thought. And harder for her to be anonymous, given how much smaller it was. Raven saw a group of tourists carrying matching shiny silver suitcases and takeaway coffee cups. They were lingering on the platform, speaking in a language she couldn't understand. Their drinks were giving off wafts of cinnamon and nutmeg.

Only six minutes until the train would depart. They were boarding very slowly. This was her chance. She hopped in amongst them and a few seconds later she was on. She tucked herself in at the back of the luggage rack. Hiding in the small gap between the plastic shelving and side wall. It was dark and claustrophobic.

It was almost 300 miles to Grantham. Three, perhaps four or even five sun's worth of flight. Going by train was much faster, but also instinctively what she felt she should do. She stood rigidly still. Not listening to the insincere announcements. She needed to change trains at Edinburgh Waverley and Newark Northgate.

She disembarked without being spotted but took a while to find her bearings at Waverley. The platform numbering didn't seem logical, and building works meant there was a constant drilling and banging. She still landed at platform six with time to spare though. For this, the longest leg, of her journey she needed a better hiding place, otherwise the cramp in her wings would become unbearable.

She used the same tactic again. Following a group of people carrying both luggage and coffee cups, her ability to go unnoticed aided by a malfunctioning computerised seat reservation system. Something that seemed to grip the passengers with either indignation or indecision.

Rather than head to the luggage rack, she went directly towards the disabled toilet. She tapped the green button with her beak. The door opened in an elegant arc, and after a few breaths, swished back closed again. After the confines of her previous journey the toilet was luxuriously spacious. She celebrated with five quick clockwise circuits of the cubicle. Although the door was closed, it wasn't locked and after her final lap, she tapped the red padlock button, before sitting back down on the sink to rest. Memorising the train calling points and times, she mulled over her options for what to do when she arrived at her destination. A tiredness was sweeping over her. The stress of her first experience of train travel beginning to take its toll. She closed her eyes.

A loud banging startled her back awake. She did not know how long she had been asleep. A man shouting. Angry. Impatient.

'Is there anybody in there? Come on out! You can't stay in there forever.'

The ticket inspector, she surmised.

'It's been occupied since Edinburgh, more than half an hour ago.' This time an older woman. Posh English accent.

'I've got a pass key, so if I don't get a response, I'll open the door manually,' said the ticket inspector, banging more loudly. 'I'll give you five seconds to come out.'

She heard a fumbling of keys and the sound of a lock turning. The toilet door was starting to open. Leaping up from inside the sink, she looked urgently for another safe place to hide. Pressing herself tightly against the base of the wall to the right of the toilet. She wished herself invisible.

'I pay my fares, so why shouldn't everyone else? Young people today.' The woman's self-righteous tone even more annoying now the door was open. The two of them had stepped inside the toilet.

'Nobody here.' The inspector sounded disappointed by the lack of opportunity for confrontation. 'I'm going to have to put the *out of order* sign on. That door shouldn't have done that. Don't want some poor bugger getting locked in and missing his stop.'

He dragged the door shut manually, but before he could lock it with his master key, Raven was up again and tapping frantically on the red padlock symbol with her beak.

'See, that shouldn't happen either.' The man sounded a little confused. 'I'll report it, but I doubt the engineer will get on board before Peterborough. Sorry, madam, but there's another toilet next to Carriage B, that way.' She heard the woman huff and her heels clicking away down the corridor.

Peterborough was further south than Grantham, Raven would have alighted before the engineer arrived. She was safe until her next change at Newark. She could relax.

Her final train was less busy. What few passengers there were glued to their phones. Their faces lit by a fluorescent shade of blue that she found cold and alien. They didn't notice her as she perched at the back of the luggage rack. The journey was brief and without incident.

Disembarking at Grantham, she stretched out her wings with glee. It was good to be outside again. She was struck at how small the station was compared to what she'd imagined. The air currents here felt unfamiliar too. It was just under a mile to the North Parade. Almost in a straight line south. Her memory of the street map she'd googled at the library still vivid. It didn't take her long to find it.

It wasn't what was there that surprised her, rather what wasn't. The place that Margaret Thatcher was born. Yet all there was to mark it was a small blue plaque more than halfway up the wall:

BIRTHPLACE OF THE RT. HON. Margaret Thatcher,
M.P. FIRST WOMAN PRIME MINISTER OF GREAT
BRITAIN AND NORTHERN IRELAND.

She hung around on the pavement with a total sense of anticlimax. Reading the plaque for the ninth time. What used to be Thatcher's family grocers' shop was now a chiropractic clinic and natural therapy centre. If it wasn't for the sign, there would be no way of knowing that she had lived there.

She wasn't the only one disappointed. Two American tourists, bedecked with expensive camera equipment, were talking loudly to a young female shop assistant. The young woman's hair was bright green and she spoke in an accent that Raven now recognised as Polish.

'That's right, she lived here as a child. But she hadn't lived here for a long time. There is a blue plaque, but they didn't want anything bigger, as it would be likely damaged.'

'I don't understand. In what way would it be damaged?' The man was loud, persistent. His camera bounced up and down on his belly as he spoke.

'Well, not everyone was a fan, you know. Anything more prominent and it would just be trashed.'

'So there must be a Thatcher museum in the town, right?'

'She hasn't got her own museum, but there's a few things in the town museum apparently.'

'A few things?'

'*Spitting Image* puppet, school records, heart of the devil, that kind of thing, you know?'

'Gravestone?'

'Not in Grantham.'

'Walking tour?'

'Not that I know of.'

'Oh, so what is there may I ask?'

'This is it.'

'No, no, no, there must be something else.'

'I am terribly sorry, sir, but I have to get on with my work. I only came out to check on the window display. There is a small tourist office in the Guildhall. I am sure they would be happy to answer any questions you have.' And that was that. After taking photos of the plaque from multiple angles the couple finally left.

Raven had wasted her time too. Travelled all this way, but still no further forward. Flying up on top of the shop she looked down on the pedestrianised area beneath her. Diagonally opposite her was a bus stop, the left-hand side of which displayed an all too familiar sign: **Nobler Age Foods.**

Flapping back to the other side of the eaves, her gaze was drawn to two other identical adverts. A large billboard near the roundabout and, closer to her, a black taxicab whose rear doors were painted with the black font on pale-blue background. The text underlined with that familiar squiggle.

She felt dizzy. For a moment she was back in her cell. The walls, all painted white except for a blue and black squiggly line across the middle of the back wall. Like a hospital heart monitor. Like an omnipresent cardiogram.

She jumped down from the roof and landed back on the pavement. And, for the first time, she saw what she had come for. It had been obscured from view by the two Americans. But now they had gone, it was clear to see. Above the roller shutter. On the first-floor window. Three words on a sticker, written in black on a pale-blue background: **Margaret Thatcher Lives.**

THIRTY-THREE

A perfect
orchestration

Chilcoat's phone was turned off. The media frenzy after the press conference had exceeded even his expectations. Trending globally on Twitter were the hashtags *#foxplague, #redmenace* and *#forrhianna.*

The car stopped at traffic lights. Chilcoat was listening to the audio of his meeting with Crull at the hunt. The day after his birthday. He knew the key exchanges off by heart now, but he never grew tired of hearing his own voice speaking such wisdom.

'It will be good sport, Farringdon and completely logical. Target the red menace and not the nocturnal badger. Maximise fear and panic. Create the conditions for an increase in armed police. A big military presence. Report every fox sitting down to have a shit to a national hotline. Flush the fucker out.'

Chilcoat smiled. Crull didn't know he was recording all their conversations. Of course he didn't. Crull thought they were equals. The fool. He knew so little, but it was proving advantageous to have a reliable fool inside the Cabinet.

Armed police on the streets of Glasgow, Liverpool and Bristol. The three cities he detested the most. The three most un-Thatcher-like cities. Glasgow and Liverpool drowning in the spittle of their trade unions and Bristol deranged with its hippy green chic.

Despite all the computer analysis, the crux of it came down to a hunch he had. He just knew that the fox and badger had stayed together. Let the public find the fox and the badger would not be far away. The car was picking up speed again. He turned his attention to checking the latest press briefing, being prepared for the lunchtime bulletins.

He wanted them alive. Wanted the opportunity to question them, torture them, dissect them. And then when their humiliation was complete, dispose of them himself. He needed to get a message out in the press to make sure that they would be taken alive. Key phrases would be repeated throughout the briefing: 'Don't approach. Don't kill.' 'Leave it to the army.' 'We need them alive to find out what has gone wrong.'

Phrases backed up by Rhianna's 'family': 'We have felt so much love and so much fear that we have been compelled to issue another statement. Due to our own loss and need to grieve, this will be our last public comment until after little Rhianna is laid to rest. Above all else we do not want any other family to experience what we have had to endure. We couldn't bear it if another family lost a child. So we wanted to say as loudly as we can: For Rhianna's sake please leave it to the authorities to approach any foxes. The scientists need the foxes alive so that they can do their tests. Report all sightings of foxes and stay safe. It is what we want, it's what Rhianna would want. Thank you.'

He stretched his legs. His chauffeur-driven car purred. Pressing a small button, the armour-plated glass screen between driver and passenger turned an opaque blue.

Pulling out his phone, he flicked open his photo collection. Bringing up his favourite. The one he had taken with the Great Lady two days after the miners' strike had ended. Drinking champagne at the Ritz. The glasses half-full, their eyes locked. Sparkling champagne, sparkling eyes. Their mouths just inches from each other's. Her lipstick. His lips. The slight crease in her blouse. Her hand holding the shaft of her champagne flute. He could smell her still. Feel her almost.

The car had slowed. Looking out of the window, he saw that the new sign that he had commissioned had now been installed. It looked good.

There is no such thing as food poverty.

THIRTY-FOUR

Strange fruit

We were walking out of Buchanan Bus Station when Marek announced, 'Let's give May Day a miss. It's too risky. The place will be swarming with police and we need to keep a low profile.'

Logan concurred. 'It's like turkeys voting for Christmas.'

I was disappointed by their sudden change of heart. Normally it was me, Blake Hardie, who was the cautious one.

The first stop on our new itinerary was a mobile phone shop. Here, Logan flirted outrageously with the red-haired shop assistant – Natalya was her name. Scottish dad, Lithuanian mum. Graduated with a 2:1 English Literature degree from Glasgow University. Decided against becoming a teacher so was doing casual work until she figured out what to do next. And that's only some of what he found out.

Logan's way of coping with the fox-plague was to turn up the volume to maximum. His chattering was non-stop. Everywhere he went he drew attention to himself. Over a lunch of falafel burgers and sweet potato wedges at Stereo, his flirting drew stony stares from both waitresses. 'As likely to succeed as an earthworm mixing cocktails at a blackbird's feast day,' Marek sneered whilst Logan was busy in the gents, preening his hair in the mirror.

Dropping our stuff at the hotel passed off without incident except for Logan's minor hyperventilation in the admittedly slow-moving lift up to our room. We took the stairs on the way back down.

I'd arranged to meet Mike for drinks at five o'clock at Mono. Without the May Day rally we still had a whole afternoon to fill. 'If we were tourists what would we do?' Marek asked me. 'Backstory, detail, we need credibility.'

'I don't know. Maybe go to the tourist office, a gallery, a museum or something.' Ten minutes later in the near empty tourist office on George Square, I was asking the young male assistant for recommendations for my two "Irish cousins" who were visiting.

'Kelvingrove Art Gallery and Museum is really popular and would be my first choice,' he replied, in an Eastern European accent.

'Kelvingrove,' growled Logan, leaning over the counter, almost eyeball to eyeball with him.

'Yes sir.'

'Was that where, you know, the fox came from which killed the little girl?'

'I'm not sure. It's not something I'm fully aware of. I've been at work so haven't heard all the latest news. But the gallery will be perfectly safe, a fox-free zone. And I've been advised that there are extra security measures in the park.'

'Get me a taxi,' Logan snapped, 'from here, to there, now.'

For half an hour we shuffled in near silence around the park. The two of them with their hands in pockets and gazes turned downwards. It was after the second loop when I suggested we go and look at some art in the gallery to help take our minds off things, that Marek said he had a terrible migraine, and wanted to go back to the hotel. He would sleep it off and phone later to meet up. I gave him thirty pounds in cash and a hug before he got into the cab. With a bad nagging feeling, I watched him climb and slump into the back seat.

'What's this Nobler Age Foods?' asked Logan, pointing at the taxi as it turned left onto the main road.

I saw the large advert emblazoned across the whole car.

'I've seen them everywhere. Just wondered what the hype is about.'

'I don't know, Logan, but you are right, they are everywhere.'

We wandered round the gallery, looking at things without looking at things and barely speaking. There wasn't so much an elephant in the room, as a bloody great Tyrannosaurus Rex.

I got takeaway teas from the cafe in the main hall and encouraged Logan back outside to sit on a bench. Not good. Two armed police walked past just as we sat down. Four men in yellow high-vis vests followed shortly behind, handing out A5 flyers with the emergency fox-line number for people to report sightings to.

'Let's go.' I stood up and Logan followed me, before they could reach our bench.

'Look man, I know you're hurting and you're angry, but we can face this together. We'll work it out.'

He turned to me as we walked.

'What's to stop me from just handing myself in to a police station and then everything will go back to normal?'

I was about to give Logan a reassuring hug when my phone rang. It was Mike. Mono was packed and service too slow, we'd be better meeting somewhere else. We settled on the CCA in half an hour. He was on his bike, we would walk over.

'We'd better phone Marek,' I said. He answered on the second ring, sounding awful.

'I'm just going to stay at the hotel. I've already picked up some food so I don't need to go out again.' I offered to come back, but he was insistent. He would sleep away the migraine, and, if feeling better, maybe watch some TV in the room so we could keep up on any developments in the news.

So Logan and I walked up through the park, past the bandstand, the skatepark, through the roses and up past the little cafe where tired-out West-End mums sipped skinny lattes and glanced anxiously at the calories on their plates, whilst their children played sugar-high games of hide and shriek. Crossing over the footbridge, Logan saw for the first time the extent of the M8 which bisected the city. He paused and stared southwards. I stopped a few paces ahead of him, waiting for him to catch up. He didn't follow so I walked back.

'What's up?' I asked gently.

He stayed quiet.

'What's on your mind?'

He sighed. 'I'm thinking, all those cars. Where are they going in such a hurry? Why so many and so fast? And what would happen if I just jumped? Would that be better than going to the police?'

I put my arm around him. 'Don't jump off the bridge Logan. That would be a daft thing to do. And besides I've grown used to having you and Marek about. Would really miss you if you weren't here. Come on. Let's go and have a drink, it will help you relax.'

Introducing Logan Fox to alcohol was a terrible idea, introducing him to my friend Mike even worse. And that's when the day started to go really bad.

The CCA's open mic session finished at midnight.

I'm a fox
In this human body
With a bounty on my head.
I escaped from a secret laboratory,
Now the government wants me dead.
I'm a fox
In this human body,
No, I'm a human
Trapped in a fox.
Some bastard has nicked my tail.
The PM wants to cull me.
But the fucker is bound to fail.
I'm a fox,
I'm a human,
I'm a freak,
A fucking foxy freak.
I've had too much to drink,
And now I'm struggling to speak.
They say that I should do it for hashtag Rhianna,
But nothing rhymes with that.
But if it was a fox that killed her
I'd happily eat my hat.
I'm a fox,
I'm a human,
I believe in a big conspiracy.
They want someone to blame
And that someone is me.

I'm a scapegoat,
I'm a victim.
NO!
I'm a revo-fucking-lutionary.
I'm doing it all for Rosa,
Who sacrificed herself for me.
I don't know what they're after,
Can't remember what they've done,
They ain't got my number,
They cannot find my bum.
I'm a fox,
I'm a friendly fox.
I'll give you a kiss,
But I won't give you a bite.
Don't listen to their lies.
Don't listen to their shite.
My name is Logan Fox.
Thank you very much and good night.'

It was unanimous. First place went to Logan. The other three finalists, all seasoned slammers, smiled with a mix of appreciation for a great performance and resentment at being usurped by a newcomer. I had to get Logan away from this and back to the hotel.

Mike was at the bar, loading up another tray of drinks. Logan was chatting to a woman, a young woman with red hair. She looked familiar. Oh god, that's Natalya, from the mobile phone shop. And they're kissing, more than just a peck. A full-blown snog. I picked up my phone to call a cab, noticing that I had four missed calls. All from Marek – the phone had been left on silent during the performances. The taxi number rang out without being answered. I hung up.

Mike sat back down, passing me a pint of Guinness. I still hadn't touched the last one. Mike Jansen was six inches taller than me. Maybe that's why he could drink so much more without falling over. Dressed in ripped jeans and a faded Clash T-shirt. His nose pierced, John Lennon-style round glasses and unkempt blonde hair. He hadn't changed much in all the years I had known him.

By now Logan was next to the stage, surrounded by people. Correction, surrounded by women. Natalya had her arm around his shoulder and one hand stroking his lower back. The two of them approached our table. Mike gave a big thumbs up.

'You don't mind, if me and erm…'

Logan looked blankly at the woman, whose grin was 42% beer and 58% lust.

'Natalya.' She laughed.

'You don't mind if me and Natalya head off to a little party she knows about? It's not often a country fox like me gets a big day out in the city.'

Mike chipped in before I could reply. 'Cool, I love parties. I'll neck this and Mr Lively here' – he pointed at me – 'can go back to the hotel to check on our migrainey cousin, leaving me and Mr Fantastic Fox to head off to the party.'

Logan shook his head. 'Afraid not. This is a very private party. What did you call it, Natalya?' Natalya blushed slightly as she whispered into Logan's ear.

'Apparently, I can't tell you that as it's a little bit rude. But I'll call you in the morning – no, make that in the afternoon – and tell you all about it.' And then they were away giggling like a pair of teenagers.

'Hey Logan!' Mike shouted. Too late. They were out of earshot.

'263 likes on Twitter inside five minutes.'

'What?' I snapped.

'Make that 275 likes, and 167 retweets.'

I gave Mike a stare.

'On Twitter. I filmed his last performance and posted it. YOU'RE GOING VIRAL, MAN!' Logan was too far gone to hear.

Mike decided he was too drunk to cycle back to the southside, so he called a cab and unlike me, got through straight away. He offered to share it, but a brisk walk through the Saturday night drunks was a better option than listening to his second-by-second update on the number of retweets, so I abandoned him on Sauchiehall Street.

As I made my way up in the hotel lift, I worried about the missed calls from Marek. I hoped he was OK. Opening the door, everything was dark but not totally quiet. Some music was coming from the corner. Nina Simone singing *Strange Fruit*. I slotted my key card into the empty holder and the lights clicked on.

'Marek,' I called. Again, more loudly. 'Marek?'

His bed was empty. I pushed open the door to the en-suite bathroom. Empty.

Panicking, I fumbled with my phone and dialled his number. A ringing tone came from the same direction as the music. Marek's new Android. Abandoned. I had no idea where he was and no way of contacting him.

THIRTY-FIVE

Wild

Logan lay motionless in the bed. The strange bed. He couldn't move. Every part of his body was tired. And there was this smell, an unfamiliar scent on him. Especially around his mouth and lips. And the scent had just gotten much stronger. Natalya had walked in. Wearing a black gown and a guilty smile. She carried a tray, two coffees, two orange juices and a pint of water. Placing the tray down on the dressing table, she bent over Logan and gently kissed him on his forehead.

Logan blushed, and closed his eyes. Not wanting to focus on the nipple and flesh that had just poked out from behind the robe. He had seen more than that last night, but at this point he couldn't remember much at all.

Natalya passed him the water, and he pulled himself up into a sitting position, and took first a sip and then lapped at the water with his tongue. After a few large slurps, the water was too far down in the glass for his tongue to reach, so he reverted to drinking it the human way. He pulled the sheet up, tucked it under his chin, and looked around at his surroundings.

The room was small but made to feel even more compact by the decor. Two walls were painted dark red, a third black and a fourth a brilliant orange. There were three bookcases, overflowing with books, a small desk with a laptop computer, an old rickety chest of drawers and a two-drawer filing cabinet as well as the dressing table on which the tray of drinks balanced. Natalya sat on the edge of the bed, smiling at him. Eventually, she broke the silence.

'That was some night. How are you feeling?'

Logan blinked back, his face full of panic.

'Do you remember much?' Natalya asked, leaning forward closer to him. Logan shook his head.

'Do you remember anything?' Again, no reply. She smiled.

'Well, I'm sure some things will start coming back to you in a bit.'

Logan again shook his head.

'I'm Natalya,' she said, laughing. She went to kiss him on the lips, but Logan moved so that the kiss was planted on his cheek instead.

'Oh, you are all shy now, are you?' She ran her fingers through his matted hair. 'You weren't so shy last night.' Still he was silent.

The pint of water was empty now, and he put it down on the bedside table. The coldness of the water had hit his stomach, causing a wave of nausea. He felt sick, very, very sick. Putting his hand over his mouth, his eyes narrowed.

Natalya grasped straight away what was happening and tugged at his wrist.

'No! Don't puke on my bed. Get to the bathroom. Quickly now.'

As he stood under the hot waves of water, some flashes of memory began to trickle back. He felt so guilty. What had he done? He stepped out of the shower and dried himself in slow motion. By the time he had finished he realised that his human clothes were in some undisclosed location in the flat. So he shuffled out of the bathroom, just wrapped in the towel.

Natalya was lying on the bed, on her stomach. Her heels kicking up in the air. She was looking at something, and she hadn't yet noticed he was there. Logan was about to ask her if she knew where his clothes were, when he heard a voice, a small tinny voice. It came from the phone that Natalya clutched in her right hand. It was his voice, his drunken voice. Last night. Oh, sweet mother of Reynard. It was beginning to come back to him now.

'Hey,' she said, turning over onto one side to look at him.

'Hey,' he mumbled back.

'Do you…'

'Do you…'

They both spoke at once. A few seconds of awkward silence followed.

'You first,' Natalya said.

'Do you know where my clothes are?'

She smiled. She had a gorgeous smile.

'I collected them earlier. They are on the sofa in the living room. But you may need to borrow a few things. Some of the clothes are, you know, a little bit ripped.'

'Ripped?'

'You know we were pretty wild last night.'

'Wild?'

'You still don't remember?'

'A little.'

Another uncomfortable pause. Logan was staring at her legs. Her long, smooth legs exposed from just beneath the thigh. And at her hair. Her red, red hair.

'What were you going to say?' It was Logan who broke the silence this time.

'I was going to ask you if you felt better for the shower.'

'Yes thanks.' This was awkward.

'And to say congratulations.'

'Congratulations?'

'You've gone viral.'

She patted the bed next to her and shuffled to one side so that there was more room for him to lie down.

Re-tucking his towel to make sure it was secure, he lay down, trying to avoid any parts of their bodies from actually touching.

'Here, take a look.' She held the phone in front of him and tapped the screen twice.

I'm a fox in this human body, with a bounty on my head. I escaped from a secret laboratory, now the government wants me dead.'

It was more than a prompt, an actual video replay. The sound quality on the film wasn't the greatest, and at times he was drowned out by cheering and laughter. But he could recall it now. Recall it all. Every word. The video finished and Natalya put the phone down on the pillow. Silence once more. She looked at him, her face just inches from his. Waiting for a reaction. Logan mumbled something.

'Will you kiss me?'

'Sorry?' she replied.

'Would you kiss me? I think it may make me feel better.'

THIRTY-SIX

The morning after

I'd eaten breakfast alone. Leaving half the food on my plate, pushing it around as I had little appetite. I'd packed up the room alone, not paying attention to what went where. I'd checked out without offering nothing more than a shrug to the receptionist when she asked if I had enjoyed my stay. I walked around aimlessly in the damp, dreich morning. I checked my phone repeatedly. Every thirty seconds at first. Then every minute. Then every five.

I stood outside the mobile phone shop, waiting for it to open. When it did at exactly 11am, I took a deep breath and summoned the courage to go in.

'I'm looking for the red-haired girl who was in here yesterday.'

'She doesn't work here anymore.'

'But she was in here yesterday?'

'Well, I'm telling you she doesn't work here anymore. Texted me ten minutes ago to quit. Something about a family emergency in Lithuania. Left me right in the shit. Now if you don't mind, I have some calls to make.'

Back outside. Alone again. *What now?* I thought. I checked my phone. Still no messages, no calls. I rang Logan's phone for the eighth time that morning. It went straight to voicemail, an automated pre-recorded message – cold and anonymous. I decided against leaving another message.

Walking back to St Enoch subway, I pondered my options. I'd arranged to meet Mike for lunch, but he hadn't replied to my text to reconfirm. No surprise perhaps, given how drunk he was last night. I was tempted to head back home, but how could I leave them alone in a strange city? I was fed up with aimless wandering. I turned around and headed back to the hotel.

The receptionist was friendly, but businesslike. I could stay another night, but not in the same suite as it was already booked. I took a twin room and left my bag at reception. They would take it up to my room when it was ready. I explained that my cousin from Connemara had not come back after going to a party and asked her to let him know about the room change if he showed. The receptionist smiled. She was tall and had black hair. She was on duty until 2pm but would let the afternoon shift know when she checked off. 'Don't worry, it sounds like he is having a good time.' She sounded kind.

I asked her if she was Lithuanian. She said 'Polish' and thanked me as not many people asked. At this point two Americans loaded with luggage appeared, wanting to know how to get to 'Edin-burrow.' I headed back out onto the street. It had stopped raining and I decided to go to the West End on foot. The walk might help clear my head.

It was coming up for midday by the time I arrived on the bustling Byres Road. Still an hour until I was due to meet Mike, that's if he turned up, he still hadn't answered any of my calls or texts. I passed time looking in *Fopp* and the *Oxfam* bookshop, but still couldn't settle. The cafes were full of people staring into their iphones. I began to resent the indulgence of it all. The whole place seemed to have an air of smugness about it.

I checked my phone again. No reply from Mike, Logan or Marek. I headed to the botanic gardens, and sat on a bench just next to the Kibble Palace. Not long after a group of teenage girls, seventeen maybe eighteen years old, stopped in a huddle in front of me. All of them were looking at their phones.

'I've already shared it on YouTube,' said the first girl, the tallest of the group.

'Me too,' said the second girl, smaller with glasses.

'Hashtag *foxconspiracy*,' the third girl said, grinning as she spoke.

'Have you seen his eyes? He's so cute,' added the fourth.

'Hashtag *sexyfox*.' The fifth laughed along with her friends.

I was just about to ask them what it was they were watching when my own phone beeped twice. It was Logan. At last. But there wasn't a message. Just links to videos. Two YouTube music videos. The first, *Going Underground.* The second, *Don't Worry, Be Happy.*

What the fuck?

THIRTY-SEVEN

Death's rattlesnake

Heading north. Uncertain how far she'd get tonight. Less confident now about her decision to fly back to Scotland, rather than take the train. She craved thinking time, hoping the flight would clear her head. She was two hours into her journey when she stopped to rest next to an old church. It looked derelict, lacking life, unlike the trio of yews that stood proud and resplendent at the entrance to the church's graveyard.

She had been in the tallest of the yews for but a few breaths, when a female blackbird landed next to her. She was a mature mother with healthy plumage, apart from her left wing that hung at a slight angle.

'I'm Debbie. I was named after my mum's favourite singer,' the blackbird chirped in a friendly manner.

'My name is Raven, even though I am a starling.' Raven was hesitant. She hadn't told anyone her name since the fire. Didn't want to explain how she got it.

'There's a bad wind coming, I can smell it.' Debbie spoke with an accent Raven was unfamiliar with.

'Thanks for the warning. I am heading north so hopefully I will be gone before it arrives,' Raven replied. This was her first bird conversation in weeks and speaking in starling tongue felt strange.

'There's a bad wind. I can smell it,' the blackbird warned again, then repeated it a third time.

Raven turned to look at Debbie more closely. Her eyes held a sadness.

The blackbird hopped to another branch and spoke in a more relaxed, cheery fashion.

'You look hungry. There are some great worms in the flower beds yonder. They've been digging the soil. Friendly soil, poison-free.'

'Thank you.'

'What's your clan, Raven? You look lonely. Where are the rest of your roost?'

Raven stuttered for a moment.

'They're further north. I've been visiting. It's a long story, but thanks for the advice. Where exactly did you say the worms were? I'm new to this area and the scents are different to what I am used to.'

'It's fifty wing flaps east of here, just beyond the row of beech trees.' Debbie stretched her wings, ready for take-off. 'Nice chatting to you. Have a safe journey.'

Debbie was right, the beds were full of bounty. Raven gorged herself on insects, millipedes and an array of earthworms. She felt properly full for the first time since she didn't remember when. The sudden feasting though, made her decidedly sleepy. 'I need somewhere to roost,' she said in her human tongue.

A noise. A loud, trundling, rumbling coming from north-west of the church. The wind was changing direction. It brought with it an overpowering smell of diesel. She thought of the blackbird's warning.

Further gusts of wind brought with them vehicle sounds. Many, many engines. She flew to the highest branch of the elm furthest from the church to get a better viewpoint. Lorries. Wave after wave. Identical trucks. Blackened windows, dark-green khaki canvas covering their loads. They looked military, she thought. Raven looked more closely as they got nearer. None of them had registration plates. No distinguishing marks.

They were passing by her now. She started counting. More than a dozen gone past already. 16, 17, 18. Still more coming. Where were they all going? 23, 24, 25. A constant earth-rattle, a loud hum of menace. 31, 32, 33. And still they came. 39, 40, 41. Hypnotic, dark, relentless. 46, 47, 48.

That's when she spotted it. On the top of the dashboard. Something other than grey. A splash of colour. The driver in truck number 48 had broken the symmetry.

Raven left her perch and flew above the convoy. From the air it was even more intimidatory. A giant snake weaving its way through the countryside. Death's rattlesnake making its way, but to where?

She glanced back and continued her count. There must be at least eighty trucks.

Looking ahead, she saw the convoy was approaching a railway crossing. She needed a chance to examine what lay on Truck 48's dashboard. A security pass perhaps? She wouldn't be able to read it unless she could get much closer.

The red lights of the crossing began to flash, and Raven quickly realised that not all the trucks would make it across. She landed on the pedestrian footbridge just a few yards north of the road crossing and looked down.

The lorries that had gotten across waited for their companions to join them. The head and body waiting for the tail. Truck 48 was the third in line behind the closed barrier.

Raven hopped as if to take off and then hesitated. She did not want to risk being seen by the drivers. If she positioned herself underneath the footbridge, she would be able to see without being visible. She heard another rumbling; a faster, more high-pitched noise. The train, the Edinburgh to London express. She hung onto some broken wire mesh that looped unevenly beneath the stonework. The speed at which the train passed shook her and she momentarily felt a loss of balance. Quickly righting herself, she hopped back to optimise her vantage point. A loud wailing noise and a flash of red light as the barriers began to rise. The sound of ignitions revving. Truck 46 passed across the line: *kerchink-kerchink-kerchink*. Wheels rattled on and off the rails and now Truck 47 was also over. The driver of Truck 48 stared ahead, his balding head catching the light. A gentle revving of the throttle, as he edged forward to rejoin the rest of the convoy.

From her footbridge perch the angle of the dashboard would obscure her view of the security pass, so Raven jumped up. She landed with a stumble on the bonnet just as the lorry passed over the crossing and moved up a gear to catch the vehicles in front. She could see it clearly now. Recognised it in an instant. The convoy, death's rattlesnake, belonged to Nobler Age Foods.

THIRTY-EIGHT

Gone viral

Chilcoat was back in Grantham. At the new depot. Harry had done well. The construction team had met their deadline. The truck boys had got the goods here safely. The progress reports were all excellent. They were ready. Nobler Age Foods was about to hit the shelves. Or rather, hit the food banks.

Traditional British Food. Made using old-fashioned British ingredients (with just a few imported US of A additives). The foods of your childhood. Tasty. Nourishing. Satisfying. An act of charity. An act of genius, genetics and eugenics. He smiled. A knock at the door. Harry.

'Come in,' Chilcoat called out.

'You look happy, boss.'

'It's all piecing itself together, Harry.' Chilcoat beamed as he got up to close the boardroom door. 'It's all piecing itself together very nicely indeed.'

Harry Turner sat with his legs crossed on the chair furthest from Chilcoat. And smiled. A wet, anxious smile. 'Is there something on your mind, Harry?' Chilcoat asked as he topped up his coffee.

'Have you been online today, sir? More specifically, have you been on Twitter?'

'Harry, you know I don't do Twitter. And when you call me *sir*, I know that something is up. Cut to the chase. What's happening in the Twitter world that is about to ruin my beautiful day?'

Harry stood up and walked over to the same end of the table where Chilcoat sat. Placing his laptop on the conference table, he adjusted the angle of the screen so that both of them could view it. 'You need to watch this, boss. Recorded Wednesday night at a bar in Glasgow. It has, as they say, gone viral.'

The audio quality wasn't that great, it had been recorded on someone's phone. Some of the lines were drowned out by laughter. The clip lasted less than three minutes. 167 seconds to be precise.

The video finished and Harry tapped on the screen to open another tab.

'It's had 858,297 views in less than twenty-four hours. And on Twitter the hashtag *manfox* is trending worldwide. Catching up hashtag *forrhianna* by the hour.' Chilcoat stood up and walked to the window. Turning his back, he stared out at nothing in particular. Lost for a moment in his own thoughts.

'Glasgow? You said it was recorded in Glasgow?'

'Yes, boss. At the CCA.'

'CCA?'

'Centre for Contemporary Arts.'

'Don't tell me. Earnest middle-class men with small beards, drinking craft beers, carrying Apple MacBooks and anorexic women sipping skinny lattes in vintage clothing.'

'Yes, boss, that sounds about right.'

'Cesspit of Cunts and Arseholes in other words. Which particular piece of shit posted this garbage?'

'A guy called Mike Jansen. Small fry, already on our books. Hunt sab, climate change activist, pisshead. He's been under obs for more than ten years, but never done anything useful until now.'

'And this video is "useful" because?' Chilcoat's tone was impatient.

'Boss, it's not the guy who posted the film who's the issue, it's the person in it.'

'And who is this ginger star of stage and screen?'

Chilcoat had turned to face Harry now. Watching him intently. Harry drew a deep breath.

'You may want something a bit stronger than coffee, boss. The ginger in the film is Alpha 1. The fox that escaped from the lab.'

'Excuse me?'

'The computer guys confirmed it less than half an hour ago. We've run the footage on seven different facial recognition software programmes. Every one of them concludes the same. 100% match. Even been onto the phone to Ivan from Spectrum this morning. Same thing. This man is our fox. He is our Alpha 1.'

The fox. Alpha 1. Escaped. The man-fox. Mutated. The fox-man. Confessing.

'Alpha 1. Alive, well and living it up in Glasgow.'

'You seem remarkably calm, boss.'

'Oh Harry, my dear child. Don't you see? This is good news. Really good news. It works. It totally works. So much quicker than I had imagined. The power of the Iron Lady. Her genes. Her pure-blooded genes. The power to transform. To be renewed. We knew its potential, but this surpasses all our expectations. The rate of regeneration is so much faster than all our computer modelling.' Reaching behind him, Chilcoat picked up a tray containing a decanter and glasses and moved it over next to the laptop.

'History, Harry. We're making history.'

He poured himself a whisky and walked over to the window. Looking out without seeing. He didn't notice a small dark bird perched on top of a stack of empty wooden pallets that lay underneath the window. Beta 3. The shadow within a shadow. A starling named Raven.

Chilcoat stared straight past her, absorbed in his own thoughts. Absorbed in the power of the forces he was unleashing. He downed the whisky in one. It was Harry who spoke next.

'I've taken the liberty of booking you a first-class carriage on tonight's sleeper, boss. A car will collect you direct from the COBRA meeting. We've got Mike Jansen in custody. Thought you'd like to question him in person. Stewing overnight will soften him up a bit.'

'Fine. I look forward to meeting him. I'm sure we will have plenty to talk about.' Stepping back to the table, he poured himself another whisky. 'Show me that video again, Harry, will you?'

THIRTY-NINE

Boxes

Box after box being loaded into vehicle after vehicle. More than 600 that morning alone. She'd been roosting in a holly bush less than five minutes' flight away. Avoiding all contact with other birds. Her eyes turned groundward, flying low, skimming the earth and keeping to the shadows. Each evening, journeying eastward to scavenge food from the bins outside the shopping mall. The KFC ones the most productive. Salty fries and overcooked chicken. Clogging herself up with grease, but still better than feeling hungry.

Each day, snatches of conversation. Phrases amidst the subterfuge. 'Regional distribution centres.' 'Tipping points in consumption.' 'Another food bank opened.' More lorries were leaving than arriving now. Two men with small computers checking them in and out.

Behind the depot, three giant accommodation blocks. Row upon row of camp beds and the smell of tiredness. Windows blacked out, her only view in through the small air vents. Midday. Two days since she had seen him in the room with the big table, laughing.

Watching and waiting, but no clearer to understanding. No closer to finding out what was happening.

Nobler Age Foods. The signs were omnipresent. **Nobler Age Foods**. On the boxes. On the vans. Emblazoned on the backs of the high-vis jackets. **Nobler Age Foods, Nobler Age Foods**.

Why did the lab get burnt down? Why did so many beasts have to die? Why are they stockpiling so much food? Why here – in Grantham? Is this all to do with *Margaret Thatcher Lives*? Why is her death so important?

Nobler Age Foods, Nobler Age Foods. Tell me your secrets, tell me your lies.

Raven was none the wiser. She was treading water, wasting time. Impatient. Frustrated. Anxious. No plan. No strategy. No bright ideas. Nothing.

Voices. A scramble of sound. Then clearer. Her mother's voice the loudest. Whispering to her. Calling to her. Summoning her. She is a fledgling, in the open field. Wanting to return. To the safety. To the comfort. To the brood.

Her mother calling to her. Distinct. Urgent.

'*This way. This way. This way.*'

Raven is drawn to three men loading up yet another lorry. Jumping off the grass verge. Flying at full pace past them. Low. Straight. They don't see her. In the back of the lorry now. Perching on the top of the highest stack of boxes. Slowing down her breathing. Blending herself into the darkness.

'*Don't move. Don't move. Don't move.*' Her mother's words dimming. Fading. Silent again. She is waiting. Alone.

Time going slowly. The air condensing around her. Suffocating now with a new sensation. The lorry fully loaded, the back doors being shut and bolted.

Her senses heightened. She can hear sounds. She can hear men speaking. A muffle of conversation outside.

'So where is this one headed?'

'Rothesay, Isle of Bute. Overnight stop in Lockerbie.' The engine starting, then hearing nothing but the rattle and hum of the machinery. Dark. Grey. Menacing.

Part Two

———————

WATER

FORTY

Island holiday

Each morning Logan made breakfast, whilst Natalya went for a run. His cooking was getting less messy; the confines of the campervan forcing him to be tidy. The food was simple, but delicious. The eggs brought from a nearby farm, the bread and tomatoes from the Co-op.

Natalya ran for five, six miles, returning in high spirits, telling him how much she was relishing getting out of the city. Enjoying the simplicity of island life and the relief of no more tortuous shifts at the mobile phone shop. For the first few days she'd grumbled to him about the intermittent Wi-Fi, but now she was delighting in being offline.

They hadn't intended to stay more than a couple of nights, but right now he couldn't imagine living anywhere else.

They were inseparable. Two peas in a pod. Or two carrots in a van, as Logan described them.

The campervan belonged to Natalya's friend Zara, a crowdsourced wedding present for a wedding that never happened. Zara's husband-to-be, Owen, was discovered having a long-term affair with Carlos Luis, a semi-professional Brazilian footballer. Found together, snuggled under a duvet watching *Match of the Day*, when Zara returned home early from her hen weekend with food poisoning. Owen had been thrown out the next day, just two weeks before the wedding.

When, the morning after their first wild night together, Natalya asked Zara if she could borrow the campervan, she was only too happy to have it taken away.

Most days after breakfast they drove into the island's main town, only town – Rothesay. Stocking up on supplies, they lingered in the small vegetarian cafe next to the castle sipping cappuccinos. Natalya reading, whilst Logan wrote.

She told him how four years of studying English literature at university had killed her enjoyment of reading, and what a pleasure it was to rediscover her love of books.

Logan began to write poetry. It was her suggestion to do so. Rhymes about his fox-life, of Rosa, his family, his everyday experiences of living in a human body. The challenges and thrills of being so very different.

At first, he wrote of the fire, of his escape with Marek, of cooking in the kitchen with Blake. Yet, as the days slipped into weeks it was easier for him to forget, to blank out the bits that caused him pain. Blake and Marek appeared rarely in his rhymes now. His poems had changed. Become more positive, more romantic. He was writing about the island, Natalya and the healing power of love.

Often, as he wrote she would sketch him. Doodles at first, then more involved portraits.

They had sex, or rather made love, at least once every day. It was more tender, less frantic than that first night in Natalya's flat. Their bodies moulding together in a symphony of pleasure.

In the afternoons they went for walks along the beach. Logan had discovered a love of rock-pooling, while Natalya collected wood and seaweed to create ethereal beach art that would be washed away with the next tide. On rainy days, they normally cut their walks short and returned to the van for an afternoon of slow love or sat in one of the hotel bars for some wet people watching.

They avoided all TV, radio and newspapers. They wouldn't go into any of the bars or cafes that had the BBC or Sky News channels scrolling on subtitled silence. At night, Logan cooked whilst she told him Lithuanian folk tales, Scottish ghost stories or often made up a mixture of both. The campervan was full of laughter. And love.

They moved the van every couple of days, but never more than a fifteen-minute drive away. They had not returned to the mainland and did not miss it. They had seen all the main tourist sites in the first week: Mount Stuart, Rothesay Castle, Ascog Hall Fernery (their favourite) and Ardencraig Gardens. Now parked up next to Scalpsie Bay, they were on the beach counting seals. Happy. Blissfully happy. But beneath this joy remained a sense of fragility. They both knew that their island holiday couldn't last forever. It was a respite, an escape.

Natalya broached the subject first on a Friday morning just over six weeks after they had arrived on the island. They were cuddled together in the campervan, rain falling outside.

'Hey, Logan darling. There's something we need to talk about.'

'What's up, babe?' he said, looking at her, sensing something was wrong.

'We're getting pretty low on money, honey.'

'How low is low?'

'I'm down to less than £800 in my account.'

'Hey, we can manage on that for ages, if we were more careful – cut out the cafes.'

'Except my direct debit for the rent on the flat is due in three days.'

'How much?'

'£580 plus another £125 for council tax a couple of days later.'

'Oh.'

'And I'm pretty much at my limit on my credit card.'

'Oh.'

'So I wondered – you know – if you had any ideas about what we should do?'

Logan shook his head, then blurted out a quick rhyme.

I don't want to go back to the mainland,

I cannot go back to the mainland.

I'll get a job cooking, cleaning.

No longer daydreaming.

There must be something on the island I can do.

To keep me happy and in love with you.'

'That's sweet, honey, but you don't have any papers, no National Insurance number, no bank account, no references. It would be easier if I looked for work.'

'But I'd miss you. If you weren't with me what would I do?'

'I know. I'd miss you too. But you know, we can't…'

'Survive on love alone?'

Their legs were wrapped around each other in a tangle. Their long limbs inseparable.

'I could go scavenging. You know that's what urban foxes do. Raid bins. Adapt. Survive.'

'That would be easier in the city, babes. It's all too small here.'

There was a brief silence. Both of them deep in thought. Natalya spoke next.

'So, I'll ask about. I'm sure I can pick up some waitressing work. It's coming up to the peak summer season.'

'Is that you want?' Logan asked gently. 'I mean, you've got so much more to give than just working in a cafe or bar. It's hardly using your full brain.'

'Well, let's see how it goes, I am sure it would be OK for the summer. It can't be any worse than Carmoan Whorehouse.'

'But love alone won't pay the bills,' mumbled Logan.

'And another thing, darling, I may need to go to the mainland this evening.'

Logan looked panicked.

'I'm really low on summer outfits, now the weather is warming up and my CV and references are all on the computer in the flat.'

'Oh.' Logan stood up. He was pacing.

'And I could buy a few more outfits for you too.'

'You don't need to do that. Besides, you just said you had no money, honey.'

'Nothing fancy. Just a few spares from, you know, a thrift shop.'

'Fine.' Logan sat down, his head on his hands, staring glumly.

'Darling, you are OK with this, aren't you?'

'Of course.'

'Hashtag *lonelyfox*?'

'Yeah. Hashtag *lonelyfox*.' Logan laughed unconvincingly.

'But it will only be for a day. Well, maybe two days, I'll come back on Sunday evening. It will be less rushed for me that way.'

'OK.'

'I'll ask in the cafes. I'm sure I'll find something.'

'With your looks, and your brains, they'd be daft not to want you. You'll have no problem.' Natalya leant forward and kissed him.

'Don't worry, babes, I'll be back in no time. You won't even notice that I'm gone.'

That afternoon, Logan stayed behind whilst she asked round the cafes. At the third one she tried, she was successful. Minimum wage, long shifts, but she could keep half of the tips. She would start on Monday morning. A week's trial.

She caught the 5pm ferry to Wemyss Bay. Logan walked into town to wave her off then meandered back up the hill, the zigzag up the steep ascent leaving him out of breath.

Natalya had moved the campervan to the campsite that morning. Logan sighed. It was the first time he had been alone for…? He couldn't remember. Turning into the campsite, he slowed his pace. He was missing her already. He was going to struggle. Time was going to go very slowly. He arrived at the campervan, and pulling the key out of his back pocket, he paused.

He heard her before he saw her. Her voice. That voice – he had not heard it since that night.

'Is there anybody else?'

This time she was quieter, calmer. There was a steady determination about the way she stared at him. 'Can I come in? I need to talk to you about Nobler Age Foods.'

The starling spoke in a tongue that was neither human nor bird. Logan said nothing, but held open the door so she could fly in. He wasn't alone, after all.

FORTY-ONE

Ghost weasel

I hadn't watched the video for three days now. I was trying to ween myself off it. Yet that two minutes forty-seven seconds was the only proof I had. The only evidence that Logan and Marek were real. That, and the assorted clothes, yoga mats and badger bedding they left behind. The cottage was so quiet without them.

I poked at the oven chips. Not done. Another five minutes at least. I speculated about where they were, what they were doing. Whether I'd imagined it all. But the video, I couldn't forget about the video. It still got new views each day, up to 3.61 million now. But far fewer new comments or retweets. Its moment of celebrity had passed. The fox-plague hysteria had died down. *Pavlova-gate* on *The Great British Bake Off* had become the new social media storm.

No new fox attacks reported for almost three weeks. And little or no news coverage of the injured children. I guess they were all making good recoveries.

It was the scientist with the white moustache who had come up with the badger theory. The foxes who had bitten the

167

children had all been linked to old badger setts. A mutated strain of bovine TB was causing them to become more aggressive, he said. The foxes had acquired the propensity to attack from a viral infection caught by being in such close proximity to badgers, perhaps from sharing bedding.

Foxes were a symptom of the problem rather than the cause. Three weeks ago a rapid extension of the badger cull passed through Parliament with a thumping majority.

Yet this somewhat complicated science was difficult to shrink down to 140 characters. The new badger threat had not caused the same wave of public fear. Most people in cities could have a reasonable chance of encountering an urban fox. But very few would stumble across an urban badger. *#badgerbites* never got off the ground.

The military patrols were still happening. But less in-your-face, mainly in semi-rural places away from large populations. The news cycle was moving on. Poor Rhianna. She wasn't mourned for long.

And just as the whole *#foxplague* hysteria had been blown in and away again like a summer sandstorm, my own life was getting back to a quiet routine. After the chaos and noise of having Marek and Logan parachuting in, I was cooking, reading, walking, gardening. A simple existence. Still not gotten around to doing any writing, but there was still over half my sabbatical from work left to do that.

I never heard back from Mike but had no inclination to speak to him now. Not after so many unanswered texts and calls. I was tired and lethargic. The short burst of vitality that Marek and Logan had brought with them faded back into the distance.

Yesterday afternoon, I visited Gran's grave and told her how muted everything had become. And I thought to myself about that day, the day that it all started. The weasel bite. I remembered, for the first time since May Day, how affectionately I had buried the weasel. And I wondered if my sadness was not *just* caused by missing Logan and Marek, but somehow linked to that moment on my bike. My fall, the bite. Crazy perhaps, but maybe there was something in it.

And so today I was in Largs library. I wanted to know more about *Mustela nivalis*, the common weasel. Their diet, their behaviour. Yet the library had no books on weasels, neither on the shelves nor in their online catalogue. The only reference was a small paragraph in a British anthology of mammals. I could look weasels up online, but I had an aversion to Wikipedia, didn't enjoy reading things on a computer screen. It was one of the many things that me and Mandy argued about.

I would go into Glasgow tomorrow. Check out Waterstones and the second-hand bookshops in Kelvinbridge. It would be my first trip into Glasgow since May Day.

On my way out, I paused at the library's community noticeboard. Amongst the usual ads for craft fairs and coffee mornings, one poster caught my eye.

Largs Food Bank Opening Soon. Volunteers Needed.

It wasn't so much the text, as the logo. That omnipresent logo. Nobler Age food banks coming to Largs.

The flyer was fixed by a single drawing pin and I found myself drawn to what was underneath: the food bank flyer had been stuck on top of another notice. Strange, given how much empty space there was left on the board.

I folded it back so I could read the one it obscured. Black and white. Old style printing. A hand-drawn quality. A beast's face. A badger's face. Its snout and eyes hovering over the monochrome text:

Stop the Badger Cull. Protest, George Square. Saturday 15th June, 12 midday.

I looked on the flyer for a Facebook page or website. But there was none. In small grey writing, almost a footnote, were five words: **The truth is out there.**

June 15th. Tomorrow, that was tomorrow. Maybe Marek or Logan would be there. I should go there instead of the bookshops. To look for them. To make things real again.

FORTY-TWO

Frustration

Chilcoat lay on the bed, oblivious to the drip of butter from the crumpet that had congealed on his chin. The TV was tuned to Channel 4 News. Jon Snow interviewing Environment Secretary Crull.

'So, Farringdon Crull. What exactly has your policy achieved?'

'As you know, Jon, the additional security measures we adopted have led to a significant reduction in harm. There hasn't been a single child injured in six weeks now.'

'Well, that is as may be, but was it proportionate? How many foxes have been killed? How many foxes experienced significant harm?' Chilcoat was still hungry. Distracted.

'Look Jon, the real issue is are our children safe? And the answer is that they are unequivocally safer now than they were one month ago.'

'At what price? How many foxes have been killed?'

'Isn't it a price worth paying to safeguard our children?'

'How many foxes killed? Ten? A hundred? A thousand? Come on, Environment Secretary, why aren't you telling us?'

God, how he hated Snow and his ridiculous ties. He was off the bed, looking in his mini-fridge. Some leftover trifle. That would do.

'Look Jon, the real issue is how many lives have we protected, how many deaths have we prevented, how much safer are our streets?'

'Over 2,400 is the figure that Animal Aid have reported. Is that accurate?' The coldness of the dessert stung. His back-left molar flared up. Not the time for a trip to the dentist though.

'It's a nonsense figure. The real statistic that matters is that no child has lost their life since Rhianna was killed.'

'And, having finished killing foxes you've been sending in badger SWAT teams? How's that going? What will that achieve? Have you the faintest clue as to what you are doing?' The trifle was finished. Still not satisfied.

'We know exactly what we are doing. We're keeping our children safe, Jon.'

He'd seen enough. He switched off the TV and walked over to the window. He stood, hands in pockets, staring. He had tried to convince himself that the missing fox and badger were an irrelevance, but he couldn't. They were proof that *it* worked. That genetic regeneration was possible. For over a month he'd kept digging away at where they could be. Like picking a scab. And it still itched and bled.

Fox and Badger. He needed to bring them in. To examine more closely their altered gene code. There would be clues, there would be evidence. The changes in their sequencing would allow him to make the final adjustments.

He couldn't accept that they had just vanished. Maybe a whisky would help. He poured himself a double.

Chilcoat was tired. He was weary of always being the

one who had to have both the ideas and the solutions. But maybe he had been trying too hard. Too busy scratching away to remember the basics. Jon Snow was right. The badger cull was achieving nothing. Alpha 1 and Alpha 2 were still at large. Chilcoat should have realised it sooner, changed his strategy as soon as he'd seen that video.

The fox-plague had been designed to capture a fox, not a human, and its mutation into *Badger Cull Plus* had lacked the simple narrative – the emotional resonance and savvy sound bites. Most people in large cities never encountered badgers in their day-to-day existence. Their concerns about badger contamination were therefore abstract.

Yet there were positives. There had to be some positives. More than ever he was convinced that it was the stress of the fire that had accelerated the fox's mutation into human form. The body tested to its physical and psychological limits. The mutated cells reacting faster, fuller and further than the computer modelling predicted.

Fear. Fear and stress. That could be the missing piece of the jigsaw. The key to transformation. The final ingredient to bringing about a full body regeneration. Mass public fear and stress, is what he needed to create in order for his experiment to proceed to the next stage.

His strategy to increase the military's presence on the streets to kill foxes and badgers may not have led to the capture of Alpha 1 and Alpha 2 but would increase the stress levels in the main cities he was targeting. And the stress would maximise the genetic impact of Nobler Age Foods on all those who consumed it. He still needed the data to confirm his theory. But it was something to cling to, make him feel more positive about his handling of the situation.

It wasn't just the fox and badger who were bugging him. Mike fucking Jansen. Still holed up in a leafy suburb of Bristol. Weekly trips to the wholefood shop and occasional bursts of yoga. The arse-wipe had given Chilcoat nothing to go on since he was released. He'd disposed of his mobile near the Severn Bridge on his first day in Bristol. Since then he had not strayed outside a three-mile radius of the shared housing he was dossing in.

Chilcoat pondered that day in the cell with him. The eight hours of questioning. He could have kept him in longer. Could have stewed him up more. Could have punctured his face more than once with the Phillips screwdriver.

But he'd known as soon as he'd seen him that he was small fry rather than mastermind. The telltale baggy T-shirt, jeans a size too big for him and haircut a DIY job with a pair of kitchen scissors. A spoilt sponger, art-school dropout. Only child. Vegan wanker.

Chilcoat regretted one thing though. He shouldn't have put so much emphasis on the tracking device they'd inserted when stitching the ugly fucker's face back up. He'd hoped it would have led him to Alpha 1 and Alpha 2 by now.

He should have known better than to rely on hope and circumstance. Should have known better than to wait for something to happen. *Snap out it, Lynton,* he told himself. *This melancholy is getting you nowhere.*

He was tired, not in the mood for drinking whisky alone. He wanted good food, good company. Picking up the room phone, he dialled for reception and asked them to arrange a taxi. A taxi to Soho, the Ivy restaurant. Quarter of an hour later, on the back seat of the cab, adjusting his tie. He hadn't time to shave, but never mind.

The Nobler Age adverts were everywhere en route. Even under the bright glare of the street lights he could pick them out. Swinging past a large church, he glimpsed the other sign, the food bank sign.

There is no such thing as food poverty.

Harry had been doing a good job, he thought, 1243 food banks and counting, more opening every day. It was a logistical achievement. Give Harry his due, he was doing just what he had asked him.

Yet he was the visions man. He was a level above everyone else he knew except Her. It was easy to set up 1243 food banks in a couple of months compared to what he had to do. It was tough being a genius, but worse having to deal with people who lacked ideas or vision. It was he who deserved to be on *Newsnight*, not Farringdon Crull.

The taxi driver had Classic FM on. Chilcoat indicated to him to turn up the volume. Piano Concerto No. 5 in E-flat major by Beethoven. The track she had chosen as her favourite on *Desert Island Discs*. February 1978. Tonight was one of those nights where he hated the secrecy of it all; the shadows, the encryption, the subterfuge. Forget about *Newsnight*. He'd love to appear on *Desert Island Discs* or better still, *The Graham Norton Show* or Jonathan Ross, or even *Strictly*. Cavort around with one of those tight-arsed, long-legged lovelies. He would love to cha-cha-cha with them for a few weeks. He deserved to be famous. He deserved to be adored. For his pure genius and for his unswerving loyalty to the Great Lady. He would be in the history books as the man who enabled her resurrection. The man who changed the political landscape, not just for a generation but for a whole century.

A late-night dinner at the Ivy was a poor substitute. The other diners, the minor reality TV celebs and has-been politicians would know nothing of the modern day Noah's ark he'd created and then burnt down on a doomed industrial site, just outside the doomed town of Stevenston, in the doomed county of North Ayrshire. North Ayrshire for fuck's sake. An animal laboratory like no other, where the genetic imprints and imported food additives were tested and retested, to the point of perfection. The Great Lady's genome encapsulated into a single E-number, a preservative added to each and every one of the food products he was distributing via the network of Nobler Age food banks.

The great unwashed, the working classes being nourished in the name of charity. The foods preparing them for the day she returned. The cleansing of their polluted souls that had to be done before she could come back and rule this land once more.

Did he care if the paparazzi did not snap frantically as he entered? Normally, not in the slightest. But tonight? Tonight was one of those rare nights where the love of the Great Lady didn't seem to be satisfying him fully.

He'd called the agency before he left the Ritz. Suzanne wasn't available at such short notice, but Scarlett would meet him outside the restaurant, and they could walk in together. She was much younger than his usual choices, blonde rather than the redhead her name suggested. Smaller too, just five foot one. The Great Lady had been five foot five and usually he insisted on someone the same height. Her ratings were exceptional though, and her profile pictures enticing. Maybe she could cheer his mood.

His taxi finally arrived at the restaurant. A quick exchange of texts and he walked over to greet Scarlett next to the entrance. Dressed in a short black skirt, white blouse and a skinny red leather tie. Red leather that matched her lipstick. Good choice, Lynton. She was hot, smoking hot. A kiss on each cheek. A hand discreetly placed on the small of her back, as they walked in together. No flashing of cameras. Seated in his usual table. Their orders placed. The staff scurrying.

A pause in conversation as they waited for their food. Tonight, for one night only, he longed to be able to tell his story. How he had swindled, embezzled, gambled and blackmailed his way to his fortune. How he used that fortune to create the perfect copy of the perfect gene, from the Great Lady herself. Imprinted now in every Nobler Age food product the length and breadth of the UK.

He could tell her how, just outside Grantham, he was creating a modern day Alexandria where offerings to the gods were brought in, manufactured and distributed. But where the *gods* were singular. A woman, whose name was Thatcher, Margaret Hilda Thatcher.

'Tell me, Scarlett, it's terribly rude of me, but how old are you?' he asked as he poured them both a large glass of red wine.

'Not at all, Dennis. I am nineteen. Twenty in August.' He smiled. *Dennis*. The name he'd registered with at the agency. It was the small flourishes he often enjoyed the most.

'Nineteen. That means you were born in 1993.' He spoke slowly now. Three years after the Great Lady was deposed. So Scarlett never knew her in power. Was not even born then. He shook his head as he realised this.

'Why do you ask?' She was holding her glass in front of her lips. Her bright red, young lips.

'I am not used to being in the company of such uncomplicated beauty.' He paused. 'But, I am savouring the occasion.' Another lull, Scarlett sipping at her wine.

'What do you do when you are not dining with old gentlemen like myself?' Chilcoat asked.

'I'm studying to be a nurse. This' – Scarlett waved her finger in a circular fashion – 'This. Is very handy for the tuition fees, you know.'

She laughed.

'A nurse. How utterly delightful. I have many ailments you could cure, my dear. A top-up?' He didn't wait for her reply, before filling her glass again.

Could he tell her now? Before the starters arrived perhaps. About the Great Lady's private nurse. About their affair. About how he persuaded her to gather dead skin and hair samples in return for the gifts he showered on her. A weekend in New York for the first time she brought him back samples of her blood. But then Scarlett would ask if they were still together or how the affair ended. And the suicide was complicated, too complicated for a night like this.

'You look deep in thought, Dennis. Is there anything I can do to help you relax?'

She had leant forward and stroked him gently above his left eyebrow.

'Oh, I am sure you can, my dear, but first we must eat. Tell me about yourself, I want to lap up every little detail. Let me…' He paused. 'Enter your world for one night.'

She started talking. He interjected at all the right moments. Asked all the right little supplementaries. Watched as she subtly stroked, twisted and played with her leather tie in the short pauses in the conversation.

'You remind me of someone,' he said, as the starters arrived.

'Who?'

'Kirsty Young.'

Scarlett's face was blank.

'She was a newsreader, now presents *Desert Island Discs*.'

Still blank.

'On Radio 4. You look very much like a younger version of her.'

'And that's a good thing, I hope? I don't really listen to the radio.' Scarlett was on to her third glass of wine now.

'It is very much a compliment. I've sometimes wanted, you know, to appear on that programme.'

Scarlett had her phone out, was googling the gaps in her knowledge. Chilcoat was smiling. Imagining himself appearing as the opening guest in a new series – the big draw, the main man. With Kirsty Young, sitting cross-legged, in a tight-fitting skirt. Staring at him with admiration.

'So how did you choose the name Nobler Age Foods?' Kirsty would ask.

'Well, I can tell you a little secret,' he'd reply. 'It's an anagram. You know how in the simpler days food additives were just known as E-numbers? Well, if you add E onto Belgrano and rearrange the letters then you get Nobler Age. And that is what we want to go back to.'

Scarlett had put her phone down. 'So if you were to be stranded on a desert island what would your luxury item be?' she asked between mouthfuls.

'Can I take two items?' Chilcoat pondered aloud.

'Of course. Of course.'

'Then the first would be a shotgun. For the foxes and the badgers.'

'How very topical.'

'And the second luxury, would be *you*.' He placed his hand on her right knee. She let it lie there.

'How very flattering.' She smiled, placed her hand on top of his and encouraged it further up her thigh.

'Suddenly, I am not feeling very hungry,' she whispered, leaning forward, her warm breath right on his ear. 'The agency has a little apartment. Only a few blocks from here. Would you care to come with me? We could carry on the conversation in more private surroundings.'

'I would like that very much.' Chilcoat's left index finger reaching further upward as he spoke. Scarlett responding, with a smile. A knowing smile.

His phone's *Maggie May* ringtone jolted them both. Looking down at the screen, he saw Farringdon Crull's name flashing. He could wait.

FORTY-THREE

Legends my mother told me

'My name is Raven. I am a starling.' She spoke slowly and confidently in human tongue. Logan stood next to the kettle, waiting for it to boil.

'From the fire,' he said.

'That's right.'

'My name is Logan. I am…' He hesitated. 'I am who I am.' Raven hopped onto the top of the campervan's passenger's seat headrest. From here she was close to eye level with him.

'I'm sorry.'

'How did you find me?'

The two of them spoke at once.

'You first.' Logan poured water into a yellow mug and dropped in a teabag. A waft of peppermint filled the van.

'I've been on Bute for – well, I've lost count of the moons now. I came in via a Nobler Age lorry that was delivering supplies to the food bank.'

'The new food bank?'

'Yes, at the back of the discovery centre.'

She watched him as he sat down. He looked uncomfortable. Confused.

'Sorry, do you want some tea? I'm not sure what I should offer you.'

'No, thank you,' she replied politely. 'I don't really like hot drinks.'

This was slow and awkward.

'What has the food bank got to do with us?' Logan was back on his feet, then sitting down again. She landed on the sofa next to him. Her eyes had a sadness within them, he thought.

'Everything, Logan. It's everything.'

'What do you mean?'

'The people who imprisoned us. Who tortured us. Who experimented on us. That logo. That squiggly line, that was the first clue.'

'Did this to us?' He ran his index finger up and down his legs.

'The people who mutated us. The people who killed all the others.' Her voice a different octave, emotional for the first time since their conversation began. He sat, clasping his mug.

'They are the same, Logan. It's all linked. The food they are giving out is poisoned. It is all part of the same experiment.'

'How do you know this?' His voice was inquisitive, fearful.

'People don't notice a starling. They think they are alone, private. They think out loud and I can hear them.' She wasn't sure if she was making sense. If she was getting through to him.

'I've been watching, listening. Using the library.'

'The li-lib-brary?' he stuttered.

'At night. The computers. Doing research.'

'You can do that?'

'Since the fire, there are many human things I can do. Even though–'

'Even though your body hasn't changed as much as mine.'

He'd finished her sentence, read what she was she thinking. 'And how did you find me?'

'It's my mum. She's been telling me things. Talking to me. In my dreams, in my sleep. Sometimes when I am awake too.'

'Things?' He was sipping at his tea. It was too hot.

'Stories from my childhood. Legends. I guess you could say.'

'Legends?' Why did he have to repeat her words all the time?

'Or ghost stories. Fairy tales you foxes may call them.'

'About what?' Logan put his mug down and was rubbing at his left eye.

'About love, about fear, about a forest; a fire, a great storm. And of a wise old fox whose cunning saved the day.'

'A fox?' He echoed her words back again.

'Yes, a fox. A fox and a badger.'

'Raven?'

'Yes, Logan?'

'You are scaring me.'

FORTY-FOUR

Details

It was tedious management speak. Blah-blah-blah strategy. Blah-blah-blah risk reduction. Blah-blah-blah private polling. Blah-blah-fucking-blah. And he'd given up an extra morning with Scarlett for this. He was regretting answering his phone whilst she had been in the shower.

Chilcoat had been sitting through this for forty minutes already. JFS, Joshua Francis Swill. A prime minister without backbone or charisma. A despicable inheritor of the Great Lady's throne. A pig farmer by birth, a weathervane politician who cocked up whichever way the wind was blowing. A man whose DNA bled compromise, compromise, compromise. An ideology-free idiot who had got into bed with the Liberal Democrats, the Liberal fucking Democrats.

For fuck's sake, how much longer would he have to listen to this shit? Seven other blank faces around the table. The PM's inner circle. Grey and useless.

Over an hour since he'd arrived at Chequers and he had been unable to get a single word in. JFS was drunk. You could tell by the redness of the flesh where his cheeky jowls merged with his double chin. Chilcoat detested him. Even more so, now he had tasted the watered-down whisky that was on offer. He couldn't stand this a moment longer. Time to intervene.

Chilcoat caught the attention of Crull, who nodded sympathetically. A minute later Crull raised his hand until the PM finally took the hint and stopped talking.

'Prime Minister, we need to stay firm on this. I hear what you are saying about negative press coverage, but I don't see that myself. *The Guardian* – since when have that pinko scum done anything else other than criticise us? *The Herald* – tartan wankers. *Channel 4* – pornographers and poofters. With respect, we need to look at the bigger picture, the longer-term impacts. The five, ten, fifteen, even fifty-year plan. And as Lynton has kindly given up his morning to join us, perhaps we should give him the opportunity to update us.'

'Yes, yes, yes, very well, Chilcott. Do enlighten us.'

'Chilcoat.'

'Sorry?' JFS spluttered as he leant forward to top up his glass.

'It's Chilcoat, sir, not Chilcott.' Lynton Chilcoat was not amused.

'Very well, that's what I said. Carry on man, we don't have all day. The Chinks are coming for lunch in a couple of hours.' Chilcoat's right eyebrow twitched.

'From what you have told us, Prime Minister, there are three details – and I emphasise details – that are troubling you. All easily addressable, if you would allow me to explain.'

Silence. At least now he had their attention.

'Detail One: increase in food banks, leading to negative headlines in *some* newspapers. Response: big society in action. Rise in food banks equals rise in civic responsibility, communities, not the state, intervening. On top of this it's British food that is being used to help those who cannot help themselves. A nobler age, a more civilised age. Boxes ticked. Critics silenced.'

He carried on without pause. Thinking to himself that the food was actually American, 82% at the last stocktake. The lack of regulations, the chlorination, the GMOs all so much better for keeping costs down.

'Detail Two: perceived exploitation of situation by tartan nationalists. Response: let them fail on their own terms. They are *too wee, too poor and too stupid* to achieve anything. If they want an independence referendum because the English have come up to Glasgow and shot a few foxes, then let them have an independence referendum and let them fail miserably. It's not a problem unless you think it into being a problem.' Chilcoat was enjoying himself now.

'Detail Three: negative reaction to badger cull amongst some, and I emphasise again *some* environmental circles. Well, what did you expect? You can't make an omelette without cracking a few eggs. Response: make a bigger omelette. Keep cracking the eggs. Send in the special forces from Section 7. Let them provoke a situation that changes public opinion. Police victims of angry mob violence. Protestors bad, police good. Dead badger, side issue.'

At this point Crull chipped in. 'Exactly – just what I've been telling you, Prime Minister. Thank you, Lynton, for summarising so succinctly.' Swill nodded, stroking his chin with his left hand, his whisky glass in the other. Chilcoat and Crull exchanged glances. They both knew that a Section 7 provocation was already in place. For that afternoon's badger protest in Glasgow.

'Very well, very well, all fine and good, but tell me, Chilcott–'

'Chilcoat.'

'Hasn't this been all a little bit messy? I've been very patient and trusting so far, but maybe it needs a firmer hand on the tiller. More oversight from my team at Number Ten?' Swill paused to top up his glass. 'So Chilcott, Crull, I'll go along with things as they are for another week. Period. After that I'll need to bring things in-house. After that, I'll be taking personal responsibility. Comprende? If the protests are still happening, if the press is still against us, then JFS will sort out the details, show you how to get things resolved. OK? End of conversation.'

JFS turned to his private secretary. A tall, skinny woman wearing a figure-hugging blue suit.

'Check my diary, will you. Come up with a Schedule B. Anything after seven days you may need to drop to allow me time to start sorting out this mess once and for all. And sort me a visit to one of these Nobler Age food banks for next week so I can see what all the fuss is about.' Turning back to Chilcoat, he added with glee, 'Deadline. You've now got a deadline. That should focus the mind somewhat. Eh?'

Chilcoat stared right into JFS's face. The prime minister blinking, almost twitching in response.

Chilcoat's distinctive ringtone cut through the room's hushed aura. 'Excuse me, this may be important.'

The prime minister waved his hand, and Chilcoat moved over to the fireplace.

'Harry. Be quick.'

'Sir, good news, a positive sighting.'

'Yes?'

'Not Alpha 1 or Alpha 2, I'm afraid, but the woman. Red-haired lover from Lithuania.'

'Red Legs?'

'Yes, Red Legs. She's back at her flat. We have three teams on her. She can't take a piss without us knowing how much toilet paper she uses.'

'Very good. Make that six teams and give her twenty-four hours. If she's not led us to Alpha 1 by then, pull her in for interrogation.'

'As you say, boss. One more thing. Mike Jansen is on the move too. He got on a train at Temple Meads, last night. Heading north it seems.'

'Interesting. Keep me posted, Harry, keep me posted.'

Chilcoat walked slowly back to the table. The prime minister had left the room.

FORTY-FIVE

Squaring up

I didn't recognise him at first. His hair was cut short, almost shaved off. His clothes, well his beige chinos and checked shirt, were nothing like I had seen him wear before. I'd been in George Square for ten, maybe fifteen minutes before he approached me. I was sitting on a bench watching the protestors assemble. It was much smaller than I'd thought it would be. Less than fifty people. A handful of whom had painted their faces black and white for badgers, and just one orangey fox-red.

A guy with a ginger beard and dark sunglasses was setting up a portable sound system. A blast of music and a staccato soundcheck. 'One-two, one-two, testing. Hey Glasgow. Stop the Cull, Stop the Crull. Yeah, that's working for once.' And back to the music. Manu Chao, *Clandestino*. One of Mandy's favourites.

That was when he had approached my bench. Now he stood directly in front of me, hands in his pockets. Looking down at me. 'Hey Blake, how you doing?'

'Mike.' Then silence. I thought of all the texts I'd sent him. The voicemails and emails. Not a single reply. Not one word.

He'd always been a bit unreliable, a bit of a pisshead. But this time he had gone too far.

'You here for the protest?' Mike asked, fidgeting as he spoke. I shrugged, then blurted out my angry reply.

'What the fuck happened to you, Mike? You couldn't be arsed to reply to any of my messages. I haven't heard from you since that night at the CCA.'

'Yeah, I am so sorry, mate. Had to get away. Keep a low profile for a while.'

'But you could have replied. Even once. Or am I not important enough for you anymore?'

'I had to lose my phone. The morning after. You know I was pretty pissed that night. Things all got a bit out of, you know, control.' He was squatting down now, so that his face was the same height as mine. Talking to me on the level. I could see a scar, a two-inch scar running down his left cheek.

'What's with the clothes, Mike? And your face. You in trouble? Where have you been?' I was unsure now whether to be worried or angry.

'Questions, questions, questions. Look, Blake, I've got to go set up. I'm doing the opening speech. But let's grab a pint, eh? After the demo is over. I'll buy you a beer and, you know, tell you about stuff.'

'You could have called me, Mike. Let me know you were all right. You just posted that video and disappeared. Like the others. Like Logan and Marek. You all just vanished. Like that. Where were you? You can tell me that at least.'

'It's complicated, Blake. I've not been about, been down south in Bristol. Getting my head together. Working a few things through.'

'Bristol? Why Bristol?'

Mike stood up. Rubbed his brow. And blinked. Blinked faster than a person normally would.

'Oh, I get it.' I got back to my feet too.

'You've been with Mandy, haven't you? I should have known. One drunk with another. Well, good luck, mate. You two. You two, you deserve each other.'

'Blake, it's not that simple.'

Manu Chao had finished. Replaced with another familiar sound. Bow Wow Wow, *Go Wild in the Country*. Another of Mandy's favourites. Was this whole playlist just designed to wind me up?

'What the fuck?' Our voices in unison. A scream. From behind me. Not a human sound, but an unearthly guttural shriek of fear and pain.

Ten yards away a woman was lying on the tarmac. Her hands folded over her face. Three men were kicking at her torso. A fourth was pulling at her hair. A fifth grabbing her left leg. There was a sixth man on his mobile phone.

A woman. A red-haired woman. A familiar-looking woman.

'That's the fox-woman.' The rest of Mike's sentence was inaudible. Drowned out by the sound of an engine and tyres screeching to a halt. A tall, dark-haired man dressed in black was jumping out of a taxicab.

And I was no longer standing still. And I was no longer angry with Mike, or afraid as to what was going to happen next. I was leaping. My mouth open. My teeth ready.

And I was flying, I was tearing, the flesh was ripping.

And the man from the taxi had a baseball bat. He swung it around his head to gather momentum. Before clubbing one, two, three of the men clear. And I had bitten one man on his face, another on his arm.

191

And Mike was standing still. His phone pointing. His phone filming. And I felt excitement. And I felt adrenaline. And I felt the power of a beast within.

And the woman was no longer on the floor, but in the arms of the man from the black cab. And I was no longer in my own body, but elsewhere. Running on all fours to get away. Diving onto the cold leather seat.

And a flash of light. And a flash of sound.

A bullet ricocheting off the glass of the phone. A bullet ripping through Mike's outstretched arm. And another following. Hitting him in the chest. Mike had fallen. His shattered mobile two yards away. The film evidence destroyed.

A crowd of seven, eight, maybe nine men swarmed around him. I shut the taxi door, numb with shock. And the engine was turned on by the man in black. And the car began its escape. I was on the back seat, breathing hard. Next to me on the floor the woman's body. Natalya's body. Twisted into the recovery position.

And behind the glass screen, the man in black drove in silence. Turning left, then right, changing lane and accelerating, then stopping at a red traffic light.

'Marek,' I said out loud, but got no reply.

FORTY-SIX

Drive, drive, drive!

I held Natalya's hand. She was still shivering, but her breathing had become more regular, less frenetic. Time was going slowly. Too slowly and too fast all at once.

After five minutes of coaxing, and with the taxi heading west along the M8 slipway, I had finally established from Natalya that Logan was in a campervan on Bute, that he no longer had a mobile phone and that she couldn't remember the name of the campsite. But it was up a steep hill. I googled campsites on Bute, there weren't many to choose from. I showed Natalya a picture of the main one at the top of the hill via Serpentine Road. She nodded.

'Give me your phone, Blake. I'll ring them,' Marek had snapped.

He clicked onto speakerphone and, driving with one hand on the wheel, made the call. 'Good afternoon, I hope you can help me. I need to talk to a friend of mine who is staying in a campervan on your site. His name is Logan, you'll recognise him by his red hair. I'm with his fiancée, I'm afraid she has just had a miscarriage and Logan really needs to be with her

BANQUET OF THE BEASTS

on the mainland.' A couple of moments later, after a muffled handover, Logan came to the phone.

'Hello. Who is this?' He sounded scared, confused.

'Listen. Don't speak. Natalya's hurt, but she's OK. She's with me and Blake. She was at George Square. On the protest. They grabbed her, beat her. But they must have had her under observation beforehand. They've got her handbag. Got her mobile. It's not going to take them long now to work out that you're on Bute. No listen. You've got to get off the island quickly any way you can and then we'll collect you.'

'Logan? Is that Logan?' Natalya struggled to sit up and speak.

'Natalya, Natalya. Our baby. Oh no, I should have been with you, it's Rosa all over again.'

'Look, calm down, Logan, you've got to be quick on this. She'll be OK, but only if you get off the island before the police find you. They'll kill you if they catch you.'

'But the baby, you said…'

'She hasn't had a miscarriage, I just said that to get the woman to get you to the phone.' And then some muffled voices and the phone being handed over again.

'Hello. It's Mrs Mcginty. From the campsite. I heard every word of that. He had the phone on speakerphone so that bird friend of his could hear.'

'Mrs Mcginty, I can explain–'

'No listen, son, don't you worry about a thing. Can you meet him at 1.20pm at Largs? He'll be on the Waverley. There's a sailing direct from Rothesay, it will be heading up to Arran, but never mind that. The police will be watching the Calmac, but they may be slower on the uptake on the Waverley. And besides, me and my mum will be going. It's her 90th today so we can keep an eye on him. Won't take me long to get him ready.'

We were parked as close as we could to the quay, outside WHSmith, about fifty yards to the ferry terminal. I held Natalya gently, I didn't want to hug her too tightly in case it hurt her even more.

'She needs a doctor, Marek. She needs a doctor.'

'I told you already. Not until Logan is safe and we are far away from here,' Marek replied in a tone that was dismissive. Patronising.

And so, we waited. And Natalya's hands felt colder. And I rubbed them harder and chatted to her about Logan. About all the good things I knew about him, about his laugh. His cooking. His bad poems. His red eyebrows. And all along I kept repeating, 'He's coming, don't worry, Logan's coming.'

Marek still hadn't told me anything. Where had he been since May Day? What had he been doing all this time? How had he gotten hold of the taxi we were now in? Where did he learn to drive? How come he had been there at George Square, just as the police came to snatch Natalya? I asked him question after question as we were parked up, waiting. All met with the same reply: 'Not now, Blake. Not now.'

I turned my attention back to Natalya. I gave her palm a squeeze and was comforted when she squeezed gently back. I still couldn't bring myself to look at her face. I thought momentarily about dashing off to pick up some arnica from the Jan de Vries health-food shop but dismissed the idea as too risky.

The dashboard clock said 1.12pm. Just over two hours since we'd left George Square. I couldn't believe it was the same day.

'There she is.' I pointed out to sea, in the direction of Cowal.

The Waverley. The world's last seagoing passenger-carrying paddle steamer. A beautiful timber deck and famous red, black and white funnels. Somewhere on board was Logan. Making his way over from Rothesay. Marek wound down his window and leant out slightly. His face was bruised, but nothing compared to poor Natalya.

'Not long now,' I whispered to her. 'Hang on in there. He'll be here soon.'

'Keep an eye out for the bird. She'll probably come ashore before he does,' Marek said.

And then simultaneously – a flashing blue light and a tap at the window. A police car driving past, stopping at the Calmac slipway. The tapping came from a bird, a small speckled bird at the window. She was now on the headrest of the front passenger seat. Raven nodded a greeting to Marek, before turning to me and saying something. Her voice was a strange pitch and difficult to fully grasp. It sounded as if she had said, 'Keep an eye out for an old woman in a wheelchair.'

The bird hopped through the hatchway to the back seat. She landed on Natalya's lap and began to sing, a strange, strange song. A warbling, echoing, lilting, dancing song. And as she sang Natalya squeezed my hand and I felt a little warmth returning.

The Waverley was docking. A cumbersome, awkward manoeuvre that seemed to leave a lot to chance. But a man on the quay caught the rope first time and began his wrapping and fastening. Then the ramps were hoisted and slowly put into position.

Another flashing light, and then another. A police van and two more cars, the last one a dark Audi with blacked-out windows. They parked in a blocking formation across the whole slipway. People on the street nearby stopped to look as two policemen tied a makeshift barrier with incident tape and cones. A checkpoint with armed police. Our view of the passengers now totally obscured.

Raven flew out of the window and perched on top of the bonnet. 'How's he going to get through that?' I asked.

'Easy,' replied Marek.

Natalya was shuffling, moving herself back up to a seated position. She straightened her hair and, licking the back of her hand, wiped clear some of the blood that had dried around her mouth.

Raven flew back inside the window.

'Start the car, Marek – he's coming.'

And the back door opened.

And an *old woman* jumped in and shouted – 'Drive, drive, drive!'

FORTY-SEVEN

Blackout

Chilcoat had told his driver told to wait indoors and then met Harry outside the warehouse. The two of them were now sat in the back of his limo. The confined space added to the tense atmosphere.

'Fucking, fucking idiots.' Chilcoat punched the car's padded leather seat three times.

He hadn't remembered feeling like this since that day in November 1990 when Geoffrey Howe triggered the Great Lady's downfall with THAT cricket bat speech. The former chancellor's resignation speech that savaged the Great Lady, falsely accused her of all sorts of ungentlemanly conduct. He could do with a cricket bat right now, to flatten the incompetent Section 7 wankers who had failed so miserably yet again.

Red Legs, snatched from the grasp of half a dozen allegedly top quality observation teams from Section 7.

Mike Jansen, aka Fox Video Fuck. Shot in full view of animal rights nutters, all of whom had smartphones to film what was happening.

Alpha 2, aka Badger Bastard: suspected to be one of the ensemble of gringos who had stopped Section 7 taking in Red Legs. Missing in action. Attacked the obs team savagely, then managed to escape from the scene in a taxi despite 326 police and security officers being within a 300-yard radius.

Harry was trotting out lame excuse after lame excuse.

'I can't control the Scottish police or account for quality control of the special forces in Section 7, boss. If it was up to me, I would have pulled in Red Legs as soon as she had been spotted, rather than risk something like this happening.' Chilcoat clenched and unclenched both fists. It had been his decision to wait twenty-four hours to pull her in.

'And the identity of Alpha 2's accomplice? The biter. Any closer to a positive ID?'

'Afraid not, boss. There's a lot of footage from the square, but as…' Harry hesitated. Then spoke with a nervousness Chilcoat was unfamiliar with. 'As Section 7 issued a Code S1-XTRA we can't fully access the files yet.'

'What do you mean, we can't access the fucking files?'

Code S1-XTRA orders allowed the scrambling of visual images and sound through new encryption technology. Photos, film, audio recorded within an area of up to a square kilometre was scrambled. Anyone who attempted to download, share or save such data wouldn't be able to. Footage would be pixelated beyond recognition and their computers or phones infected with both a tracking device and destructive malware.

'Apparently, the home secretary needs to sign something, before an unscrambled version is released and he is waiting for the PM to tell him it is OK to do so. It was in the legislation, you know, something the Liberals insisted on.'

Chilcoat slammed his glass of whisky onto the foldable table. A big crack appearing in his glass, two ice-cubes leaping out onto Harry's lap.

'And the problem is?'

'Apparently, the prime minister is in Birmingham for a special recording of *Celebrity Great British Bake Off*.'

'He's doing what?'

'It's his wife. She is a contestant, and the PM is going along, for, you know, moral support. I'm just repeating what I've been told, boss.'

'So, when will we get clearance? After he's done a few episodes of *Countdown*? Asked for some help with sudoku off Carol Vorderman?'

'She doesn't present *Countdown* anymore, boss.'

Chilcoat glared.

'I'm still waiting to hear back, boss.'

'Waiting, Harry. We haven't got the time to be waiting.'

'I know, boss, I know.'

Chilcoat was examining the crack in his whisky glass, wondering if it was still safe to drink from.

'And the coma camcorder cock?'

'You mean Mike Jansen, boss?'

'I know what he's called. I was asking for an update on his condition.'

'He's in a coma, boss.'

This was getting him nowhere. He threw the glass across the car, this time smashing it. Fragments of glass rebounded across both their laps.

'Mike Jansen's condition is unchanged, boss. He is still in a coma. Last medical bulletin' – Harry glanced at his phone – 'was obtained twenty-four minutes ago. Next update in thirty-six minutes' time. Estimated chance of survival remains at 75%. Percentage chance of permanent brain impairment 60%. Any other details you require?'

'And the evening bulletins, Harry. What have you got prepared for that? How are you explaining that an unarmed protestor got shot, because some nonce of a copper mistook a mobile phone for a firearm?'

'We could run with one of two angles, boss. We've fully prepared them both but wanted your sign-off before proceeding.'

'It's lucky my wife isn't appearing on *Celebrity Bake Off* then, isn't it?'

'You aren't married, boss.'

'Harry!' Chilcoat had leant forward so his face was just centimetres from Harry's.

'Harry. You have succeeded in telling me not one thing I did not already know except that our useless pig-suckling prime minister is too busy asking Mary Berry for a blow job to worry his soggy little bottom about allowing us immediate access to files that are central to everything we have been working on for – how many years?'

Harry was silent.

'I repeat. What have you prepared for this evening's news bulletins?'

'Two scenarios. Suicide or terrorism.'

'Suicide or terrorism. Meaning?'

'Mike Jansen shoots himself as an act of suicide or is a victim of a terrorist attack.'

'Hardly very nuanced, is it, Harry?'

'We haven't had much time, sir. Everything has been a little hectic.'

Chilcoat noticed the change from *boss* to *sir* and hit Harry in the face hard with the back of his hand.

'Not good enough, Harry. Not good enough. I will not sign off on either of those options. Maybe you could ask the prime minister for his opinion? After he's finished nibbling on his wife's sweet muffins on national TV, that is.'

A pause, then Harry asked, 'So what would you suggest?'

'A news blackout, Harry. A total and utter blackout. No foxes. No badgers. No protests. No news whatsoever. We need to shut this thing down.'

'Agreed, boss. I'll get onto it straight away.'

'Harry. I'm watching you closely on this one. Another fuck up, and it won't just be Mike Jansen lying in a coma.'

FORTY-EIGHT

A familiar journey

The fifteen-minute drive from Largs to Cardwell Garden Centre was long enough for me to tell Logan and Raven about what had happened in the square. The screams. The snatch squad. The fightback. The sharp rattle of gunfire. The escape.

Logan was a little calmer now. He had removed the old woman's clothes that Mrs Mcginty had provided, along with the wig and slippers. Naked except for his boxers, he was cradling Natalya, caressing her hair gently and whispering things that I couldn't quite make out.

The garden centre car park was nearly three quarters full. Marek parked the taxi on the far right end of the upper slope. It wouldn't be visible from either the road or the shop entrance. He carefully described to Raven the car we were to transfer to and it didn't take her long to find it. The small green hatchback was situated on the lower level. Nobody asked him how he had got hold of it. Like me, I guess they felt relieved that we would soon be out of the taxi.

My next worry. How on earth we could get Natalya from the taxi to the hatchback, a distance of some fifty yards. She could hardly stand let alone walk. I started to open the door. I'd seen a trolley next to the shop with an abandoned cheese plant that stood over five feet tall. I began to get out when Marek stopped me.

'What you doing?'

'That cheese plant over there. Natalya and Logan could hide behind it as we walk over to the hatchback.' Marek laughed, a cruel, mocking laugh, and put his hand over his mouth to stop himself reacting further.

'So should I go and bring it over? Then we make a dash for it?' I asked.

'I was thinking that I would just move the cab right next to the car, that way we don't need to walk anywhere.' Marek snorted.

I smiled nervously. 'Yeah, guess that would be easier. I hadn't thought of that.'

The transfer to the new car was quick. Logan lifted Natalya from one back seat to the other. I saw the pain wrinkle across her face as he did so, and again fretted about the need for a doctor.

Marek grabbed a holdall from the boot of the hatchback. 'There's clothes, a first aid kit, arnica and wet wipes in here,' he said, passing the bag to Logan. 'Get your make-up off and get dressed quickly. If we get stopped with you looking like that, it'll be hard to explain. There's some painkillers in there too.'

In less than two minutes we were on the road. Logan stayed on the back seat next to Natalya, even though the lack of legroom made it difficult for him to get changed, especially as we giddied our way round multiple roundabouts as Gourock turned into Greenock. Natalya swallowed two pills; one blue, one white followed by an arnica pellet. She whispered a thank you to Marek, though I wasn't sure if he heard. Raven perched just behind her on the rear shelf. She would occasionally add guttural clacks and clicks of reassurance to Logan's continual sweet mumbles of affection.

We were going north-west now, through Greenock where they used to build ships, but now where anonymous retail parks competed for attention with oversized roundabouts and concrete tower blocks.

'Where are we going?' I asked Marek.

'I've rented us a cottage. It's about two hours' drive from here. It's safe. Remote. There's a forest nearby.'

'What about a doctor for Natalya?'

'It's in hand, someone will meet us there. I need to call her when we are half an hour away. Give me your mobile.' Marek slowed the car slightly as I handed him my phone. There was a blast of cold air, the driver's window opening wide.

'Hey, what you doing?' Marek had let my phone slip down onto the carriageway. The whir of the window sealing back closed.

'Marek!'

A white van overtook us, its wheels must have gone straight over the phone.

'I thought you needed my phone to contact the doctor?'

'Use your brain, Blake. It wasn't secure. They could be tracking us. It's a nurse and not a doctor, and I will call her on *my* phone which is properly encrypted.'

I found myself shrinking back, avoiding shouting or confronting Marek. Somehow, he made me feel scared rather than angry. Unsettled rather than reassured. My mind was so full of questions.

For the first time since leaving George Square, I wondered about Mike. Was he really shot, or had I imagined that?

How badly was he injured? Did I care? Should I call Mandy? Could I face ever speaking to her again? Was I better off just not knowing, just not thinking? I closed off my mind and focussed on nothing. I stared out of the window. The car was accelerating. A brief sprint on the motorway before heading onto the Erskine Bridge and the A82. One of the main routes out of Glasgow that took us past Clydebank before skirting Dumbarton.

Marek drove carefully, but confidently. He didn't once ask for directions, use a satnav or hesitate about his route. I turned around to look at the others on the back seat. Natalya was sleeping now, her head spooned on Logan's chest as he gently stroked her hair. He had wiped much of the dried blood from her face, but there was little he could do to camouflage the bruising and grazing. The bird too, looked sleepy, if that's something starlings can do.

I started to speak, but Logan lifted a finger to his lips to hush me. He didn't want Natalya to be woken. The journey continued without conversation. The only sound was the continual hum of the engine and the rumbles of passing trucks. The traffic heading out of the city was just as busy as that heading inward. Day-trippers to Loch Lomond and tourists heading to Glencoe. For half an hour we were stuck behind two large campervans, before we branched off at Tarbert, joining the A83. Heading along the banks of Loch Fyne, through Inveraray. We were following the signs to Campbeltown now, heading into the heart of the Kintyre peninsula. The journey was a familiar one.

Mandy's 30th birthday. April 2011. We'd stayed in a white cottage on the banks of the loch in a small village called Tayvallich. Mandy's idea to drive this way. Cheaper, she said, than having to take the two ferries, from Gourock to Dunoon and then Portavadie to Tarbert, though that would have shortened the driving for me.

I was a nervous driver. Always had been. Ever since I'd written a car off at the age of seventeen, not long after passing my test. Not my fault. Someone in a Land Rover jumped a red light. They never stopped. I wasn't hurt, but the car was a write-off. Left wedged in the traffic-light pole until the police came to tow it away.

The loch at Tayvallich was the one where they had released beavers. I hadn't seen them, but Mandy had done so on her birthday, as I drove back from a magical walk along the beaver trail. The new tourist trail, that was to allow visitors a circular walk round the loch but had been closed by flooding caused by the beavers themselves felling trees and changing the water course so it ran directly down the new path. An ironic reclamation, as if the beavers were saying *this land is our land* and *we* will decide who comes to visit.

That afternoon we had found a tree felled by the beavers and collected the shavings that were grooved and carved by the beavers' teeth. There was something both beautiful and cartoon-like about them. The next day though, Mandy told me she had lost the bits of wood. Probably left them in the pub, where we were until closing time, so I wasn't able to take them home like I'd wanted to.

Was she already seeing Mike when we were living together? Flirting with him by text? Having drunken conversations after I had gone to bed?

At Lochgilphead now. Not far from Kilmartin Glen. Where my gran took me on her 75th birthday. Celebrated it among the ancient standing stones and cairns.

Here, Marek pulled in momentarily. He pulled a phone from his jacket pocket. I could hear only one side of the conversation.

'It's me. We're at Lochgilphead.'

'She's doing OK. Slept most of the way.'

'We'll be in Tayvallich in about half an hour. It's the small white cottage next to the loch, just after the pub. We'll meet you there.'

FORTY-NINE

Iron Lady lullabies

He had watched it four times in a row. It was beginning to work. Her words were familiar, soothing. His blood pressure one or two points lower on the Richter scale. Chilcoat leant forward and pressed eject. The DVD came out slowly and he wiped it with the sleeve of his dressing gown, before placing it carefully in its case. He had collated the contents himself, back in 1997, not long after that charlatan Tony Blair had come to power.

He called it his ILL collection: Iron Lady Lullabies. Thirty of the most relaxing of her speeches; just snippets, each around 45 seconds long. Some were famous: Francis of Assisi on the steps of Downing Street; rejoicing at the Falklands triumph. Others less so, including some simply divine performances at Prime Minister's Questions.

He poured himself a whisky. The laptop was set up for the video call with Crull. He was using Vector 12 encryption for the first time, so would need to keep the call short. Its stability on longer calls was not yet fully tested.

Crull was travelling back from a climate change summit in some swamp-infested Latin American jungle. As was customary with these bore-fests, the negotiations overran. He'd missed his connecting flight and was now overnighting in New York, before returning to the UK.

Radio 4 was on quietly in the background, and the familiar pip-pip-pip alerted Chilcoat to the time. Midnight. He pulled the collar of his dressing gown closed and tightened his belt. He'd set the webcam to its narrowest angle as he was not in the mood to get dressed for such a short call. Two minutes past midnight. He was late. Chilcoat despised lateness. Then the laptop beeped a harsh, high-pitched, incoming call alert.

'Lynton.'

'Crull.'

Niceties over, they got down to business. Crull spoke first.

'I know time is limited, so I won't waste it bemoaning the incompetence of Section 7, but what this basically boils down to is JFS not having a full set of balls.'

Chilcoat nodded.

'Hughie is a perfectly adequate blank page home secretary, but his energies go into wagging his tail in front of the PM. He won't do anything without getting a teacher's note first.'

'Exactly,' said Chilcoat, taking a sip of whisky. 'JFS is too risk-adverse. No ideology, no personality and in thrall to liberals. We simply can't let him get his hands on Nobler Age. He doesn't understand it. He never will. He is the blockage we need to remove—'

'I don't know if Lance King is still giving him a weekly handjob,' Crull interrupted, 'but to me that's the most logical explanation as to why our great leader's face lights up every time the head of the *Liberal Demoh-crats* walks into the room. King is an execrable excuse of a politician. He only agreed to being foreign secretary instead of deputy PM so that he could wave

his hyperactive dick about abroad without his wife finding out.'
Chilcoat smiled. Lance King's Spanish wife was quite a looker
and he wouldn't mind spending some time with her whilst her
husband was away.

'You've done well, not trusting JFS with the real motivating
factor of Nobler Age Foods. If he found it, it would short-
circuit his pig-infested brain. And Lynton...'

Chilcoat had leant forward closer to the camera, his face
occupying the full screen.

'I can honestly say that what we are doing excites me.
Eliminating the poverty gene through repeated exposure to
GM foods at food banks. I wish I had thought of that.'

'Thank you, Crull. I am glad you are still enthusiastic.'

'It will take bold leadership to pull this off though. Someone
able to step out of the comfort zone of Middle England. A
communicator, a populist and not a compromiser. It's reached
a critical point, don't you think?'

'Exactly, Farringdon. Tomorrow is the day I get the data.
The first month's data. Give me a few days to analyse it and I
will know more about how quickly we will need to act. When
the point of no return is.'

'Exciting days ahead of us, Lynton.'

'Indeed. Time on this call is short. Can I ask you a theoretical
question? If our friend JFS was, for some unexpected reason, to
become incapacitated, who would step into his shoes? In normal
times it would be the deputy PM, but since the coalition that
role was done away with. As you said, in order to allow Lance
King to play away from home.'

'Well, the chancellor is, as you know, not without many
skeletons in his closet. That rules him out. Hughie doesn't have
the ambition, so that leaves three contenders.'

'The three E's: education, energy.' Chilcoat paused. 'And environment.'

'Very impressive, Lynton. You read the situation well.'

'And again, speaking theoretically, how would the environment secretary fare in such a theoretical contest?'

'Well, the environment secretary would be very keen to be ready for such an unfortunate situation arising.'

'How very noble.' Chilcoat smiled. Leaning back, he adjusted his gown slightly to avoid any of his chest showing on screen.

'And talking of *Noble*. I hear that JFS will be visiting staff at one of the new flagship food banks on Saturday morning. In Glasgow. 10am. City Chambers at George Square.'

'How very interesting. I think we should talk again before then, don't you, Mr Crull?'

'Yes indeed, I think we should.' Chilcoat closed his laptop down and picked up the desk phone.

'Room service, how can we help, Mr Chilcoat?'

'I need a steak. Cooked rare. Very rare, and brought to my room.'

'Indeed, it will be with you in less than half an hour.'

Perfect. Just enough time to watch the DVD again.

FIFTY

Relapse

We had been in the cottage for three days already. Marek was in the forest. He was spending more time as his badger self during the day. He was quiet, sullen almost, whilst in his human form. He had said nothing of where he had been for the weeks since he'd walked out of the hotel back on May Day. I sensed that he didn't want me to ask him anything, so I didn't. I still wondered about Mike, if he was OK. But every time I did, I thought too about Mandy. And my emotions were complicated, so I tried to channel my thoughts away to something else.

The cottage was cosy. Old-fashioned. Filled with eclectic furniture, it had an olde worlde charm. The lounge had a wood burning stove, a purple sofa as well as the dark-green sofa bed, an oak dining table with six slightly scruffy chairs, and a large dresser that was full of second-hand books, maps and strange antiques. The best room, however, was the conservatory. This modern extension, filled with wicker furniture, padded nicely with rainbow-coloured cushions, was bright, light and gave us stupendous views over the loch.

The cottage backed directly onto the loch, we had our own jetty even. There were two bedrooms – Logan and Natalya took the double. Raven and I shared the twin. Marek had the sofa bed in the lounge, his request, so he wouldn't wake us with his nocturnal ramblings.

Not that I had slept much. As soon as my head hit the pillow my thoughts went back to George Square, my mind racing backwards and forwards. Thinking of Mike, of Mandy, of Natalya, of Marek. I would doze fitfully, finally getting into a deep sleep at around 4 or 5am, not long before Logan's singing in the shower would wake me.

I headed downstairs with my head clogged with tiredness. Natalya was sat up on the sofa, propped up by a couple of particularly large cushions and wrapped in a duvet. Logan had pulled a dining chair next to her so that he could hold her hand as they talked.

The day we arrived, Jocelyn, the nurse who Marek phoned, had brought Natalya pain relief and had done a manual examination for broken bones.

Jocelyn was tall, sporty-looking. Her jet-black hair was tied in a ponytail, and the edge of a tattoo poked out from the bottom of the right-hand sleeve. I wanted to ask her how she knew Marek, where they had met, but I never got the chance. She was rushing, didn't want to be interrupted and was in the cottage for less than ten minutes.

Her words still echoed in my head each time I saw Natalya's bruises. 'I'm hoping that it's just badly bruised, rather than broken ribs, but without an X-ray it's hard to tell for sure. The main worry is if she has any internal bleeding. If there's any blood in her pee or if her temperature starts to rise, she really needs hospital care.'

Logan took her temperature. Initially on half-hour intervals, then hourly. Now down to every two hours. So far, it had remained stable. The nearest hospital was at Lochgilphead, a thirty-minute drive away. Jocelyn had said if we drove her in on a day she was on shift then she might be able to book her in under a false name, but if we rang an ambulance the paramedics may pass on her details to the police.

None of us except Marek had a mobile phone – not since the Erskine bridge. He was controlling everything, I thought. He seemed to have changed so much since that first day in my cottage when he was friendly and warm. Logan too was a changed man (or should that be fox). All he cared about now was Natalya. She used up 100 per cent of his attention. He spoke calmly, gently. He hadn't spoken in verse once since we arrived in the cottage.

On the first morning, I stood in the kitchen with him, waiting for the green tea to brew. 'It's lovely to see you and Natalya so close.'

He smiled as he stirred the tea in the pot with a spoon. 'I know what you're thinking. How come I'm Rosa this, Rosa that, and now I'm all loved up over Natalya. Well, I'm just as surprised. I think that Rosa was my fox-love and Natalya is my man-love. Both equally wonderful. I'm a different person now. Rosa wouldn't fall for me looking like this, but Natalya has.'

Marek spent at least an hour each morning writing in his notebook. He'd join us for breakfast but talk little and eat even less. Soon afterwards, he'd head out to the woods and then not be seen until late afternoon. So, with Logan and Natalya ensconced and Marek missing, it was Raven who I spent most time talking too.

'I'll tell you what I told Logan in the campervan,' she said. It was the second day in the cottage, and she was beginning to relax more. Her sentences were longer, more coherent and she hopped about less frequently. She was sitting on the coffee table in the lounge, so she could make eye contact with me as I lay on the sofa.

'The laboratory, Nobler Age Foods and Margaret Thatcher. They are all linked. There is a company called MTL – Margaret Thatcher Lives – which is the real trading name behind all this.'

I sat up to sip at my Earl Grey tea, before placing the mug back down on the coaster to the right of Raven. My movement made her hop up a few inches before landing back down.

'I travelled to Thatcher's birthplace, to Grantham. That's where I followed a convoy to the warehouse. At least two moons came and went before I climbed inside one. That brought me all the way to Rothesay.'

'Weren't you scared in the lorry?'

'Not really. Nothing is that frightening after the fire.'

Raven's voice was still a little mangled, but the more time I spent with her the easier she was to follow. Most sentences she would intermingle clicks and clacks with her words. Her speech had a lilting rhythm. Her small frame and limited volume made her both captivating and hypnotic. She too, was growing used to me. You could tell by the way her beak tilted when I walked into the room. But it was still only Natalya who she directly perched on.

'In Rothesay, I watched them unload the lorries and I heard snatches of conversation. That this was one of hundreds of food banks. That the food wasn't like what you got in the supermarkets. Then, on the island, I used to go into the library in Rothesay after dark and look things up on the computers.

Like I did in Largs, but I couldn't find anything. I guess I was stuck. Waiting for something to happen. And it did. I found Logan. I didn't recognise him at first, but I was following him, he seemed familiar, you see. He didn't notice, nobody ever notices a starling.'

'What are they up to, Raven?' The question was semi-rhetorical. I stood up and wandered into the kitchen with my now empty mug. Raven followed me and landed on top of the microwave.

'Do you mind me calling you Raven?'

'I'm getting used to it. It's better than *Sturnus vulgaris*. I know I am a starling. You know I am a starling. Marek, Logan and Natalya all know that I am a starling. The humans in the laboratory couldn't work it out. Labelled me *Raven*. I sometimes think that's what saved me. They dosed me up wrong, as if I *was* a raven.' She flew from the microwave to the tap.

'In a way it helps. Separates out the old self from the new.'

She moved from the tap to the work surface. Its black marble finish contrasted to the pale pine in the rest of the kitchen. I ran the tap, waiting for the water to run hot before rinsing my mug.

'I was pretty lonely before Logan and Marek burst in on my life. Do you get lonely too?'

She did not reply straight away and hopped back on top of the tap before tilting her head to make sure I was paying her full attention.

'I miss my roost. I miss my mum and sisters too. It's OK here, with new friends, but it's not the same.'

I walked back into the lounge and she followed. She landed back on the coffee table. She clacked – it took her a few attempts to get her human voice working – by which time I had leant in closer.

'It was dark. Very, very dark before. Now I can see some light.' I leant back on the sofa and to my surprise and delight she hopped onto my lap.

'Now it's my turn to ask you something.'

'Sure.'

'How long have you been part weasel?'

'Sorry?'

'How long have you been part weasel?'

'I don't know what you mean.' I was uncomfortable, fidgeting, and scratched at my left ankle where I had a stubborn patch of eczema. My movement prompted Raven to flap back up and land again on her preferred spot on the coffee table.

'The weasel. From the fire. Walinska. Whenever I see you, I think of her. Whenever you move, I can see her movement.'

A key at the front door. The conversation paused. In walked Marek, in his human form. Looking tired.

'Good walk?' I asked, happy to steer the conversation away from me.

He mumbled a non-committal reply and headed to the kitchen. I heard the sound of the kettle. Logan emerged from the conservatory, stretching his arms, his fingers interlocked over his head. He yawned and did a couple of gentle side bends.

'How's Natalya?' I asked.

'Much the same. Much the same. She's awake. Go and say hello. She'll be pleased to see you.' Logan headed into the kitchen and Raven hopped up into the air to follow him.

I went in the other direction and stepped into the conservatory.

Natalya was still on the sofa. Still propped up with cushions. Still wrapped in a duvet. Her eyes were closed and she looked sleepy. Peaceful. Her head though, was at an odd angle. I thought that it looked uncomfortable, that she'd get a crick in her neck.

'Hey,' I said gently.

'Hey.' A little louder, this time right next to her.

'Hey sleepy.' This time more urgently and combined with a firm tap to her shoulder. Her head dropped forward.

I felt my breath catch in my throat and at the same time a wave of nausea rippling through me. I touched the side of her face. It felt cold.

'Natalya. Come on, wake up.' I shook her firmly.

'Logan! Quick. Someone. It's Natalya.'

Raven was first in the room, she cawed a guttural shriek as she saw Natalya slumped. Logan was next to arrive. He paused at the doorway. The colour drained from him instantly and he stood as if nailed to the floor. Frozen. Silent. Lost.

Marek came in last. What seemed an age was only seconds. He carried a bright yellow mug with a grinning cartoon beaver on it.

'She's not breathing,' I said. 'She's not breathing.'

FIFTY-ONE

Life-changing

'Time of death, 3.29pm.'

'Never regained consciousness.'

'Internal bleeding too severe.'

The words echoed down the phone but were not registered. The sterility of a hospital death. The anonymity. The loneliness. The discord between the body's internal, red bloody miasma and the white, antiseptic hospital walls. So familiar.

It was little more than an hour since Harry had rung him with the news. Not unexpected, but nevertheless not exactly welcomed.

'A corpse can't answer questions,' had been Chilcoat's only comment, before holding down his thumb on the red phone icon to terminate the call.

Mike Jansen was dead.

Another cul-de-sac reached. But Chilcoat was unmoved by this latest news. He had not slept since he had received the food bank data. The first month's data from four key cities: Glasgow, Liverpool, Bristol and Brighton.

The *volunteer* trials. Their take-up rate so much higher than he had anticipated. Free food in return for a weekly sample of saliva, urine or blood. The size of the food parcel linked to the type and number of samples. Food banks with no need for vouchers or referrals. Just participation in an experiment. His experiment. The Great Lady's experiment. No, he had not slept for more than forty-eight hours. Yet he did not feel tired, far from it.

It wasn't frustration or anger that kept him from sleeping, but excitement. It was so much more definitive than he could have imagined. He had to make sure that he wasn't missing something. Had to go over the data again and again. He couldn't waste time not being awake.

He had no difficulties administering the injections himself. The same time. The same dosage. The same method that the Great Lady's nurse had done for all those years in Number Ten. Adrenaline. He could manage without sleep, for a week maybe, until after the visit to Glasgow. The full-length mirror in the bathroom of his hotel suite, the bright overhead light. The needle finding the vein in the top of his right thigh.

He had fixed a white bed sheet to the wall, using a mix of drawing pins and plasters. On it now was scrawled a series of numbers:

92%
94%
88%
36%
2345
1297
1566
1101

Below these a series of words, barely legible:
saliva

mutation
nutrition
smear
psychometrics.

Arrows led off these words into a large, hand-drawn table. Longer numbers, some with decimal points. A second table, a repeat of the first though, with the final column in red ink rather than blue. Then a third table, some numbers crossed out. An extra column added with comments also crossed out.

Check this
Cross reference Glasgow
Cross reference Liverpool
Cross reference Brighton
Cross reference Bristol

Then more arrows and asterisks and a series of seemingly random numbers that was repeated across four lines. And on the fifth a different formula, repeated seven times. Each formula beginning with the same three letters: *MTL. Margaret Thatcher Lives.* The endgame. The date he was working towards. And then in the centre of the sheet, a pattern. A repetition. A recognisable and reoccurring chorus of numbers. Circled three times in red.

Chilcoat's phone rang. He ignored it.

The room felt hot, uncomfortably hot. His phone rang again. This time he picked it up to see who was calling. Harry. He could wait. After ten seconds it went to voicemail. He let the phone slip to the floor, where it clunked against a discarded Bell's whisky bottle. Chilcoat stared again at the numbers he had circled. And smiled. A chilling, wide, face-enveloping smile.

'Not long until we will be together again, my love,' he blurted out, before draining what was left in his whisky glass. His phone beeped twice. Harry again. Texting this time.

Leaning over to pick up the phone, Chilcoat stumbled from his chair and fell in a crumple on the floor. The glass broke under his weight and cut the side of his left arm. He inspected the wound. Nothing too major. Nothing to lose any sleep over.

Standing up, for a brief moment he leant against the hanging sheet to aid his balance. A line of blood imprinted its way across his data. Chilcoat felt dizzy, disconnected.

'Jesus.'

He must have drunk more than he thought. Or the injections, maybe he had overdone the injections. He sat back down on the floor for a few seconds to regather his balance. His phone beeped again. He scrabbled on the floor to find it.

Harry, another message. This time Chilcoat read it.

MJ death leaked by hospital. Protest planned Glasgow Saturday for PM visit. All over Twitter. Pls call. URGENT.

FIFTY-TWO

The return

It was Rosa... Rosa's voice... calling to him.

'Not again.'

'Not again.'

'You mustn't let it happen again.'

The voice bounced off the cottage walls. It echoed off the floor, the ceiling, the windows. It danced in, and danced out. Marek was pumping at her chest, both hands splayed. His eyes bulging.

I was counting, but the numbers were getting too high. 24, 25, 26. Raven was warbling; unintelligible alien cackles, repeated rhythmic sounds.

Natalya was not responding. It was taking too long. It was a thirty-minute drive to the hospital. Too far to even consider. Unless. Unless we could get her breathing again.

56, 57, 58.

Marek paused. He stood up, banging his shin against the coffee table. He grimaced and scrunched his hands into tight balls in front of his face. Logan was in the far corner now. He was pleading with something or someone. The voice in his head. Louder and louder. Rosa's voice. Pleading with him.

'Fight back, Logan.
You have to fight back.
Don't be so passive.
Remember what it was like to be alone.'

Raven had stopped her warble. I had stopped my count.
Marek had not resumed his attempts to resuscitate her.

'Let me in, Logan.'

Rosa's voice was calm, reassuring.

'Let me in, Logan.
Breathe, just breathe.'

Natalya lay on the sofa. Her frost-white flesh. Cold. Lifeless.
Her red hair, tangled, knotted. Her mouth, her lips. Dry. Closed.

I looked beyond her through the window over the loch.
She was a shadow within a shadow. A misted reflection in the
summer glass. I could see the mirrored image of Logan moving
forward and Marek stepping back. I placed my arm around
Marek's shoulder. He gripped me hard on the elbow.

Raven was flying. Small circles over the sofa. Clockwise.

I watched in the glass. As she looped, a repeated circle. Her
wings. The beat of her wings. A steady rhythm; a *thwap, thwap,*
thwap of beating wings breaking the silence. I watched in the
glass. As Logan clasped Natalya's hand in both of his. He was
kneeling in front of the sofa. His face pressed close to her chest.

'Will you be with me forever?
Will you guide me and love me?
Will you be with me forever?'

And still Raven flew. The beating of her wings coinciding
with the gaps between Logan's words.

'Will you be with me forever?
Will you guide me and love me?
Will you be with me forever?'

And the beating of her wings.

And in the glass I saw the sun over the loch. The orange glow of light reflecting. The room was filled with an oak tree scent. Logan was whispering.

'Breathe. Breathe, my darling. Come back to me. Come back to me.'

And Raven's wings beat a steady rhythm. And I felt a pulse of energy rising within me. And the grip on my elbow fell away. I looked to my right. Marek was in his badger form. On his back legs, his front limbs outstretched. And Logan was whispering.

'Breathe. Breathe. Breathe.'

There was a crack. The lightbulb above me shattered. The cottage fell orange in the sunset glow. And the weasel within me let out a shriek. A high-pitched shrill scream.

And Natalya sat up. Choking, gulping, swallowing. She sucked in the air, six or seven deep breaths. Panting. Her eyes bloodshot and dazed. Her breathing rasping, slowing, returning to something more normal now.

Her gaze catching on Raven's wings. Concentrating, she breathed in rhythm with her as she flew round the sofa in a steady circle. And Marek, still on his hind legs, started to applaud with his paws.

And Logan stared into her eyes. Her brilliant, green fox-eyes. And Natalya laughed. A beautiful laugh that smelt to him of moss and lichen.

'Welcome back, my darling.' Logan kissed her gently on the forehead.

'Welcome back,' I repeated in a voice that may not have been my own.

Natalya clung to Logan, her arms wrapped around his neck. Pulling him closer, she held him in a tight embrace.

FIFTY-THREE

A darkness descending

Mosses, ferns, lichens. Their scents invigorating. The rainwater dripping from the branches overhead trickle down her back. Freshening and cleansing. Before her is a rock, a grey rock. It seems incongruous. Raven flaps her wings once and lands on top of it. From her elevated position she can see the trees more clearly. It is beautiful. Her first visit to the forest. Normally, she had flown around the loch, but today the rain had made her seek out shelter.

The trees here are ancient; wise. They speak to her in a tongue that is unfamiliar yet reassuring. One tree in particular caught her attention. A wild service tree. Its bark clipped, as if someone, or something had been scratching. She hops down off the rock and lands at the root of the tree. A smell, a scent which she knows well. Badger. Marek. So, this is where he has been coming.

She glances up to the high branches. It is a magical place; the atmosphere feels electric. Behind the tree there are scats and behind them signs of digging. Hopping forward, she stares for a few seconds. That is when she spots the entrance to the sett.

The dappled light had made it difficult to see. She hops forward three times and peers into the dark entrance.

'Hey!'

Startled by a flash of light she calls out in alarm. Two eyes are peering out at her. She opens her wings, as if to fly, but hesitates. The scent has changed.

She can smell burning; fire. Is this her? A reflection? A mirror? The eyes are at the wrong height. Too small for a badger. Too low down for a starling.

If it is not her own self she is seeing, then who?

A voice. A quiet voice.

'Is there anybody else?'

'Is there anybody else?'

Raven looks up at the sky. The light is changing. She ought to return to the cottage for dinner.

'Is there anybody else?'

The voice is faint, echoing. The shadows beneath where the voice comes from are receding. The shape is consolidating.

It is her. The weasel. From the fire. Her shell. Her spirit. Her soul. Her ghost.

'Is there anybody else?'

Why has she come? Why now?

'Is there anybody else?'

This cannot be a good omen. It is a warning. Taking her back to that moment. 'What is it that we should be afraid of?' Raven calls out. Trying to camouflage her fear. Flapping her wings to take off. She lands on the freshly-dug earth. The damp soil is cold under her feet. She repeats her cry.

'What is it that we should be afraid of?'

There is no answer. A third time, her question differs slightly.

'Who is it that we should be afraid of?'

Looking directly into the sett's entrance. The weasel has gone. The lights from her eyes extinguished. There is nothing before her but darkness.

FIFTY-FOUR

Midsummer Feast

I'd gotten up after 10am. Another night of disturbed sleep. It must have been 4 or 5 in the morning before my mind cleared enough to allow me to sleep. I felt wrecked.

Logan greeted me in the kitchen, handing me a coffee and a bowl of muesli. 'You've got fifteen minutes to eat your breakfast then the kitchen is out of bounds.'

I stared at him blankly. 'Here's your shopping list. Marek's car keys are in the hallway.'

'What's this for?' I asked. 'There's enough to feed a dozen people.'

'I'm cooking a solstice feast to celebrate Natalya being saved. It's a fox tradition to dine in style at midsummer.'

'But do you really need all of this?'

'Yours is not to question the wisdom of the fox-chef.' Logan flicked me with a tea-towel. 'Don't hang about, there's a lot of cooking to do. Quick, quick, get to it.'

There were to be six courses. All of which were vegan. A starter of red pepper houmous on black olive crackers, followed by a celeriac, fennel and orange zest soup. Then a carrot and parsnip loaf served with new potatoes, berry coulis and a crisp green salad. This was accompanied by sweet and sour kale muffins with a cucumber raita. And for dessert, rhubarb crumble with vanilla custard and chocolate and beetroot brownies.

Despite my tiredness, the drive to and from Lochgilphead passed without incident. I went to both the Co-op and Tesco as well as an old-fashioned greengrocer. Stopping to get a takeaway coffee before my drive back, I spotted a small shop whose display had a mix of second-hand electrical items, including mobile phones.

I had a flashback to Natalya in the mobile phone shop, that first day, May Day. If something happened to me in Lochgilphead, I had no way of communicating with the others. Despite what Marek may think, we each needed a mobile phone. I took a deep breath and entered the shop.

The woman working there could not be more unlike Natalya. Scottish, plump, brunette and sullen. She did me a deal on three pay-as-you-go phones, each with £20 credit for £180 in total. Not wanting to pay by card, in case it got traced, I went to the cashpoint opposite and paid with cash.

The whole trip had taken around three hours. A light, persistent drizzle was falling as I parked outside the cottage. Back inside, Natalya was up but still in a dressing gown. She leant against the kitchen door holding a cup of what smelt like coffee.

'Good to see you,' I said, dropping down the last of the shopping bags.

'You too.'

'How are you feeling?'

'Surprisingly OK. A little achy, but I'm surviving.'

'At last, at last. What kept you?' Logan emerged from the kitchen. 'I've got to get started if you want to eat before

Lammas. Out my way. Out my way. Everyone out, only Logan the masterchef and his sous chef Marek Dogovsky allowed in here now.'

Shooed away into the conservatory, myself and Natalya sat side by side on the two-seater sofa. Looking out over the loch.

'It's good to have you back, Nat,' I said, smiling.

'It's good to be here.'

'You scared us all you know, with stopping breathing like that. How are you really?'

'Tired and sore, but… you know. Alive and kicking.'

'Good.'

'Funny thing is. How much stronger everything smells. Garlic, rosemary, cinnamon. Coming from the kitchen just now. It's like I've got a whole new nose.'

'Strange. Heightened senses. I guess it's a reaction of the body somehow.'

'They have oranges and lemons out now.'

'I've never been that strong at smelling. Always a bit sinusy.'

'Yeah, I noticed.'

'Can you keep a secret?' I asked.

As I spoke, a loud 'Ow! Sweet mother of Reynard' came from the kitchen. Logan swore repeatedly.

'Shall I see if he needs help?'

'No. He'll be fine. He's probably just grated his knuckles. He was always doing that in the campervan. Not quite used to having opposable thumbs. What's this secret you want to tell me about?'

'This.'

I laid out the three mobile phones on the coffee table. 'Don't tell Marek, but if something happened whilst I was out shopping there would be no way of contacting you or Logan.

They are old-fashioned ones, not smart, no GPS, no Wi-Fi. So, chances of being tracked are much less.'

'Cool. That's a good idea. Can I have the red one?'

'You can have whichever one you want, Nat.'

She had leant forward to pick up the phone. I tried not to look at the long, white sliver of leg that was exposed. Was I envious that Logan had found her before I did? I always found it so easy talking to her. Daft, I was being daft. Pull yourself together, Blake. She was too young for me anyway.

'Listen to that rain,' Natalya said as she leant back. A strand of her red hair tickling its way close to her mouth.

'Typical Scottish midsummer,' I mumbled.

'Oh, here's Raven. Can you get the door?'

I felt a sense of relief no longer having to be alone with Natalya and watched as Raven shook rainwater from her wings and took a moment to settle. A brief silence, then Natalya spoke. 'Fancy watching some DVDs? I found some great ones in the bookcase.'

'Cool,' squawked Raven.

'A duvet day. Let the badger and fox do the work for a change.' Natalya was heading to the lounge. My eyes followed her as she moved.

So, whilst Logan cooked, Marek chopped and scrubbed, and we watched three films back to back. *Watership Down, Flash Gordon* and *Muppets Take Manhattan*. I wasn't sure if the DVDs came with the cottage or if Marek had got them. Funny, as they happened to be three of my all-time favourites. As the credits rolled on Kermit and Miss Piggy, the rain outside stopped and blue sky finally began to appear.

I opened the conservatory door for Raven to stretch her wings and then heard Marek shout, 'An hour. Dinner will be served in an hour.' Turning around, I saw how red and sweaty he looked. 'It's like a sauna in there. I'm off to get showered.'

'I'd better get dressed too.' Natalya followed him, though more slowly. My gaze drawn to her as she rubbed the back of her left leg with knuckles as if trying to get the circulation going again. Her gown scrunched up, revealing more flesh and a large purple bruise. She turned around, and I blushed slightly, wondering if she had sensed me looking at her.

'It's lovely out there now. Let's eat outside.'

'Great idea,' I said, beginning to pick up the glasses and cutlery. A freshened-up Marek helped me carry the table out to the patio. He rushed back to the kitchen after Logan shrieked for his assistance. By the time the table was fully set, Raven was back and perched herself at its head.

'I've been chatting to the beavers up on the loch. They told me it is going to be clear all night and they are having a midsummer feast too,' she said.

Natalya sat opposite me. Her wet hair revealing a jagged scalp wound near her left temple. The bruising underneath her eye was camouflaged with fresh make-up. Marek emerged with the first of the dishes on a tray, a tea towel over his arm. He unloaded his goodies with uncharacteristic flamboyance and charm. Logan followed, carrying two bottles of wine.

Seated at last, Marek cleared his throat with a dramatic cough. 'Dinner is served, but before we eat, we must make a toast. To the spirits of the forest!'

We all raised our glasses, except for Raven who was sharing Natalya's and joined in by tapping her beak on the glass.

'To the forest!' shouted Marek.

'To truth and justice!' Raven called out.

'To love and peace.' Natalya this time.

'To the wheel of the year turning,' I called.

'To the food of the land nourishing us all.' Logan's turn.

'To the solstice!' All of us in unison.

The sixth and final toast complete. One toast for each course about to be served, finally we could get started.

How glorious the food was. Fresh tastes, delicious smells, beautiful textures, a rainbow of colours. Logan was a genius cook. I had never tasted food so divine.

Before it came to the final dessert, Logan drew himself up to his feet and waited for the conversation to subside. Myself and Natalya simultaneously banged our glasses with spoons and shouted, 'Speech, Speech.'

Marek let out an overdramatised groan and playfully buried his head in his hands, and Raven flew up and landed on Natalya's shoulder.

Picking up his glass of wine, Logan milked the moment, before Natalya's 'get on with it, sexy fox' prompted him to start. I felt another unexpected pang of jealousy. I leant over the table to top up my glass, resisting the temptation to interrupt Logan.

'Friends. Tonight is midsummer's eve. The longest day. The brightest day. And we have much to celebrate.' I looked up at Raven. She was nodding her agreement.

'I don't know what really happened. Without a doctor we can't really know for sure. But my true love came back to me and made me the happiest...' Logan paused. 'Made me the happiest mutant fox-man in the universe.' I glanced at Natalya, she was both blushing and beaming. 'The happiest, the luckiest and the humblest. For as you know I have already loved once and lost. And when it looked like I might lose again... Well, I don't need to go there, do I.'

Raven had hopped down off Natalya and perched instead on my shoulder; her presence was reassuring.

'And so, Natalya, my beautiful foxy woman. You have made me the happiest foxy man alive. Not just by breathing, but by believing. Believing in me. Our future will be blessed with great joy and I cannot wait to share it with you.'

Natalya now stood and embraced him across the table in a firm hug. She was crying. Logan waved at her to sit back down.

'But it is not just her I need to toast. Please refill your glasses.'

A wee commotion as glasses and bottles moved amongst us.

I looked at Raven. She mouthed – well, beaked – something to me, but I couldn't catch what she said. Logan had started again.

'To the badger-man, Marek. My soul brother, without whom I would have perished. His courage and determination got us to safety, and he brought us together in this' – he waved his arms across a 360 degree arc – 'little piece of paradise and he is simply the best kitchen assistant a mutant fox-man masterchef could ask for.'

'To Marek!' Natalya's shout drowned out all our other voices combined.

Raven had jumped down off my shoulder and was back on the table, just as Logan started his next toast. 'To Raven. The bravest and wisest amongst us. Without her we would have died in that fire and none of this would have happened.'

'To Raven!' This time it was my voice which was the loudest.

A pause and then Natalya spoke.

'And to the weasel-man, who gave us shelter and who never judges. A beautiful creature who too has known sorrow and loneliness. But he has warmth in his heart that like this midsummer day burns forever brightly. To the host with the most, weasel-man.'

'To weasel-man.' It was Logan whose voice resonated the strongest on this toast.

I was blushing. Embarrassed by their description. Not knowing where to look. By the time I had refocussed, Natalya was back on her feet.

'I can't let this evening pass without a toast to our fantastic foxy cook. To the one who has lit up my whole world and brought me back to life. He has enchanted us all with his food. But he has also magically captured my heart. To Logan – please everyone – raise your glasses to Logan.'

'To Logan.' Our voices rang out as one, but I felt an echo of sadness as I watched the two of them again embrace. Then silence, a single moment of silence, before Logan shouted, 'Time for pudding.' With a dramatic click of his fingers, Marek stood and followed Logan to the kitchen. Natalya also stood. 'I need a piss after all that excitement.'

Just me and Raven were left. She was pecking at the tablecloth, her body language appeared awry, awkward. As if, now the others had gone indoors, she could stop pretending.

'Sorry, Raven. Are you OK? You seem a little on edge.'

'It's nothing, it can wait.'

'No, please, tell me.'

'I don't want to ruin the moment. Everyone is having such a lovely time. I don't want to spoil it.'

'Spoil it?' I held out my finger for her to perch on, but she stayed on the table.

'I have a bad feeling, that's all.'

'A bad feeling?'

'That this will be the last time we will all be together.'

'Sorry?'

Logan and Natalya had re-emerged. He was singing to her. Oh God, where did he get that song from? Renée and Renato, *Save Your Love*. Logan, please.

They were kissing now as they walked. Finally disentangling as they reached us. They sat holding hands across the table.

'Pudding is served.' Marek put down the tray. The crumble was in a large, green, oval dish, its topping a golden brown. A separate plate held eight perfect squares of dark chocolate brownies.

'Have they really got beetroot in them?' Natalya asked.

'One hundred per cent full-fat beetroot, my long-haired lover from Lith-uania,' sang back Logan, in a decidedly un-Jimmy Osmond growl. As he leant over to kiss Natalya again, his right hand clunked heavily onto a dessert spoon that catapulted hot custard over the table. Some of it landing on Raven's feet.

'Sorry, sorry, sorry,' he whispered. I whisked out a tissue from my pocket and mopped at the mess.

'I'm going in,' Raven squawked.

'Oh please, it was just a wee accident, my friend.' Logan's speech was a little slurred.

'And you haven't eaten your brownie yet,' added Natalya.

'I'm full, Logan. I'm not used to such rich food. I'm tired, it's been an emotional couple of days. I need to rest before my journey tomorrow.'

'Journey?' I asked.

Natalya had leant forward so that her head was level with Raven's beak. 'Are you going somewhere without us?' Her tone was playful, but Raven did not seem amused. We were all seated now, except for Raven, who was perched on top of an empty wine bottle.

'I'm sorry to interrupt your festivities. I need to roost, I'm tired.'

'You said you were going on a journey?' I tried to sound sympathetic and non-judgemental, but I too had drunk much more wine than usual, so I wasn't sure how I sounded.

'I'm flying to Glasgow.' Raven sounded angry.

'Glasgow?' Natalya and Logan in unison. 'Glasgow?' I repeated a fraction behind them.

Only Marek stayed silent.

'There is something happening which we should witness.'

'What's happening?' Logan asked, leaning forward to pick up a chocolate brownie as he spoke.

'It's complicated. I only know snatches from what the other birds have been saying.'

'I didn't know you'd been chatting to the birds,' I said, also helping myself to a brownie from the plate.

'I hear their conversations as they fly past, and sometimes they stick.'

'You've been listening to their tweets, in other words,' Logan said, his mouth half-full.

Raven ignored the joke.

'There is a gathering tomorrow in George Square to protest against the prime minister's visit to a food bank, a Nobler Age food bank. And also...' She paused. 'To remember the protestor who was shot.' Raven stared at me. Waiting for me to react. Mike. They were gathering for him. Why? I was confused. Struggling to follow the implications of what Raven had just said.

'I was going to fly over and take a look,' Raven said, still in her human tongue.

'And when exactly did you plan on telling us this?' Marek

stood up from the table, his chair scraping, ripping the napkin from his chin. He threw it down on the table next to Raven. She hopped down off the bottle, and turned her back on Marek, starting to preen anxiously.

The scraping of another chair. This time it was Natalya.

'Look, we have had a tremendous evening. A beautiful feast. But we need to be open with one another. With none of this secrecy...' She then turned to Marek. 'Or petty gesturing.'

'I am not gesturing, Natalya. I am just pissed at Raven for not mentioning this sooner.'

'And you tell us everything, don't you Marek. You tell us everything all the time.' Raven was circling the table now, clearly distressed.

'Look everyone, let's calm down,' I said, pulling myself up from the table. Making eye contact with Natalya.

'Calm down, calm down.' Logan was chiming in a fake Scouse accent, his arms waving.

Natalya glared at him. 'You need to sober up, Logan. Go in and make some coffee. It's getting cold, so I suggest we tidy up out here and meet inside in five minutes. And I mean all of us. No sulking off into your badger costume, Marek.' She turned to me. 'You can bring in the crumble and brownies. There's no way I'm going to miss out on them.'

FIFTY-FIVE

Anomalies

'Fucking irrelevant,' Chilcoat snarled. Harry was regurgitating anomaly after anomaly in the food bank data. Inconsistencies in methodologies, the absence of peer review and the rapidly increasing rate of hospital admissions.

'You are missing the fucking point, Harry.' The two of them, sat in the boardroom. Opposite sides of the table.

'Look, boss, even Franklyn Whitlock is with me on this. He emailed me again this morning about the risk of cross-contamination of genetic samples in the lab.'

'The *Chief Grovelling Government Scientist*. You dare quote that man to me? For fuck's sake, Harry. That man is so wet he could drown in his own spittle. What he thinks is irrelevant.'

'Boss, but what about the suicides? Wasn't that one of the alerts we talked about when setting out the research parameters?'

'Look, Harry, the Americans aren't providing all this food for us to come up with anomalies. A few suicides can be expected. Collateral damage, as they say.' The conversation paused. Chilcoat watched as Harry leant forward to sip at his coffee, which must have been cold by now.

'I can live with some anomalies, boss, let the data run its course so we can properly assess the risks, but there is something else.'

'Yes, Harry. I am all ears.' Chilcoat's tone was sarcastic, dismissive.

'I think JFS needs to know about the security risks of tomorrow's visit. Section 7 are advising it should be postponed, or moved to another city. Not Glasgow. Not with the protests planned over Mike Jansen's death.'

'Section 7 are a bunch of lily-livered cunts, Harry. Are you really saying that their judgement is more informed than mine?' Chilcoat leant across the table, his chin resting on the outstretched thumb of his left hand.

'I've had three missed calls from Hughie. Wanting an update on the security arrangements. I need to know what to tell him.'

'Fuck the home secretary. The visit is going ahead, Harry. You know the schedule. You know the plan. I've looked at the data. It's fine. It's all on track. But we need the PM's visit tomorrow to help reinforce the normality of the Nobler Age brand. It's a staging post. A midway point.'

'To what, sir? With respect, I am no longer clear about the endgame. The data to me is clear and I don't reach the same conclusions as you. Neither do any of the scientists. The food bank trials reveal nothing reliable about the genetic causes of poverty.'

Chilcoat stood up quickly, knocking his chair over in the process. He circled the table and lunging forward, grabbed Harry by his shoulders. Expecting a headbutt, Harry instinctively covered his face.

'Come with me, Harry. I have something to show you. Something that will stop you from whingeing on about data.

242

This is not about understanding and curing poverty. It is something bigger. So much bigger.'

Out of the boardroom and into a corridor. Turning left and then right. Walking in silence. Reaching a fire door. A warning sign saying it was alarmed. Chilcoat pushing at the grey bar, opening it, but no alarm sounded. Another corridor. Darker. No windows, no doors. And at its end, a staircase leading down. Heading further down. Into a basement within a basement. A locked door. Three keys and two bolts to open it. Still no words exchanged.

Standing in a low-ceilinged room, perhaps twelve foot wide and ten foot long. Dark. Cold.

Chilcoat flicked on a light switch, a single bulb casting a pale yellow glow over the grey walls. The room was bare except for a single red-leather armchair. And a small foldable card table on which sat a frosted glass and an empty whisky bottle.

'There's only one seat in here, we can stand,' said Chilcoat.

'It's freezing in here, boss.'

Chilcoat pointed at the wall opposite the door.

'What am I looking at boss? It's a bare wall.'

'Use your eyes, Harry. Engage your brain.'

Harry stepped over to the wall, anxiously looking up and down.

'There's nothing there, boss. It's just a wall. Can we get back to talking about the data reports? What did you mean it wasn't about curing poverty?'

'Fuck the data, Harry. You need to start using your imagination. Have I got to spell everything out for you?'

Chilcoat slipped his right hand inside his jacket's inner pocket and pulled out a pistol. A compact Smith & Wesson.

He waved it around three times, before pointing directly at Harry's forehead.

'Examine the wall, Harry. Use those brilliant blue eyes of yours. If you can't find what you are looking for then you'll be joining Mike Jansen sooner than you think.'

Harry blinked rapidly. 'The wall… i-it's, um…' Stuttering now and breathing heavily. 'It's not one solid wall. It's made up of eight, no, nine different panels.'

'Very good, Harry. Carry on.'

Harry turned around and started to search the wall again. The pistol now pointed at the back of his head.

'And the middle panel, to the right of it is a small button. A metallic circle.'

'Press it, Harry. Press the button. See what happens.'

Chilcoat was right up against him now. The gun tight against his right temple. Harry gulped for air as he pressed the button. A twelve-inch metallic rod emerged, extending out at a right angle. At the same time a red light in the ceiling panel started flashing. On the top of the rod was an LCD display and a scrolling message.

'Read what it says, Harry.' Chilcoat pushed the point of the pistol harder into his temple.

'It's a-asking…' Harry stuttered, 'it's asking to enter a security code.'

'You've got thirty seconds, Harry. Thirty seconds to enter the code. If you don't, then the alarm will go off. And that may cause a reaction.'

'But I don't know the code, boss.'

'You don't know the code?'

'No. Please. Lynton. I don't. I'll do anything you want. But I can't do this.'

'Pathetic.'

Chilcoat pushed Harry out of the way. 'Allow me the honour.'

Then entered the eight-digit code. 13101925. The Great Lady's birthday. The red light in the ceiling stopped flashing, and the room returned back into a synthetic yellow glow. A loud rumbling, then a metallic sound. The middle section of the wall was opening. A large metal chute emerged like an elongated drawer of a filing cabinet. Chilcoat held the gun to Harry's throat.

'Get down on your knees. And pay your respects.'

The slow-moving drawer had stopped. Chilcoat stood next to Harry. The gun now pointed directly into his right ear.

'Now, Harry. Take a look inside the drawer.'

Chilcoat yanked Harry up. Pulled him over to the open cabinet and thrust his face into the portion furthest away from the wall. It was that part of the coffin which was open. It was that part of the coffin where the Great Lady rested her head. Her skeletal face rested on a purple and gold cushion. Where she waited. Until the conditions were right. Until the work was done. Until she could return.

'Now Harry, tell the Lady that everything in the data is fine. That everything is getting sorted. That there are no anomalies.'

FIFTY-SIX

Secrets and lies

I was pacing round the lounge. Pawing at my eyes, rubbing them, scratching them. 'How long have you known?'

'Marek. How long have you known?' Silence. Marek stared at the floor; he looked sullen, angry. He refused to answer.

'And the rest of you? How long have you known that my friend Mike was killed? My friend. Not your friend.' I paused. 'How long have you known?'

'This morning, when you were out shopping. That's when Marek told me and Logan.' Natalya's voice was sympathetic, apologetic. I had sat back down, and she leant forward, touching me gently on the elbow.

'And you, Raven?' I shrugged off Natalya's hand, not ready to accept any comfort.

'Only tonight. In the forest. Before I came here. From my conversation with…' She hesitated. 'With the birds.'

'Tweeting again, Raven, I see.' Logan grinned.

'That's not funny, Logan. None of this is fucking funny.' I was back on my feet again. I wasn't upset by what Raven was saying, wasn't concerned about her hiding information from me. It was Marek who had been concealing too much for too long.

'And when did you first know about this Marek?' He looked straight at me, but stayed silent. I couldn't read what he was thinking, couldn't see any emotion in his face.

'WHEN?!' I shouted, my face six inches from his.

'I didn't want to upset you,' he said finally, lifting up a half-empty wine glass from the coffee table and swilling the contents round his mouth.

'Upset me? And you think this isn't?'

Silence. A group of friends suddenly feeling like strangers.

'Look, this isn't helping any of us.' Natalya the peacemaker again. 'Just tell him won't you, Marek? How did you find out?'

Marek put his glass down, empty.

'I've been researching.'

'Researching? What kind of researching?'

'Online. At night. Here in the cottage, whilst you were sleeping.'

'But you told us there wasn't Wi-Fi? And besides, I tried on both your laptop and iPad and no connections showed up.' Logan's turn to enter the conversation.

'They are both fully encrypted and you need three levels of code to get online. A novice wouldn't know how to.'

I glanced at Logan. He looked angry.

'Great. You have an all-singing, all-dancing IT with secret internet connections, and I just get this crummy Nokia that can't even check the weather forecast.'

He dropped the phone I had given him on the coffee table. It rattled against the empty wine glass.

'And where did you get that?' For the first time Marek look agitated.

'I bought them this morning. They are not smart, so not traceable and I paid in cash. We need some way of keeping in touch when we are apart.'

'They can still track our calls, you idiot, and these phones are too basic to be encrypted. After all I've done to keep us safe. I can't believe you've been so stupid.'

'Go fuck yourself, Marek.' I was pacing again. My head buzzing.

'Look, this isn't helping. We are all on the same side, we have got to trust one another. Marek, you were wrong to keep information about Mike to yourself. Blake had a right to know.' Natalya sounded close to tears now. Marek stared at her. His fingers on his nose. He wouldn't change, not now, would he?

'Look, Blake, you're upset, you're tired. We are all tired. It's been a long day. Let's not argue. It's what they would want, for us to fall out. Fall apart.' Natalya again speaking the most sense. 'Agreed,' Raven called out from above us, before fluttering down onto the top of my head.

'I'm sorry about your friend.' She spoke gently, her beak close to my ear.

'Yeah, me too.' Logan embraced me. Patting me hard on the back. 'If it wasn't for him I may not have had the confidence to ask Natalya out on a date. What do they call it? Dutch courage? I owe him at least three pints of Guinness.'

I snorted. 'If I remember rightly, it was Natalya who made the first move.'

'Yeah, let's not go there,' Natalya chipped in. 'The main thing is to decide what we are going to do tomorrow. Should we go into Glasgow? I don't think I could face it.'

'I'll stay with you, babes.' Logan hugged her as he spoke.

'Myself and Raven can go.' Marek was by the kitchen door. His wine glass no longer empty. 'The rest of you can make the tribute video.'

'The what?' Natalya and I spoke in unison.

'A video tribute to your friend. A follow-up to the CCA video. To post online ahead of the demo. I can show you how to encrypt it so it's safe to post.'

'Where did you learn all this, Marek?' Natalya asked. He didn't reply. He was rubbing hard at his nose. It wouldn't be long until he was badger again.

FIFTY-SEVEN

Phobia

It had been thirty-one years since he had been on a plane. An inconvenience rather than a fully-fledged phobia, he would say to people. But tonight he had no choice. A private jet. Just him and the two pilots. He needed to be in Glasgow early. Before first light. Couldn't rely on the sleeper train. Couldn't face a seven-hour car journey. He stared at the tarmac and then up at the plane. It seemed small, fragile. Its white chassis devoid of any markings.

Lynton Chilcoat. What would the Great Lady think? Just get on the fucking plane. He laughed at himself.

He had contemplated calling the agency. A girl for the flight to take his mind off things. But he didn't want anyone to witness him like this. Or drugs. Morphine. Cannabis. All easily arrangeable. No, he needed a clear head for the morning.

Lynton Chilcoat, just get on the fucking plane. He was already wired after his meeting with Harry. Wasn't wise to risk another adrenaline shot.

Lynton Chilcoat, just get on the fucking plane.

'We're ready for you now, sir.' The pilot beckoned him.

Gripping hard on the handrail. Eight steps and then in. Was this as bad as it would get? After all these years? A blue curtain separated the cockpit from the cabin. There was space for six passengers, but he was the only one. Three rows of two. He sat in the back row, closest to the emergency exit.

'How long is the flight?' he asked the pilot

'Just over ninety minutes.'

'And weather conditions?'

'All calm. Very little wind.'

'So no turbulence?'

'Nothing to worry about, sir. Now, can I get you something before we get ready for take-off?'

'A whisky? Bell's if you have it.'

'Of course.'

Chilcoat belted himself in. Glass of whisky in his hand. Staring ahead.

A loud whirring. The engine started. Vibrating. Loud. So close. Taxiing along the runway. Gaining speed. Take-off. Gaining height. No longer horizontal. The plane rising sharply. One of the most dangerous parts of the flight accomplished. Statistically safer now. Grasping the armrest. Still not taken a sip from his glass. A change in pressure. Was there enough oxygen in here? His eyes closed.

Two faces. Their faces.

'Are you all right, sir?'

The co-pilot, out of his seat. Leaning over him. Smelling of chewing gum. Chilcoat ignored him. Too lost in his memories to answer.

In the hotel. Showering. Hot jets of water. Cascading off his body. Calming down. Washing away the images from his mind.

BANQUET OF THE BEASTS

Forty, maybe fifty minutes since they landed. Unable to recall anything of the car journey from the airport.

The anonymity of it all. A chain hotel. A lone business traveller. Nothing unusual, nothing untoward. Arriving in the middle of the night. No witnesses save for the duty manager on reception. He'd transfer to the Hilton tomorrow, after JFS had been dealt with. He wasn't thinking about that now.

Their faces in his mind. Her face. His daughter's face. Fading into the background. Where it needed to be. Where she had to be.

A busy day in front of him. No time for distractions. No place for wasted thoughts. No time for sentiment. Too much to do. Not time for her. And besides, he had to be ready to enjoy the day ahead.

FIFTY-EIGHT

Approaching midday

She'd been anxiously hopping the whole journey. From the passenger seat to the dashboard and back again. The closer to Glasgow, the jumpier she became. She and Marek had exchanged but a handful of words on the ninety-minute journey. She found him disconcerting. His flash of indignation at the dinner table. His refusal to reveal how he knew what he knew.

She wished that Blake, the weasel one, was with her. She felt safe with him, she could trust him. With Marek you never knew what mood he would be in. How he would react. He'd disappeared once and he could do it again.

Where had he been all that time after May Day? Where did he get his money from? The car, the cottage, the laptop, the iPad? Logan was straightforward. What you saw is what you got. Marek? She did not feel safe around him.

She hopped back onto the passenger seat, they were approaching the Erskine Bridge. Traffic was busy but still moving. An orange campervan, similar to the one Logan and Natalya had on Bute, overtook them. She thought back to her journey to Rothesay, in the back of the Nobler Age truck. Why did she feel the same now as then? She had a bad feeling about today. A very bad feeling indeed.

My phone beeped. Marek. *Crossing Erskine Bridge. On Schedule.*

Not much detail there then, but at least he'd texted as we'd finally agreed. Agreed to text each other on an hourly basis. He was two minutes ahead of schedule, in fact. It was Natalya who had won him round to the importance of keeping in touch over breakfast. The need to act as a team, not just individuals. I texted back *In woods, all ok*, pondered whether I should say anything else, then hit *send*.

Logan gave me a big thumbs up. 'We're ready. Start filming, Batman.' I held up Marek's laptop in front of me and after double-checking the encryption settings, began recording.

'My name is Logan Fox. I am a friend of Mike Jansen. Mike was a peaceful protestor. Mike was a gentle person. He never hurt anybody in his life. He loved making people happy. He stood alongside the badgers and foxes and those without a voice. He wanted a better world. A kinder world. He was shot by someone who is doing bad things to the animals. Mike's killing was not an accident. They wanted him to be quiet, wanted him to go away. Wanted to cause suffering, fear and terror. I am not alone in missing Mike. We are all grieving for his loss. Without him our life will never be the same again. But they will never stop us remembering our friend Mike and all he stood for.'

Chilcoat stood at the entrance to the City Chambers. In just over an hour everything would change. He sucked in air in deep breaths, savouring the taste of it, wanting to remember the enormity of this moment. Today would go down in history. The first time in over a century that a sitting British prime minister would be assassinated. Nobody remembers 11th May 1812, when John Bellingham shot dead the Right Honourable Spencer Perceval as he entered the House of Commons lobby. But everyone would remember where they were when Joshua Francis Swill was shot, in the same way they remembered where they were when JFK got a bullet through his head.

The square was filling up. Two, maybe, three-hundred protestors, more coming in. They were tightly controlled by the police whose numbers almost matched them. A single entrance, protestors channelled into a 'protest zone' fenced off from the rest of the square. Visibly armed officers patrolling the zone's perimeter. Searching protestors as they entered, confiscating megaphones, loudspeakers, anything that could make the crowd heard over the incessant buzz of the helicopter overhead.

Traffic was slow as they approached the city centre, almost down to a crawl. Raven hopped from side to side on the passenger seat.

'I could get out and fly to the square quicker than this, Marek.'

'And I could walk there faster too.' There was something in his voice that rattled her. Was it nonchalance or was it arrogance? She found him hard to read.

'I could go ahead and meet you there?' Raven asked.

Marek grunted. Pressing a button, the passenger window opened and she flew out, landing on the wing mirror of the now stationary car.

'I'll find you in the square,' she squawked as the window closed.

We were back in the cottage. Logan in the kitchen reheating leftovers for an early lunch. Natalya and I sat side by side in the conservatory. I was hungry, the brisk walk back had given me an appetite.

'I'm really sorry about Mike. He seemed like a good guy.'

'He was. He could drive me a bit mad at times, especially after a few beers. But he was really sound. You know I can't believe he's…' My sentence trailed off into nothingness.

'It can't be easy for you. Being on your own and so soon after you split up with your wife and all.'

'We weren't married.'

'But you lived together?'

'Only for two years.'

'That's still a long time.'

'It seems too short to me.'

'I'm sorry, that came out wrong.' Natalya leant forward, her face close to mine. I saw tiredness in her eyes.

'You don't really feel comfortable talking about this, do you?' she said, leaning back a little. Silence. Natalya stretched out her hand and gently rested it on my shoulder. 'I would like to have met her. You must miss not having her around.'

I didn't reply. Thinking of my last encounter with Mike. The way he blinked when I asked him about Mandy. Which was hurting me more right now? His betrayal, or him being dead? Was it selfish of me to no longer care? Did I miss Mandy? Or was I feeling guilty at my fondness for Natalya? My longing for something, somebody I knew I could not have?

'Well, Logan used to miss Rosa, but he got over that,' I half-whispered, not sure if Natalya heard me. My phone beeped.

'Was that Marek?' Logan had re-entered the room, carrying a tray of kale muffins and three mugs of Earl Grey tea.

'Yes, it's Marek.'

'Well?' Logan asked, balancing the tray on the coffee table. *Traffic bad, Raven flown ahead. All OK.*

'Is that a good thing?' Natalya asked, helping herself to a muffin.

'I'm not sure,' said Logan, 'let's see if any of the protest groups have set up a live-stream we can watch. I can't believe Marek didn't tell us there was Wi-Fi.'

'Do you think we should? He told us not to use any sites he hadn't screened for us in advance.'

'Ah, he's not here, so he won't know. Ten minutes won't hurt.' Logan was opening up the laptop as he spoke.

She flew low. It was her sixth circuit and still no sign of Marek. The square was full. The protestors were penned in, more than a thousand people, she reckoned, perhaps nearer two thousand. Police surrounded the fence four-deep. Traffic passed slowly on three sides of the square, but the road in front of the Chambers was blocked off.

She glanced up at the clock tower. Almost midday. This didn't feel good. This didn't feel good at all.

FIFTY-NINE

Impact

Chilcoat sipped at his whisky. His car was parked on North Frederick Street, about a hundred yards from where JFS would be hit. Behind him were half a dozen police vans. In front, two unmarked armed response vehicles. Tapping the remote control, the screen flickered into life. Four displays. Screen One: inside the Chambers; Screen Two: the front steps of the building; Screen Three: a close-up of the protestors; Screen Four: an aerial shot of the whole square.

Not long now. He slipped on his headphones, grey wireless headphones, extra padding for comfort. An approving nod, the sound quality was exceptional. Zooming in on Screen One. He could hear people's whispered asides from within the Chambers' press conference. The Labour leader of the Council, Kyle Gordon, a tedious and odious man in an over-tailored pinstripe suit, bullshitting about how sometimes it was better to do things together.

He switched to Screen Three. Protestors chanting. Same old, same old. Back to Screen Two. An empty podium; this would capture the final moments of JFS' life. His head exploding with the impact of the sniper's bullet. Chilcoat smiled, he would come back to this view shortly. And Screen Four, the 360-degree aerial shot, complete with helicopter whirr.

Tap, tap, tap. It took him a few seconds to realise that the noise was coming from outside the car.

After lowering the window, he saw Harry, pale and breathless.

'Boss, sorry to interrupt. I've been phoning, but you didn't pick up.' Chilcoat pointed his left finger to his headphones, now lying around his neck.

'Is there a problem, Harry?'

'No, boss. Good news. A positive sighting of the gringo-biter from the square. The one with the eyebrows who helped to snatch Red Legs. He's been spotted at a mobile phone shop in Lochgilphead.'

Chilcoat stared blankly.

'It's in Argyll, sir, about fifty miles north-west of Glasgow.' Harry paused. Shuffling his phone from one hand to the other, he leant further into the car.

'We've been monitoring all mobile phone shops within a 100-mile radius of Glasgow. Our man bought three phones yesterday. Description spot on. More interesting still, CCTV footage analysis confirms a retina match with an audience member at the May Day mutant fox performance. The phones have been traced to Tayvallich, a village eleven miles west of the phone shop.'

'Very good, Harry. A precise address in Tayvallich?'

'We're working on it. We can narrow it down to fifteen, maximum twenty houses. Village isn't big and besides, five minutes ago someone in Tayvallich started watching *IndyLive* web stream. Chances are that's them, but their signal will be stronger once we are in position.'

'And your plan?'

'Permission to go to level nine, boss.'

'Permission granted.'

'Very good. I'll keep you posted.' Harry sprinted away from the car, his phone held to his ear, issuing instructions.

Chilcoat closed the window, smiling broadly as he put his headphones back on.

On Screen Two a man was soundchecking the microphone. He tapped onto the visuals from inside the Chambers. Environment Secretary Crull's speech was coming to an end. It was almost time.

'I've got a live-stream on Facebook,' said Natalya. 'BBC News channel are covering it after the midday bulletin when JFS does his speech. The live-stream's a bit boring, just lots of blurred close-ups and muffled chanting.'

'Anyone want the last muffin?' Logan held it out in front of him on the tray.

'You have it, I'm not hungry. I'm about done with the edit. Do you want to see it before I post it?'

'No, we trust you, man,' Logan replied, his mouth already half-full. 'Any joy with accessing Mike's Twitter? It would be so much better if we could post it from his account. A voice from beyond the grave...' Logan trailed off, perhaps aware that he was being insensitive. I'd noticed this more since we'd been in the cottage. He hadn't yet become fully tactful but was heading in the right direction.

'I've tried, but without his password it's no use. I'll have to set up a dummy account.'

'*ForFoxSake2013* is my guess,' said Natalya, still fiddling away at the laptop. 'Capital Fs. Reckon he would have changed it after the video went viral.'

'For fox sake, Natalya, that's worked. You are a genius.' I leant over the table and kissed her on her forehead. 'Logan Fox, you are one lucky man,' I said, blushing as I spoke. Logan was still eating. He started to speak but paused until there were just a few crumbs of the muffin left to chew.

'And she, my weasel friend, is one hell of a lucky lady. Budge up, babe, let's see what's happening. Any sign of that mutant badger arriving yet?'

Raven rested on the lamp post directly opposite the City Chambers. There was still no sign of Marek. The sound levels had increased. The chants were getting angrier, louder. The police numbers swelled too. An uneasy equilibrium that wouldn't last, she thought.

Chilcoat too, was watching. He had taken off the headphones. He had rolled down the window. He wanted to hear the screams himself. In real time. Less than a minute now.

Raven heard it first. The sound of an engine, then the shouts, a hysterical cacophony of sound.

'Get out of the way. For fuck's sake.'
'Watch out. What's he doing?'
'What the fuck? What's that car doing?'
'It's not stopping. Oh my God. It's not stopping.'
'Who's driving that?'
'Watch out. Watch out!'

She could hear every word, every scream. The sounds travelled fast. She heard them instants before she saw the car. The green car. The same colour, the same size, *the same one* that Marek had been driving. Heading across the square, in a perfect straight line through the buffer zone the police had created. The penned-in protestors just yards to the right. It was going fast; forty maybe fifty miles an hour. Everything else seemed to be frozen still.

Raven glanced ahead of her. A group of people had emerged from the Chambers and were gathering at the podium by the main entrance. The car was speeding straight at them.

I sat in the middle, laptop on the coffee table. Natalya on my left, Logan on the right. Watching *IndyLive* and the BBC simultaneously.

Chilcoat saw the car on the aerial shot at the same time as he heard the shouts. At the same time as the doors revolved open and Prime Minister Joshua Francis Swill stepped out in front of the gathered press.

A loud knocking at the front door. A heavy, persistent, angry knocking. And a voice, a woman's voice shouting from within the conservatory.

'What the fuck?' Logan and Natalya leaping to their feet, a clattering as the laptop and table were knocked to the floor.

The car just yards from the wall of the City Chambers, mounting the pavement. Raven flapping her wings, gaining height. The angle of her flight path for the briefest of moments allowing a view in through the front passenger window. She saw him. On the driver's seat. A black-and-white shape. Huddled. Waiting for the impact. Marek. In his badger form.

The sound of gunfire, the cracking of metal, of glass shattering.

A blank computer screen. No picture, but still sounds. Me, Logan and Natalya being pushed and shoved out of the back door.

The ripping sound of metal on brick, on flesh. The crumpling of the car. And then for a solitary second an eerie quiet. Then the scent, the dark and toxic scent of death ascending. She flew higher and higher to escape its grip. In her head she was back there. The fire, the laboratory. The horrific burning smell of animal flesh.

And Chilcoat repeatedly pushing the button to shut the window, swearing at how slowly it closed. Unable to shut out the noises of the square. 'Just drive!' he shouted.

And the three of us sprinting, zigzagging as fast as we could towards the jetty. Not stopping to look back, too afraid to turn round.

SIXTY

Sirens

She had flown to the river and back again three times now. It was maybe twenty minutes since the impact. The car had been travelling so fast, it had hit the wall head-on. Marek could not have survived. Yet she still sensed his presence, felt him here, somewhere in the square.

The noise was deafening, wave after wave of sirens. The flashing of the blue lights bounced off everything, creating a strange, suffocating flickering, that sucked the warmth out of the air. She flew up to the top of a lamp post just a few yards from the impact. The crumpled car lay embedded in the brickwork, six feet to the left of the entrance. A large screen was being erected so that people at street level could not see. She watched as two spaniels – sniffer dogs – held on leashes, inspected the car. Their tails wagging, they were the only ones acting without a sense of panic.

The press had been herded into a nearby hotel, their faces white with shock, their phones and cameras recording everything as if that was the only way to make things real.

The protestors now largely silent. Behind the lines of armed police. Guns pointing directly into the crowd. Dozens and dozens of guns. A distinct smell of sweat and fear. The police closing in, kettling the crowd tighter. A tall uniformed man with a greying beard held aloft a loudspeaker.

'You are being held here under Section 24 of the Crime and Public Order Act. This entitles us to detain both witnesses and suspects for questioning for up to twelve hours without requiring a court order. We are setting up facilities so that each and every one of you can be questioned here in the vicinity of George Square. Under Section 24 we have the right to confiscate any materials that could be used to incite further public disorder, including telephones, laptops and other electronic devices.'

Raven turned her gaze back to the City Chambers. Behind the screen, around twenty people were on their hands and knees searching the ground. For what she did not know.

She flew up to the roof of the building itself. A pigeon landed next to her and shuffled up closer to start a conversation.

'Coo-coo. (What a carry on). Coo-Kuparoo. (So much noise). Koo-Cupparoop. (No bread).'

'Kreepac, kreepac. (Indeed, indeed),' Raven replied in starling tongue.

'Coo-coo. (What a carry on). Coo-Kuparoo. (So much noise). Koo-Cupparoop. (No bread).'

Raven found herself half-smiling. She had forgotten how repetitive pigeons were.

'Kreepac, kreepac, wrandinggrihjjflkk? (Indeed, indeed, what's going on?)' The pigeon looked back at her, but flew off without answering.

SIXTY-ONE

Boxed-in

The van was getting darker. Box after box, like Lego bricks being stacked in front of us until they reached just short of the ceiling. Then a snapping shut of the door and the dusk-light glow, just short of full blackness.

'What's in the boxes?' asked Logan. He sniffed out loud twice. 'Smells like cabbage.'

'I heard one of them mention kale,' Natalya replied. 'Are you OK?'

It took me a few seconds to realise she was talking to me.

'Where are we going?' I asked, ignoring her question. My voice getting cut off as the engine started.

'I counted fifty-six boxes, that's one hell of a lot of kale,' Logan said, raising his voice over the sound of the van's vehicle-reversing alarm.

We were moving now, a steady hum from the engine as it went up in gears, and increased speed. Swaying from side to side as the van weaved its way around what must have been tight and windy roads. We continued like this for five, maybe ten minutes before the vehicle started to slow. It edged forward

266

a few feet at a time, before coming to a halt. The engine ticked over and was then switched off. There was the sound of muffled voices. The rattling of metal and a blast of cold air and light.

'Roadblock. Don't make a sound,' whispered Natalya.

'So what have you got in here?' A male voice. Unfamiliar. Brusque.

'Kale.' A friendlier voice, with a broad Highland accent.

'That's a lot of boxes. Where you headed?'

'Glasgow. Farmers' market there tomorrow.'

'You see any of these characters on your travels?'

'Let's take a look. No. No, sorry officer, can't help you there, I'm afraid. What's this in connection with?'

'I can't tell you. Suffice to say it's serious. I do need to search the van. How many boxes you got in here?'

'Fifty-six.'

'That will take too long to move. Brian, bring Jiffy over, we'll get her to check.'

'Jiffy?'

'Jiffy the sniffy, here she is. Best sniffer dog in Scotland. Come on, girl. The queue is backing up so do your stuff. I'll make a bit more room so you can get a proper smell.'

A little more light entered the back of the van as boxes began to be moved. My heart pounding as the sound of claws and panting inched closer. Natalya's hand grabbing mine. Her fingers ice-cold. The dog was a few feet away. An excited, almost gleeful sound of heavy canine breathing echoed off the tight walls. The thwap, thwap of her tail against cardboard.

I brought Natalya's hand up to my heart and I thought of Walinska. The weasel. And I felt a warmth. A strong reassuring feeling. And I found my breathing slowing. And the pounding of my heart quietening.

'No, nothing in there, girl. Very well. You can go, sir. But if you happen across any of these individuals, don't approach them. Phone 999 immediately. They are somewhere in the locality. Maybe hitching for lifts.'

The van darkened again as the boxes were put back. The door closed and the reassuring sound of the engine started. It wasn't until we were back up to full speed that Logan broke the silence.

'Well done, everyone. The Silent Team.' His voice gave way to the sound of him and Natalya kissing, and her fingers slipped from mine as she gave out a large sigh followed by laughter.

'Well, that proves my theory,' she said.

'Which is?'

'None of us are human, otherwise the dog–'

'Jiffy,' interjected Logan.

'Otherwise Jiffy the sniffy would have smelt us out. She's trained for finding humans.'

'Not genetic mutants,' added Logan.

'Exactly.'

The possible significance of what Natalya had just said was bouncing around in my head, when the van stopped abruptly. Its engine still ticking over.

'Not again,' I said, gulping for air.

Footsteps and the sound of the van door opening again. A voice. A male voice. A friendly voice. It was Spike, the driver. Jocelyn's cousin. Speaking over the top of the boxes in an exaggerated whisper.

'Don't worry guys. All OK. Just queuing to get onto the ferry. Hold onto your stomachs though. Could be a bumpy ride, the wind is getting up.' Then he was gone. The door closed and the engine switched off.

'Where are we?' asked Natalya.

'In the back of a van, darling. Nice, but not as good as our old campervan.'

'Very funny, Logan. I meant, where are we?'

'As opposed to what are we?' I said, stretching out my left leg. It was feeling cramped.

'Sorry?'

'What you said, none of us being human. What did you mean by that, Nat?'

'Fox-man, woman-fox, man-weasel. We are all hybrids.'

'Masters of disguise and enemies of the state,' chipped in Logan.

'That's why the dog couldn't smell us, we don't smell like normal humans.'

'Jiffy the sniffy couldn't get a whiffy.'

'Logan, shut up, will you,' Natalya snapped. 'We're having a grown-up conversation here.'

'My guess is that it's the Tarbert to Portavadie ferry. We haven't driven that far from Tayvallich.' I was happy to steer the conversation away from hybrids.

'Portavadie?'

'It's on the west coast of the Cowal peninsula, the mainland, though pretty remote. Less than an hour's drive to Dunoon.'

Logan had started scratching his ear with the knuckle of his middle finger.

'You got fleas, dear?' asked Natalya.

'Very funny. Oh, here we go. We are moving again.'

The van crawled forward. There was a metallic clunk as it went up the slipway, then the engine cut out again. There was a gentle rocking now. We were on the boat.

'This will be fun. Know any good sea shanties anyone? What's that Rod Stewart one? Something about sailing?'

'Please, Logan, you are not singing that in here. I'd rather hand myself over to the police.' Natalya laughed. I had a flashback to May Day in Glasgow. When Logan was nervous his volume switch turned up to maximum. I was relieved there was no alcohol on board.

'Whoa, that was a big one, as the actress said to the bishop. Hold onto your hats, this is going to be one hell of a bumpy ride.'

'Hashtag *clichéfox*.' Natalya gave Logan a lovey-style air kiss.

'Fuck, that was close.'

A box of kale had tumbled from the pile. Logan quickly outstretched his arm to stop it hitting Natalya in the face.

'Lightning fast reaction saves the day again. Don't call me cliché, I am not French.' Logan sounded like a cross between Inspector Clouseau and Danny La Rue with his camp accent. Another box fell, this time I diverted it.

'Whoever packed this lorry didn't know shit.' Logan again, this time in a fake Bronx accent. 'We are going to drown in a sea of kale. What a way to go.'

'How long is this crossing?' Natalya asked, sounding anxious.

'About half – oof – an hour.'

'That last wave lifted my butt clean off the floor. You could pay good money in Soho for that.'

A car alarm had started. 'Great. Now there's two of them.'

'Two of what, Natalya?' asked Logan, back in his usual voice.

'Wailing noises.'

'Very funny… very funny.'

For a few minutes Logan managed to stay quiet. It was Natalya who spoke next.

'I wonder how our tribute video is doing?'

'I don't know. It had already been shared one hundred times before we left the cottage. Fuck.' A box had landed straight on top of me.

'We still don't know what's going on.' Natalya was sounding tired. The rocking was subsiding slightly.

'It was just lucky that Jocelyn had a home visit in the village. If she hadn't seen them setting up the roadblock, she couldn't have gotten us out so quickly,' I said.

'That Jocelyn is one cool lady. The nurse in the boat who gets my vote,' Logan said.

'But how does Marek know her? And Spike, her cousin. Was it just a helpful coincidence he was just waiting for us with his van or what?' Natalya had asked out loud the questions I too had been pondering.

It seemed so long ago. But it was maybe just ninety minutes, two hours maximum since we'd left the cottage. Jocelyn's boat speeding north across the loch, the three of us covered under blankets. The three of us twisted into a space too small. My head resting on Natalya's lap. Now again, the three of us compacted together. Natalya leaning against my shoulder.

'You all right, Nat, you sound weary?' I asked.

'I'm not too bad considering. Just, you know, a little worried about what happens next. Once we are finally out of this van.'

SIXTY-TWO

Gridlock

The traffic was gridlocked. He would have been as quick walking. His mood was darkening as every minute passed. He had not heard from Crull since impact. Harry too, had gone silent.

He flicked news channels on his iPad. The same images repeated. The same inconclusive scrolling headline. **Major security incident in Glasgow. Prime Minister critically injured.** Its seriousness emphasised by the black banner that surrounded the text.

Was JFS dead? He wanted confirmation. He needed confirmation.

That car. Could it be a counter operation? Someone trying to stop him shooting JFS? But how could that be, unless there had been a leak? Only two people other than himself knew: Crull and the sniper. It made no sense.

Tapping the larger screen in front of him, he brought back the moment of impact. The car's registration number was fake, the first thing he'd checked. Swiping with three fingers he slowed the footage down. Tapping it quickly four times increased its magnification. The time code showed 12.59.31. He hit pause and, bringing up the control panel, changed the footage so that it would inch forward frame by frame.

His car also stuttered forward in slow motion; stop-start-stop-start-stop.

Zooming in to maximum, refocussing and recentering. A view through the back window. Blurred, but not impossible to see. The moment the car hit. There was nobody in the driver's seat. The car was empty.

Rewind to 12.59.26. Five seconds before impact. The same viewpoint. The car edging forward in spasms, mirroring again his own movements through the gridlocked streets.

A flash of light at 12.59.27. The driver door opening.

A blur. A dark blur. Pause. The traffic outside stopped again. Moving the screen focus to the right. Changing the pixelation and the colour contrast. Now 12.59.28. A distinct shape. A black-and-white shape. Moving, rolling. The glint of something blue and green. Zooming in on that spot of colour. Eyes. Two eyes. A face. A non-human face.

A rev of the engine and a change of gear. Moving at normal speed at last.

The car door held open. They had arrived. Hilton Glasgow Grosvenor Hotel, Byres Road. What was normally a ten-minute drive, had taken almost two hours. Chilcoat stepped out onto the pavement, a little unsteady on his feet. Pausing a moment, he leaned one hand on the car's roof.

'Are you OK, sir?' his driver asked.

Ignoring the question, he picked up his pace and strode into the hotel lobby and straight to the reception desk. There was nobody there. Waiting a few seconds, he turned his gaze to the right of the desk and saw a dozen, no, maybe twenty people standing in silence in front of a TV screen. He was a little too far away to be able to make out what was being said. A female receptionist was positioned at the back of the crowd. Young, dark hair, nice legs, tight ass. She turned around. Not quite as good from the front, he thought, noticing her small chin and overplucked eyebrows.

'I'm terribly sorry to keep you waiting, sir,' she said from back behind the reception desk. Her voice sounding a little anxious.

'Has something happened?' Chilcoat replied innocently, gesticulating towards the TV.

'Yes, sir. They think the prime minister may have been killed. A terrorist attack. Here in Glasgow, George Square. I'm afraid everyone is a little in shock.'

'Oh my, that is terrible news. I have suite ten booked. I trust everything is in order?' Bending down slightly to look at her computer, the young receptionist exposed a small white square of lace between the buttons of her blouse. Chilcoat's gaze lowered.

'Yes sir, everything is in order. Do you need any assistance with your luggage?'

'No thank you. My driver will take care of that.' He leant forward to read her name badge.

'Melanie?'

'Yes sir?' The receptionist was uncomfortable, perhaps concerned he was about to make a complaint about her not being behind the desk when he arrived.

'That's a beautiful name. How old are you?'

'I'm twenty-six, sir.'

'You have such a lovely figure. A man could look at you all night and just smile. Are you working late tonight?'

'I'm finishing at eight o'clock, sir.'

'And then?'

'Excuse me?'

'Do you have a boyfriend or husband to go home to?'

'I'm sorry, sir, I feel a little uncomfortable with your questions.'

'Forgive me, it's just... Oh, never mind. An old fool like me. I sometimes forget I am not young anymore. An attractive young lady such as yourself would have no possible interest in being with such a gnarled old dog as me. Do enjoy the rest of your day, my dear. Whatever you get up to.' He turned and headed towards the lift, the room key in his left hand.

She would remember. If anyone asked about him. She would remember him clearly now. What time he checked in, what he was wearing, what he said. But she would also keep her distance for the rest of his stay and advise her female colleagues to do likewise. More privacy. No interruptions. A tried and tested routine. A little reckless, but satisfying nevertheless.

SIXTY-THREE

Wanted

Spike had parked on the driveway, as close to the house as he could. He opened up the back door of the van, whistling something that sounded very familiar. *Love Shack* by the B-52's perhaps or maybe The Soup Dragon's *I'm Free*. Neither song seemed appropriate.

My legs did not want to work. I managed to stand, aided by Logan who looked relieved to be finally getting out of the kale van. Natalya was pale and although she did not complain, I reckoned she was hurting more than she let on. The air was cold but refreshing. I saw the sign. *Bed and Breakfast*. Gold font on white, all lower case apart from the two Bs. I heard Spike say something about how we were using the side door, rather than the guest entrance.

I paused to glance around before going in. A three-storey Victorian building, red-brick. Substantial, with a well-maintained garden by the look of it too. A plump, cheery woman greeted us in the kitchen. She held out her hand to me and Logan, her handshake was firm and businesslike. She gave Natalya a hug.

'I'm Joan. Joan Wilson. Friend of Mrs Mcginty from the campsite. Spike here is my daughter's husband. We'll tuck you upstairs in the attic room. You'll be safe here. You must be hungry. I'll give you half an hour to freshen up and then see what you fancy. You all look done in, poor things.'

Logan mumbled a thank you and the three of us followed Spike upstairs.

Our room was a family suite. A large, bright room, though two walls had bare plaster. There was a smell of paint and a breeze from the window which was open.

'Sorry about the half-done decor,' Spike said. 'Leak caused by dodgy guttering, been trying to get the job finished for weeks, but you know how things are.' He opened the bathroom door. It had a full-sized bath with an old-fashioned shower, the type where you had to fiddle about with both taps to get the temperature right. As well as the double and single beds, there was a two-seater sofa, a writing desk and a large, flat-screen TV. Apart from the missing paint, the repairs looked pretty much done.

'It's fine, don't worry,' I said. 'The room is great, just what we need.'

Natalya had dashed into the loo. As she emerged Spike asked, 'Anything else you guys need? I've got to catch the next ferry onto the mainland.'

'A change of clothes would be good,' I said. 'It was a bit hot and sweaty in the van.'

'Some loo roll too. There's not much in there,' Natalya added.

'And a laptop. We may want to go online, check on a few things,' added Logan.

'No bother. I'll get Joan to sort all that for you.'

Natalya stepped forward and hugged Spike.

'Thanks, Spike. I don't know what would have happened to us if you and Jocelyn hadn't got us out when you did.'

'No worries. Anyone who is a friend of Marek's is a friend of ours.'

'Yes, thanks Spike.' I looked out the window, recognising the view over the harbour. The wide promenade and the Calmac noticeboard. 'We're in Rothesay?' I asked, seeking confirmation.

'Yep, that's right. Tarbert to Portavadie ferry, then a short drive to Colintraive to get the wee boat across. Things have gone pretty mental in Glasgow, we figured it safer to keep you away from all that for now.' Logan was quiet. He was holding Natalya's hand and swaying forward on the balls of his feet.

'Once we got to Portvadie there weren't any more roadblocks. But there's plenty of them on the A78 so I'm not looking forward to my drive to Glasgow. I've gotta go. Don't want to miss the next ferry. Got a vanload of kale to sell, you know.'

Logan stepped forward and embraced Spike. A strong, solid bear hug. He stood back in silence. I was more circumspect, shaking hands, whilst Natalya kissed him on both cheeks, continental fashion.

'Tea anyone?' I asked, wanting something to do to fill in the silence that had enveloped the room. A few minutes later there was a knock-*knock, knock, knock*-knock banging at the door and in walked Mrs Wilson.

'Thought we needed a door code, just in case. So, it's one loud, three quiet, one loud.' She repeated the pattern.

She carried three white bathrobes and an IKEA bag. 'Stuff folks have left behind, so it's a bit of an eclectic mix. Anna, that's

Spike's wife, she will bring more clothes over this evening. She is similar build to you, my dear,' she said, glancing at Natalya, 'so I am sure that there will be something you can wear.'

'My, you *do* all look done in. Not surprising really. I find Spike's driving stressful enough even when I'm sat in the front. So what do you want to eat?'

'We're all vegetarians,' I said.

'Oh that's easy. I wasn't sure, what with Logan being a fox and all, that's what he'd eat.'

'I like all vegetables,' Logan said, his voice flat.

'Except olives,' added Natalya.

'OK. No olives. I'll remember that. There's plenty of nice dishes in the freezer, it won't take me long to defrost them in the microwave.' She paused.

'If I was you, I wouldn't turn the TV on until after you've eaten. Need to build your strength back up first. I'll bring a laptop up for you later. Wouldn't want what they're saying about you on Twitter to interfere with your appetite.' I exchanged glances with Logan.

'So an hour until grub's up? Should give you all time to shower. Shut the window if you get too cold, I was just airing the room to get rid of the smell of paint.'

Ninety minutes later. The three of us sat on the bed in identical white bathrobes, Natalya in the middle. The mugs of peppermint tea going cold on the table. The laptop unopened at the foot of the bed. BBC News channel. 17.35 hours.

The scrolling headline: **Major security incident in Glasgow. Prime Minister seriously injured. Police probe animal rights terror video link. Press conference expected at 20.00 hours.**

And the images of a car. A green car. A familiar car. Our car, apparently driverless, crashing into the wall at forty, fifty miles an hour. The footage stopped seconds from impact. To the right of the entrance, a subdued crowd of protestors kettled in by the type of wire fencing you normally see around building sites. A screened-off blue tarpaulin erected in front of the City Chambers. Then the film cut away to an external shot of a hospital with a chaotic scramble of press outside.

The time on-screen was 17.37. It was a video. Our video. Our tribute video to Mike. Logan staring straight at the camera.

'My name is Logan Fox. I am not alone. They will never stop us.' The video tampered with. Logan's words heavily edited.

'Terror. Killing. Fear.' His voice slowed down.

The camera zooming in. 'Life will never be the same again.'

Now, stills of our faces. First Logan, then Natalya and finally myself. My hairline receding, my distinctive large eyebrows. Certain phrases echoing in my mind: 'Do not approach', 'Likely to be armed and extremely dangerous', 'Phone this number if you see them'.

'Turn it off. Turn it off. Turn it off. TURN IT OFF!' Natalya shouted before Logan pressed the button that made the screen flicker into grey nothing.

SIXTY-FOUR

Loose ends

'He's dead. There will be a press conference, this evening at eight o'clock. It will be announced officially then.' Chilcoat remained silent, swapping the phone to his left ear, he leant down to take out a bottle of whisky from a leather case on the armchair.

'You there, Lynton?'

'Yes, I'm here.'

'Just the line went quiet.'

'There's a lot to think about.'

'Of course.'

'Are there any indicators, you know, as to who…'

Chilcoat was interrupted by the voice on the other end.

'Lynton, what the fuck happened there? It wasn't, wasn't, it wasn't…' the voice stuttered, 'it wasn't like you described. The car, who was driving the car?'

'Everything is under control, Farringdon. Just you do your part and I'll tidy up any loose ends.'

'Loose ends?' Crull spat out with anger.

'It was, I agree, a somewhat unexpected turn of events.' Chilcoat balanced the phone in the crook of his neck, pouring himself another drink. 'But the outcome was the same as we discussed.'

'Look, Lynton, I don't know what games you are playing with me. That car nearly killed me. As it is I'm loaded with codeine, with an arm in a sling and about to tell the world that the British prime minster has been assassinated.'

'You'll be fine, Farringdon. Just don't let the press badger you for too many details at this stage.' Chilcoat was grinning.

'I need to know who was driving that car. You need to be straight with me.'

'Don't worry, everything will be sorted.' There was a loud knock on the door and a voice called out, 'Room service.'

'I've got to go, there's somebody at the door. Goodnight, Acting Prime Minister.'

'That's not funny, Lynton.' Another knock on the door as Chilcoat ended the call smiling.

'Room service.' An Eastern European accent. A male hotel worker pushed a trolley into the room.

'Just leave it by the table. I have some work to do, so don't want to be disturbed. I'll leave the trolley in the corridor when I am finished.' The man muttered a polite acknowledgement and retreated. Chilcoat locked the door behind him and walked over to the table.

Pulling up the lids on the plates, he found himself sniffing at the crisply-cooked lamb. The smell of charred flesh was simultaneously overwhelming and reassuring. He was looking forward to this.

SIXTY-FIVE

Disguises

I watched as Logan took the scissors and cut tentatively at first and then a little more confidently, until finishing with a flourish.

'I can't look,' Natalya cried.

'It will grow back, babe. Do you want any more off?'

'Logan, there's nothing left to cut.' She gave him a look, then turning to me she said, 'Pass me the dye. I need to get this over with and then I'll do your eyebrows.'

It was more painful than I thought having my eyebrows plucked. The shaving of my head, easy by comparison. Natalya was perched on the edge of the bed, about to do her big reveal. 'I can't look,' she repeated as she unwrapped the towel.

'Gee.' Logan exhaled. 'You're blonde. And. Erm. Beautiful.' Getting up, he gave her a hug.

'You look great, Nat,' I tried to reassure her.

We had made plans for the disguises when Joan came to clear the plates after dinner. Of the three of us, it had been Logan who was most insistent that we must get to the mainland, to look for Marek. Joan was vocal in trying to dissuade us from going. But I had backed Logan, fearing the consequences for Joan if we were found here. So the plan was to catch the first ferry in the morning and brazen it out on public transport. Joan had asked us what we needed.

The list scrawled in Logan's barely decipherable writing was read out loud by Natalya before Joan went back downstairs: hair dye, clippers, glasses for Logan. Costumes – Lycra and bikes for me and Nat, and for Logan a suit, shirt, tie and briefcase. The cyclists and the businessman.

'You suit being blonde,' I said.

'It's not really me. Look, Logan, I don't think a pair of glasses and a suit will fool anyone. Me and Blake have had haircuts, how come you are getting away without a makeover?'

'Believe me, my disguise will work. It's all in the mind.' Logan tapped the side of his head, but his words failed to reassure.

It had been Joan's idea for Logan and Natalya to travel separately. 'They'll be looking for you as a couple. A pair of redheads, plus a smaller, brown-haired guy with big eyebrows,' she'd said to an unconvinced Logan. Allowing him to keep his red hair was the compromise to get him to agree on being separated.

Knock-*knock, knock, knock*-knock. Joan was returning with the costumes. 'The bikes are in the garage ready for you to collect in the morning. Here's the gear to go with them.' She handed us helmets and a very small pile of brightly-coloured clothes.

'If someone is wearing Lycra, the face is the last place you look. So it's the perfect disguise,' she added, smiling.

'You seem to be enjoying this, Joan,' Natalya said.

'Well, it takes me back.'

'Sorry?'

'To South Africa, in the '70s and '80s. I was in London running a safe house for the ANC. Until I fell in love with a Scotsman and moved here.'

'Your husband. We've not met him,' Logan mumbled.

'No, love, he passed away, four years ago, cancer. Miss him terribly, but what can you do?' Nat leant forward to embrace her. I was noticing how huggy she was and thinking how good it would be if I could be more like that.

'Don't worry about me, pet, it's you who we've got to take care of. I'll bring your breakfast up at six before the other guests get up. I've already got your tickets, so you won't need to queue up. Now, how's about a dress rehearsal. Make sure you have everything you need?'

The three of us exchanged glances.

'You first, Nat,' I said to break the silence. She picked up her small bundle of Lycra and headed into the bathroom.

'Wow. You look stunning,' I said as she emerged a few minutes later.

'Hashtag *TourdeForce*,' blurted Logan.

'It doesn't exactly leave a lot to the imagination.' Natalya plucked at the outfit that clung to her with a shimmer.

'You were right about not looking at faces,' Logan added. 'I can't take my eyes off you.'

'Enough, Logan,' Joan snapped. 'Who's next?'

'You go,' I said, my Lycra remaining neatly folded on my lap.

And so in the style of the kid's TV series, Mr Benn, into the bathroom-cum-changing room went a scruffy old punk-fox, and out came a suited and booted businessman.

'Logan the Lawyer!' shrieked Natalya. 'You look ridiculous, honey.'

'But do I look different?' he asked. 'Do you know it's me?'

Nat brushed a speck of something off his shoulder pad. 'Just concentrate on keeping your mouth shut and you will be fine.'

'You've only got one contact lens in,' Joan commented.

'It's the Bowie look,' said Logan. Then quickly added, 'I'll do both in the morning, honest,' after Joan gave him a menacing glare.

So it was my turn. The black Lycra leggings and the sky-blue top. Even without moving, I felt uncomfortable, exposed.

'Very good. Very good. Hashtag *Bradley Wiggins*. Somehow, you don't look so small in that.' Logan was fiddling with his tie as he spoke.

'You all look good. But a disguise is only as strong as your attitude allows it. That's the main thing you need to concentrate on.' Joan looked us over like a proud mother hen, her green eyes sparkling.

'You don't have to go, you know? You can stay here until things blow over.'

'It's not going to blow over, Joan,' I said. 'Especially if JFS is dead. They will never give up until we are found.'

'But you are safer here than in Glasgow. You could just lie low. Who knows? Maybe they will catch the real bad guys for once.'

'I'm tired of hiding away,' Logan said, backing me up. 'And besides, Marek and Raven are out there somewhere and we can't just abandon them. Those guys are family to me.'

'Logan's right. Marek saved my life not so long ago, so I owe it to him to check he's A-OK,' Natalya added quietly. A united front, the three of us in agreement.

'I know, dears.' Joan staring at the carpet now. 'I'd be doing the same if I was you. I just worry. I'm not sure what you're going to do when you get to Glasgow – that's if you get there OK to begin with, the police and army will be everywhere. I just don't want anything bad to happen to you.'

Natalya was next to Logan's side, her arm wrapped around his shoulder. 'You just keep this room ready for us. Once we've sorted out what needs sorting out, we'll be back for more of your beautiful hospitality.'

'Of course, of course. There's something bad happening and you kids are caught up in it through no fault of your own. There'll always be a room for you here, and your badger and starling friends too. If you find them.'

'*When* we find them, Joan. *When,* not if.' My voice was calm, confident.

'Well, I wish you goodnight then, I'll bring your breakfast up in the morning. Try and get some sleep.'

I had picked up the TV remote control, my finger hovering over the on/off switch. Joan stepped over and one by one, gave us each a hug.

'Your ferry tickets are in Logan's briefcase. You need to be onboard for ten to, so best to leave here by a quarter to seven at the latest. You rest now, no more TV. It will only wind you up. Goodnight, my dears. Sweet dreams.'

SIXTY-SIX

Faces in torchlight

The temperature had dropped, but at least it was dry. The hemmed-in protestors huddled together. Some hugged, some cried, most stood or sat, a few lay down. Many just stared. Ten hours they had been here now.

Could Marek have been amongst them all that time without her noticing?

She flew down and landed on top of the left-hand side of two Portaloos that had been delivered an hour ago. Even with the door shut, there was a bad smell – half chemical, half human. A semi-permanent queue of around fifteen people formed in front.

How much longer would they keep them? The announcements explaining what was happening had long since stopped.

She landed on the ground and pecked at some crusts. Debris from sandwiches that had been thrown over the fence in green refuse sacks. The bread tasted stale, cheap, plasticky. Then, spotting a discarded packet, she paused. *Nobler Age Foods.*

Don't eat them! Don't eat them! she wanted to shout, but somehow the words would not come out.

She flapped across the square. The crowd had thinned very slightly. Perhaps not enough to be noticed by a human eye, but she was used to judging the size of flocks and she was sure there were less people than there had been. The police were processing people, but only a handful each hour. She calculated it would take more than a week to clear the square at that rate.

Half the encampment was in shadow, half-illuminated by the floodlights that had been set up for the investigation team in front of the Chambers. There was no sign of Marek. He could be in the shadows, but she doubted it. She had to face up to it. He was gone.

As she shuffled amongst the protestors, she caught snatches of conversation.

'I need to be at work tomorrow, Sian is on holiday and nobody else can cover.'

'My mum will be freaking out.'

'I don't know who is going to feed Milligan.'

'I still can't get a signal.'

'Nobody can get a signal.'

'Do you think they will keep us here all night?'

'I'm cold, so cold.'

She saw no sign of Marek.

She hopped around the feet of the protestors for ten or fifteen minutes then flew up again, over the Heras fencing, to the top of the floodlight pole. It took a while for her eyes to adjust to the brightness. The car was still there, its windscreen and doors removed to allow the forensic teams inside.

The front of the Chambers was quiet. A small huddle of men stood on the steps. Groups of armed officers were positioned along the pavement. Three mobile incident units, large caravans had been set up on the road heading east. In two of them protestors were being questioned, in the third the door had been closed for some time, a dim yellow glow just visible from within.

Back in the encampment, a murmur of song had started. John Lennon's *Imagine*. A few voices at first, then more joined in. A spattering of applause, and then some laughter.

Next up. The Proclaimers: *I'm Gonna Be (500 Miles)*. Louder. Cheerier. There was movement amongst the guards. Raised voices. She couldn't make out what was being said.

And then a scream. A woman's scream. Loud. Piercing. A woman being dragged by the hair, along the ground by two men. A third shining his torch into the faces behind. A line of faces; scared, angry. Flickers of torchlight, casting, searching for any signs of resistance. The crowd formed into an arc of bodies, arms linked. A single body, a single beast, putting on its protective shell as the searchlight scanned the faces.

It was then that Raven saw him. Third row back, fourth from the perimeter fence. Tall, dark. His eyes, his unmistakable eyes. His spikey hair messed up. His face grazed and bruised.

And then darkness. The searchlight switched off. The police's attention back on the woman, silent now at their feet on the other side of the perimeter. They picked her up and carried her like a carcass of meat, towards a waiting police van. The back doors opened and the darkness enclosed her.

The searchlight flicked back on. Moving across the crowd row by row, looking to see if anybody else dared to sing. Third row back, fourth from the left. A young woman with pale skin and hair streaked with green and blue. Marek was nowhere to be seen.

SIXTY-SEVEN

Special delivery

The hot water rinsing away the oil. She had been good. Not as firm as Suzanne, or as hot as Scarlett, but a pleasure nevertheless. He had tipped well and would use her again next time he was in Glasgow and had something to celebrate. Sinead. It was always the ones with names beginning with S that he took a shine to. He smiled as he turned off the shower. He allowed the water to drip off his body, before stepping out of the cubicle and into his bathrobe.

His mobile phone was charging on the table. He glanced at the screen. 4.37am. Too late to sleep now. Three missed calls. All from Crull. He could wait until after he had eaten. His *massage* had given him an appetite. Sitting on the edge of the bed, he picked up the room phone. It was answered on the third ring. He ordered a full English breakfast, no tomato and extra black pudding.

A chortle. Silly bitch had left her knickers behind. Red, a bright scarlet. Picking them up, he enjoyed the softness of the lace. He opened his bedside drawer, hesitated, then placed them back on his pillow.

At 5.02am there was a quiet knock on the door. By now he was dressed. Dark suit, white shirt, black tie. Funeral outfit. A day of national mourning, after all. Ready for the breakfast press conference scheduled for 7am. He sat on the edge of his bed. The attendant placed his tray on the table and asked if there was anything else he needed.

Chilcoat glanced behind him. At the red lace that rested on his pillow still.

'An envelope. I have an item to courier to London. Delicate item. A5 padded envelope should be sufficient.' He licked his lips as he spoke. Perhaps unconsciously, perhaps all too aware.

'No problem, sir, I will have one sent up immediately. Anything else?'

'Can you book me a taxi for 6.30am to the Scottish Exhibition Centre.'

'Of course, sir, consider it done. It will be waiting for you then.'

At 6.25am Chilcoat handed the envelope to the receptionist. A female receptionist; mid-twenties, brunette, overweight. *Tamsin*, her name badge says. *Student,* he thinks. A scent of perspiration and cheap perfume. Not a patch on the one who checked him in yesterday.

'This needs to be couriered immediately. Signed for delivery.' He handed her the package, addressed to the Ritz hotel.

'Very good, sir.'

I couldn't eat my breakfast. I nibbled on the toast and potato scone, but the rest I left untouched.

'You not having that?' Logan looked at my plate eagerly. I nodded and he pulled it over onto his lap and started tucking in. Natalya was quiet, also picking at her food.

'You all right, love?' Logan asked, his mouth half-full with mushrooms.

She didn't reply.

'You OK, Nat?' Logan repeated, wiping his mouth with the back of his hand. 'What's up?'

'I don't know if I can go through with this.' Unlike me and Logan, Natalya was not dressed in her outfit. She was still in her T-shirt and dressing gown. Until now that hadn't seemed significant. 'It's madness. We're safe here and yet we are just going in blindly without a plan. They'll shoot us as soon as they see us.'

Silence.

Logan had put his plate down and half knelt, half squatted in front of her. 'I've got to go for Marek. He saved me in the fire. I can't leave him now and I can't just sit here and hide.'

'But we don't have a plan.'

'We've managed so far, haven't we?' Logan looked at me for support. Natalya was crying.

'Last time I was in George Square they nearly killed me. It still hurts. Everything still hurts. And that was before yesterday, before they thought we…'

She paused, unable to bring herself to say what we had been accused of.

'You know they are just going to ramp everything up ten thousandfold. It's a deathtrap. I don't want to die, I don't want to die, Logan. And besides…' She paused again. Her hands cradled in front of her, she began rocking, her eyes turned down to the floor.

'Besides what?' I asked.

She looked up.

'You were going to say something but stopped.'

293

'Nothing, Blake. It's nothing. I just don't think we should go.'

Logan was pacing, to the window and back again.

'What's changed, Nat? Last night we had it all sorted and now you wake up and just throw everything up in the air. Tell me what's changed?'

'Nothing has changed, Logan. I've just had some sleep. Had time to think, to get my brain back in focus after yesterday.'

Logan had stopped pacing. 'I've got to go,' Logan repeated five, six times. And then a final, 'I've got to go,' now in a whisper.

'I notice it's *I* and not *we*, Logan. It's no good being a martyr. That doesn't bring you back to me. I don't want you to go. I thought we had something special. I thought we were partners, equals. But obviously not, you are just caught up in your own world, your own self. Stay with me, Logan. I need you to stay with me.' Natalya's eyes looked different. Was it fear? Was it anger?

'I've got to go. I've got to go,' he repeated again.

Logan turned away from Natalya and looked over to the window. 'The ferry's there, it will be going soon,' he said, 'and we need to be on it.'

'There is no *we* if you are dead, Logan.'

Natalya looked at me. Her face as pale as I'd seen it since that day we had rescued her in George Square. She stared at me, waiting for my response. Could I stay with her? Comfort her? Be with her? Was this my chance to make her fall for me and not Logan? I shook my head. Why was I thinking like this?

'Sorry, Nat, I'm going with Logan. I've lived my life regretting not doing things. I can't not go now.'

'Then go. Be heroes. Save the world. Just don't expect me to come to your fucking funerals.' She kicked hard at the coffee table, toppling it over. The breakfast plates skidded across the floor, smashing with a loud clatter. The bathroom door slammed shut. Logan leant forward and started picking up the pieces of the plates.

'Leave it, Logan. Go talk to her.'

She had flown back and forth, back and forth. The air was still, with little current. The area around George Square remained cordoned off. A circle of armed police manned temporary barriers. Unarmed officers were directing what little traffic there was.

'Everyone is at home watching on TV,' she heard one officer say.

She was hungry. It had been a long time since she had eaten. When was it? The car journey. She had pecked at some fat balls that Natalya had prepared for her. On the floor of the car, in front of the passenger seat. That must have been around 11am, was that only yesterday? And then last night in the square, pecked at some crumbs, then felt no desire to eat at all after realising they came from Nobler Age.

Had that been Marek she had seen in the crowd last night? Was that his face? Was that really him? She couldn't think straight.

It's 6.42am. The taxi pulls up in front of the SEC. A new temporary drop-off point, behind concrete barriers.

She carried on flying, instinct now guiding her towards an eating place. The city was stirring. Sauchiehall Street was rich with pickings, the discarded takeaways from the confetti of student bars and fast-food outlets. A council street-sweeper was sucking up many offerings as she approached. A newsagent at the top end, not far from the dental hospital, was unloading papers from a white van half-parked on the pavement, its driver looking anxious. Perhaps affected by events, or maybe just on the lookout for traffic wardens, who could be vicious even at this early hour. The newsagent unfolded a poster for the window, displaying the day's headline for the world to see.

Prime Minister Assassinated. Hunt for Animal Rights Killers. NEWS SPECIAL.

And on the front pages, split photos. The scene of carnage from George Square. And the face of one of the main suspects. Logan the Fox.

'There isn't time for this.' Those were Logan the Fox's words as he headed for the stairs. Natalya stood by the bathroom door. Leaning into its frame, both her eyes puffed red with tears. She looked as if her legs would buckle at any moment.

'I've got to go, Nat. Are you going to be OK?' I asked.

She shrugged, pulling her arms to her chest.

I stepped forward to give her a hug and she clung to me uneasily.

'Don't let him do anything stupid,' she whispered.

'I'll bring him back safe, I promise.' I picked up my bike helmet and the small backpack that Joan had prepared for me.

'I've got to go, catch the ferry.'

Natalya forced a half-smile. 'You look good in Lycra, weasel-man.'

'You too, Nat.'

And that was it. My last exchange. The last time I saw her. In her human form.

The final security check at 6.53am. A third inspection of his papers, a second scan of his briefcase, another quick pat down from a security guard who also runs an electronic scanner up and down his leg. He is finally cleared to go in.

Taking his seat at 6.55am. Two rows from the back. A full, but remarkably hushed audience. 6.57am. He spots Harry's shaved head, three rows further forward. 6.59am. *These things never start on time*, he thinks, only to be surprised by the appearance of three men at the head of the room. Taking their seats just as the clock turns to the top of the hour. Farringdon Crull to the right of the podium. A dark shirt, white suit, black tie. His left arm in a sling. The white of the bandage catching the light. Chilcoat leans forward, this is going to be fun.

At 7am the ferry leaves, exactly on time.

SIXTY-EIGHT

Crossing over
to the other side

The crowd of protestors sat uneasily on the concrete. Exhausted. Almost silent. Raven watched as thirty armed soldiers entered the square and circled three times before leaving. The soldiers said nothing, but succeeded in intimidating the protestors further into themselves. After they left armed police delivered the food. Egg and bacon rolls, teas and coffees. Wrapped in the all-too-familiar Nobler Age packaging. The protestors – was that the right description for them anymore? – the protestors were too hungry to question and tucked in.

A large mobile screen on the back of a flatbed truck had been trundled in through the police cordon. Like those portable cinemas you get on islands showing out-of-date films, the screen was manoeuvred slowly to the left, and the right, before finding its spot in front of the Chambers. Pixelated at first, then a horrible bright blue, then flickering into life, the clock on the screen turning from 6.59am to 7am. Then came sound.

Voices. The speakers reverberated around the whole square. Set to the BBC News channel, they were about to broadcast the press conference live to the protest camp.

A crowd had gathered around the TV. The rest of the passenger lounge was empty, save for a small group of pensioners and a spattering of people glued to their smartphones. I hadn't seen Logan, though as I was on my bike, I'd embarked with the cars rather than the foot passengers. I caught a glimpse of the scrolling headline.

Press Conference, LIVE, Glasgow.

Deciding I'd rather not know what was being said, I headed to the small shop.

'Earl Grey tea, please.'

'That's one pound eighty.' The man serving me was overweight with a neatly-trimmed goatee and a friendly demeanour. He smelt of HP Sauce.

'Shocking, isn't it?'

'Sorry?' I asked hesitantly.

He pointed at the newspapers on the rack next to the till. The headlines screamed out at me.

Assassination... Nation in Shock as PM Slain by Animal Rights Terrorist...

Foxhunt.

There was Logan's face, a still from yesterday's video. Smiling, but in a kind of menacing manner. I paid the man and picked up my tea. I had to get away. Which way was the observatory deck? I wanted fresh air. A man's voice shouting after me. Fuck. Not already. We were barely out of Rothesay.

'Excuse me!' he repeated loudly. I stopped. What was the point of running? Turning around, I saw it was the HP-Sauce man. 'Your change, you forgot your change.' He handed me three pound coins and a twenty-pence piece.

'Sorry, I mean, thank you. I didn't sleep well, what with everything. The news, you know.'

He patted me gently on the shoulder. 'No problem, sir. Everyone is a wee bit jumpy today. Only to be expected under the circumstances.' I pocketed the change and watched him return to the shop. I headed for the stairs and out onto the deck. A gust of cold wind greeted me. The second-floor observatory deck. Deserted? Not quite. There was only one other person though. Out at the front, peering over the railing. A man in a suit. It took me a few moments to recognise him.

Raven flew back up onto the lamp post in front of the Chambers. Despite all the police, the army, the guns, the cameras, she was invisible. Coming and going as she pleased. The man's voice boomed out across the square. She listened, not to what he said, but how he sounded. The slight throatiness, the occasional hesitancy, the tendency to say 'f' instead of 'th'. She had heard this voice before. He was familiar.

'Following an emergency cabinet meeting last night, it is with both huge honour and great sadness that I have accepted the role of acting prime minister for an initial free-month period. Up until our autumn conference.' The man paused; his right index finger scratched momentarily at his eyelid. 'As you know, I was with the prime minister at the time of the attack. And immediately afterwards in the hospital.'

Another pause. He blinked. Composing himself. Was this emotion genuine? Chilcoat turned, a late arrival in the row behind him caused people to stand and chairs to be scraped. He glared at the dark-haired reporter seating himself. Turning his attention back to Crull, he saw how tired he looked. A clever move not to wear make-up. He was performing well.

I took a few steps forward, wanting to go over to him. To speak to him. To ask him what he was thinking. To discuss what we should do. Whether or not we should get the return ferry back and hide out with Natalya and Joan. I paused. Thinking back. How long ago was it? That night in Glasgow. Seven, eight weeks maybe? En route to the CCA. Logan stood at the motorway, staring out in the same melancholic manner. Was he thinking the same now? Was he regretting abandoning Natalya? Should I persuade him to go back to her?

I didn't know that Natalya had already left our attic room. That she had left whilst Joan was busy cooking breakfast for the four Americans, two Austrians and an IT consultant from Scunthorpe.

I turned back and walked round to the other side of the boat. I looked back to Rothesay, at what we were leaving behind. Logan stared out to Wemyss Bay and what lay ahead. My gaze followed the curve of the hills above the town and was drawn to a line of trees to the south of the golf course.

I was too far away to see her. Even with binoculars she would have been an invisible speck of red. A fox. A beautiful vixen in the prime of her life. Exploring territory that was both unfamiliar and reminiscent of home. A vixen with a bleached blonde tuft of fur at the back of her neck. A vixen who stood and watched the Rothesay to Wemyss Bay ferry making its way to the mainland. A vixen who for the first time that day was feeling the kick, the kick of new life within her belly.

Raven heard only phrases not full sentences.

'Emergency powers... Unprecedented attack... Nation comes together at difficult times... Police and security services spared no resources... Bring them to justice.'

I'd returned to the passenger lounge, standing at the back of the crowd round the TV. Twenty or thirty people in front of me. Staring at the screen, well it was more of a computer monitor, really. Volume turned up fully, the sound was distorting slightly.

The new acting prime minister had sat down now. George Carter was on his feet. The policeman in charge of the investigation had a voice which was flat and emotionless. I listened to his description of the attack; the cause of death, the lines of enquiry, the detention of the protestors, the video posted by the "main suspects", the police raid at Tayvallich, the roadblocks, the manhunt – I could sense a giant red arrow swivelling over my head. *I'm here*, it said. Squeezing my eyes shut, the arrow faded and when I reopened them a few seconds later, everybody's attention remained on the screen.

They showed photos of Logan and Natalya. Stills from the video. Then footage of the CCA. That performance. And then. My photo. The photo of me and my gran, Charlotte-Ann. Where did they get that? New Writers Award 2010 at the Scottish Storytelling Centre in Edinburgh. My grandmother's finest hour. The oldest-ever recipient for her debut novel, *Resistance*.

Charlotte-Ann's fist in an ironic black panther-style salute. Her face contorted with mock anger. And me, stood behind her, eyes staring drunkenly. An ill-fitting tuxedo and a single piece of A4 paper held up above my head. *We will resist!* in a dark-green font that looked almost black. I hadn't seen that photo since... Oh my.

I felt dizzy. I felt like fainting. I felt like I had all my breath taken away from inside of me.

The room was swaying. The boat was spinning.

And then it stopped.

In my head, a new calm. A female voice. Not anybody I recognised. Whispering, reassuring me. *'Don't be afraid. Don't be afraid. Don't be afraid.'*

Raven watched the face on the screen. The large eyebrows unmistakable even given his strange attire. Blake Hardie. And beside him an older woman. A familiar woman. A strong presence about her. An unmistakeable presence. A starling-woman. In her human form. Before she passed. Before she was born. The woman holding a book. Words written in green. A dark green. The colour of starling feathers in the sun.

And still, the voice on the screen was alien, accusatory, angry.

'Terrorist. Killer. Assassin.'

'Suspect. Ringleader. Dangerous.'

She couldn't take this. She couldn't watch. She couldn't accept this. She started flying. Anywhere. Away. She wanted out. She wanted *out*.

SIXTY-NINE

Out of time

The Calmac voice. Its familiar Highland lilt had announced that the ferry was reaching Wemyss Bay. I climbed down the stairs to the car deck to exit with my bike. My first public test passed. Nobody had given me a second glance or made the connection between my new eyebrowless face and that on screen. My mind though, was in turmoil. Why that photo? Why drag my gran into all this?

I collected my bike in a fog, not noticing the cars embarking or hearing what the fluorescent-bibbed boat crew were discussing. I was the last to leave. The foot passengers would be on the concourse already. The train was due to leave at 7.54am, arriving in Glasgow for a quarter to nine.

Logan was one of five people queuing in front of me at the small ticket office. The station clock showed 7.42. Still plenty of time, no danger of missing the train. I heard him ask for a single and watched as he pocketed his ticket and change and headed towards the platform.

'A return to Glasgow please.' I hesitated. I would be coming back, wouldn't I?

There were renovation works at the station. A new roof replacing the slime-ridden glass. I lost sight of Logan behind the towers of scaffolding as I headed towards the platform. The train from Glasgow had just pulled in.

The first carriage had a white bike symbol on its door. I got on and strapped my bike into the space next to the folding seats, then paused at the table by the window. After checking I was on the side with the view of the coast, I sat down. I felt self-conscious. Not so much the giant red arrow, but everyone else in the carriage was staring into their phones. The lack of a smartphone made me stand out. The Lycra too, was disconcerting me. I would wait until Paisley Gilmour Street and then get changed in the toilet.

Chilcoat's attention was waning. The questions were going on for too long and George Carter had nothing interesting left to say. He wondered if he should go back to the hotel or head straight to Grantham.

He could do with a second breakfast. The bacon at the Hilton was always overdone. He could find somewhere in the Merchant City for a decent fry-up, but the traffic would still be chaotic. He could always walk part of the way and cut through the square. Get to see the faces of the great unwashed for himself. Watch the body collectors come and sort out the ones to be taken to the lab.

No, Grantham and indeed London, could wait. He would spend another night in Glasgow and see what developed. He looked ahead and noticed Harry was on his iPad, no doubt equally bored by this bloated press conference.

'I'll take one last question. From the back of the room. There has been a hand up for some time. The lady in the red dress.' Crull pointed immediately behind Chilcoat.

'Prime Minister. Can I ask you...?' A male voice.

'Sorry, not you, sir. The lady to your right?'

Chilcoat's attention perked back up. Turning, he could see two people on their feet. A woman in red and a man in black. The one who had come in late.

'The lady in red, please. Final question. We are almost out of time.'

'Leanne Sutherland, *STV News.*'

'Can you,' the man was continuing, oblivious to the angry glare he was getting from both Leanne and Crull. 'Can you explain the link between Nobler Age Foods and a fire at an animal laboratory on April 8th?'

'Not you, sir, Leanne. Please, your question. Sit down, will you. Can someone get the mic to Leanne from STV?' Crull's voice suddenly agitated.

The man was continuing. His voice loud enough to be heard without a microphone. 'The link between a fire at an animal laboratory on the day that Margaret Thatcher died and over 300 cases of–' Chilcoat turned to look at Harry. He was no longer looking at his iPad but staring directly at the man in black. Leanne spoke with a broad Aberdeenshire accent.

'Prime Minister, thank you very much. I wanted to ask you quickly in relation to the protesters in the square, how long you think–'

An angry shout. The man in black had snatched the microphone from Leanne.

'I'm afraid we are out of time.' Harry was pushing his way to the aisle. Chilcoat was also on his feet and pointing something directly at the man who was still speaking.

Raven did not witness what happened next. I did not witness what happened next. Logan did not witness what happened next. Natalya did not witness what happened next. Over 31.4 million people watching on live TV in the UK witnessed it. Over 800 million people worldwide on cable TV and live-stream witnessed it. A crowd of 1,984 people kettled in George Square witnessed it. The moment when the man in black, the man with the short spikey hair shouted into the microphone.

'My name is Marek Dogovsky and I am a badger. And I want people to know that what you are putting in Nobler Age Foods that is making everyone so sick.'

I did not witness the acting prime minister of less than twelve hours being thrown to the floor by a phalanx of security. Logan did not see the people in the conference room start to scream and push. Natalya did not see Chilcoat fire three shots at the man in black. Raven did not see Marek Dogovsky shrink down from his human self into his badger form. None of us saw each of the three bullets passing over him and into the head of Leanne Sutherland from *STV News*. She was catapulted into the arms of a skinny Arabic man from *Al Jazeera*, who collapsed into the lap of a shaven-headed reporter from the *New York Times* whose chair gave way with a terrible ripping sound of metal and cloth.

Logan did not see Marek bound from the room on all fours, knocking over a line of security staff at the door like skittles.

None of us witnessed any of this, but plenty of other people did. Though that was the last they saw because after that the TV screens went blank.

SEVENTY

Full force

There were gasps in my carriage. The woman opposite me screamed.

'What's happening?' I asked.

'Someone has just shot an STV reporter in the head on live television!'

'Not someone. Some thing,' the skinny man dressed in double denim interjected from across the aisle.

'Some *thing*?' I was trying not to display too many signs of panic.

'Yes. A badger. A badger just shot an STV woman because she interrupted him. Splat. Just like fucking that.'

Denim Man was hyper, acting out what had gone on.

'Jesus, this is all getting too weird.' The woman next to me had starting dialling. 'Did you see it? Did you see it?' she shouted at whoever was on the other end of the phone.

I had to warn Logan. But not here on the train. It was too enclosed, too public. I would change out of this insufferable Lycra and wait until we reached Glasgow and warn him then.

Raven was in Glasgow's botanical gardens. A ten-minute flight from George Square, but a different world. She remembered the grand greenhouse from growing up. The Kibble Palace, they called it. It was always warm in there, and there were always good crumbs to be had outside.

She felt cold. Hesitant. She wanted her body back. Her old life. Wanted out from this hybrid shell. Wanted away from the confusion that was overwhelming her.

Morning commuters mixed in the park with students, joggers and dog walkers. There was an unfamiliar intensity to the morning. A silent intensity. People huddled in whispered conversation grouped around their phones. A man sat on the bench closest to the food kiosk, his MacBook Air balanced on his lap, his mouth wide open. Small, tinny voices were barely audible.

She hopped parallel to the main footpath. Snatches of conversation were everywhere. The air was full of it. The Wi-Fi, the information, the constant flow of data. The scramble of sounds. The blue lights. The channels shifting. Raven hopped faster.

'Badger.' Up onto a branch now.

'Badger.' Back onto the grass.

'Badger.' Snatches of conversation. But always returning to this one word. All ages, all sizes. Men, women, children. She was invisible. She was not on their screen. She was not on their TV. They had not picked up on her signal.

'Badger.' Over and over again.

The killer. The suspect. The terrorist. Guilty. Already condemned. And she could sense Marek, here in the park. And she could sense Logan, here in the grass. And she could sense Charlotte-Ann, here in the trees.

'Badger.' It was just a word. A collection of letters. A random mumbling of data.

'Badger.' What was his name? Who was he? When did he live? When did he die? When was he reborn?

'Badger.' His scent, his voice. Everywhere. In everything.

'Badger.'

That night. The fire. The laboratory. And the kiosk. The food kiosk, here in the park. With the sign. That sign. That emblem. That everywhere-you-look emblem. The same lines, the same distinct pattern. The same damned pattern.

She was inside the greenhouse now. Pecking at the floor but tasting only gravel. There was nobody in here. No Wi-Fi, no signal, you see. They were all outside. They were all outside, lost in a world that did not exist.

Who was she? Who was *she*?

Raven. Starling. Human.

Deceased so many times, but always reborn. But never so alone.

She was tired. Despite the heat from within the glass-domed greenhouse, she felt cold. A park attendant came in, carrying a trowel and watering can. As he opened the door, she flew back out.

The air was less static, but still she could hear them speaking. 'On the run... killer... terrorist.'

The Wi-Fi signals. Everywhere she went the data bombarding here. And then his voice. Marek's voice. The man on the bench, replaying, retweeting the final seconds that were broadcast from the press conference.

'...fire at an animal laboratory... Nobler Age Foods... making everyone sick.'

Was she really so alone?

No Marek. No Logan. No Natalya. No Blake. Just her.
Just her.

Her hair, the speckled black and green of a starling feather.

No, she was not alone. She never had been. She let out a shriek. A startled collection of guttural sounds that reverberated, that echoed, that bounced, that flew. Like data from the cloud, the call was spreading faster now. Up the trees and out across the branches. Up the trees and along the river. Up the trees and over the bridge. Up the trees and into the sky.

Travelling further. Repeated. Echoed. Loud. Resonant. Defiant.

'We must gather. We must gather. We must gather.'

Three times she summoned the roost. Three times they heard her call. And now where there had been a single starling, there were four, five, six. And now where there had been six starlings, there were a dozen, fifteen, twenty. In the grass, next to the rhododendrons, in the flower beds they gathered.

The humans remained oblivious. Faces down in blue screens. Arthritic thumbs and stiff necks as they watched events unfolding. Unaware of the gathering, the great gathering that had begun. At its centre, a solitary bird, caught up in her own grief, her losses, her desire to return back to the love of her roost.

SEVENTY-ONE

Blood and resistance

The train pulled into Central Station at 8.47am, two minutes late. Many passengers were slow to disembark, remaining seated, watching events unfold. Others left the train in small huddles. Or walked in zombie-like states, eyes fixed on the screens they held out in front of them, pausing only to excavate their tickets from pockets and shuffle through the barrier.

With my bike I was slow and the crowded concourse awkward to walk through without bumping ankles. The ticket inspector waved me towards the wide access gate and I had to rejoin a queue twice as long as the others. I glimpsed a man in a suit who could have been Logan walking through a gate to my right. But I was not sure. I was to meet him at the Gordon Street entrance. That was the arrangement. But the man in the suit was heading to the escalator, towards Argyle Street, the opposite direction.

My attention was drawn to the rows of armed police who stood behind the ticket barriers. Guns. I had never seen so many guns. The man in the suit was no longer in sight.

It took me five minutes to battle through the logjam and reach Gordon Street. The announcement was still echoing in my head I had heard it so often. 'Due to a serious incident all trains are subject to delay or cancellation. If your journey is not essential please consider delaying your departure until tomorrow. Please wait on the concourse for further announcements.'

Was my journey essential?

I headed to Hope Street and found an empty bike rack next to a deli cafe. I was relieved to offload the bike, and immediately felt less conspicuous. In vain, I looked around for Logan. He could be anywhere by now. Shuffling back along Gordon Street, the crowd interweaving with taxis parked at the rank. Everything was stationary.

The air smelt of burnt eggs, and the sound of sirens was getting louder.

I spotted a flash of red hair, but the body shape was all wrong; short and squat not tall and skinny. I took out my phone and called up his number. No signal. I rebooted. No signal. Great. I had no way of finding him now. A brief flurry of movement and then outside the Co-op, a stalemate of human bodies. Not moving again.

'What's happening?' I asked a young woman who was carrying what looked like an art portfolio.

'The police have stormed the square, is what I've heard. Everything is shut off.'

'So there is no way to get there?' She shook her head. Her face looked older and more tired than it should.

'My phone can't get a signal, I've got a friend in the square I'm worried about.'

'They are blocking everyone's signal. Nobody can get through.' A new rush of sirens, and the whirring of a helicopter. The woman leant into me. This close up, I could see that her hair was shimmering with streaks of blue and green.

'Resist.' Her voice was soft and quiet. The same one I heard on the ferry. 'Be brave.' She spoke in a barely audible whisper.

A jolt. A push from the crowd. I glanced behind me for the woman I'd been speaking to. She was no longer there. A small, suited man, sipping at a takeaway coffee, stood in her place. He was too busy staring at his Blackberry to give me any attention.

Armed police everywhere. Dogs barking. A chaotic evacuation. They had been put on lockdown. Only the injured and the politicians had left. Mobile signal and Wi-Fi jammed. The world's press trapped in a bubble of silence.

The bloodstained seats, floor and walls. A sharp splatter of colour in an otherwise grey room. A circle of upturned tables cordoned off the worst of the red.

Then an abrasive announcement blasted out over the PA. 'Please make your way to the emergency exits immediately.' In the pushing and shoving, Chilcoat took his opportunity. Brushing alongside Harry, he had stretched his left arm around his shoulder, and with Harry stuck between two American journalists, he'd lowered his arm and slipped the gun into the side pocket of Harry's suit. The 3D-printed digital stealth gun had served its purpose. Deadly at close range, invisible to X-ray, and complicated to explain.

'You owe me one, Harry,' he had whispered, before branching off rightwards in a gap that had emerged next to the fire exit. His left heel was leaving a faint imprint of blood as he moved to the top of the stairs. The marks had ended by the ninth step down.

Back on the move, his mind was racing. *Damage Limitation.* He mentally repeated the phrase as his attempt to focus on the face of the Great Lady was repeatedly swallowed up by the image of Leanne Sutherland's last moment. The ripping apart of her eye socket, the explosion of her skull, the snapping back of her neck with the force of the bullets. There was no way she could have survived.

As horrible as that image was, it was still preferable to *his* face. His words. The badger. Dogovsky. How had he gotten in? And how the fuck had he gotten out?

Damage Limitation. Another step down. *Damage Limitation.* Another step. *Damage Limitation.* Until finally, there were no more steps and the light began to change.

SEVENTY-TWO

No man's land

Heading south down Union Street the crowds were less claustrophobic. But they started building up again outside KFC. Turning left onto Argyle Street, I paused for a moment at Waterstones and noticed that there were throngs of people sheltering inside. Next to the doorway a young homeless woman sat up in her sleeping bag, and stared directly at me for a brief moment, before she turned her gaze back down to the kerbside.

Ignoring her, I edged along the pavement then ground to a halt opposite St Enoch subway. A police line blocked the way ahead. I stood for perhaps three or four minutes before a surge of energy erupted behind me, picking my legs up from underneath me.

I was being carried towards the police line. I didn't dare risk turning around to see what was pushing at me for fear of tripping over my feet or those of the people in front. Then as quickly as the surge started it stopped.

I was closer to the police line but more to the right.

Reinforcements arriving. The police five, maybe six deep. What were my options? Could I skirt through the St Enoch shopping centre? That could be bring me out onto Queen Street, closer to the square. Then before I could think any further, movement.

'Move back,' a single voice shouted.

'Move back.' This time the call amplified on a loudhailer.

But we weren't going back, but forwards. A tide of people being evacuated from Central station had nowhere to go but into us. My legs propelled forward and lifted off the ground as a swathe of human flesh enveloped me.

The police line separated, batons raised. A loud roar. The charge had begun.

I stood, eyes closed. Expecting the onslaught of pain from their truncheons but I felt nothing. The police had run straight past me, as if I wasn't there. As if I was invisible.

I was in no man's land, a sterile zone on Argyle Street. Behind me, I could hear screams as truncheons and shields hit flesh. Had nobody seen me? Was nobody coming to get me?

People who had locked themselves in shops stared anxiously out. The flickering reflection of blue lights on tinted shop windows added to my sense of disorientation.

I walked at a normal pace, reaching the junction with Queen Street. As I turned the corner, I felt a gust of wind and smelt burning. The scent of bonfire night. I looked up the street but couldn't see any flames.

A heavily-pregnant woman with a buggy stood outside Next with a mobile phone glued to her ear. She rocked the buggy back and forth. To her right an Asian man, a security guard holding a walkie-talkie, peered at me from the doorway of Primark. There was nobody else on the streets. No police, no protestors, nobody.

I stopped at the pedestrian crossing. A junction normally busy with cars and buses, but today there was no traffic. The automatic display counted down the seconds until it was deemed safe to cross. Despite the absence of vehicles, I hesitated in crossing until the seven had become six, become five, become four and onto zero.

At the familiar beeping I darted across. I looked up towards the square. A line of police vans strung along Queen Street, zigzagging up from outside the Gallery of Modern Art. Their lights flashed, but there was no sign of anyone either in them or behind them. A droning noise, like angry wasps, seeped its way towards me.

And a voice. That same female voice calling to me. 'Get inside quick.' A hand grasping at my arm.

She wore a tabard over a white-and-beige-striped shirt. Her face was pale, her hair black, but streaked with blue and green.

'I'm Amy, Amy Carson,' she said a few seconds after she'd shut back down the roller blinds.

'Hi,' I replied, wondering if I should give her my name. Decided against doing so.

I spotted a large art portfolio propped up against the counter. And somehow sensed that inside would be paintings of birds and trees.

'You OK?' Amy asked. She was holding a pricing gun and a 500g pack of dried apricots.

'I think so. It's pretty crazy out there. Any idea what's happening?'

'Roadblock. Riot. Revolution. The three Rs. You don't mind if I carry on pricing stuff? We had a big delivery yesterday, haven't yet got it all sorted. Megan the Vegan – that's my boss – couldn't get in so it's just me in the shop today.'

Amy had paused her pricing and was holding up two packs of kale crisps. 'You look kind of familiar?'

I took a deep breath before replying. 'My name is Blake Hardie and I am a friend of Logan the Fox.'

SEVENTY-THREE

Taxi for Mr Chilcoat

Cameras everywhere. *BBC. ITV. Channel 4, Fox, CNN. Russia Today, Al Jazeera, Sky.* Jostling for position along with French, Japanese, Turkish, Greek. A cacophony of language; excited, frantic, confused.

Alpha 2. The badger. The deviant. Where was he?

The TV crews were saying the same thing in multiple ways. The prime minister's assassin breaking into a press conference and running away disguised as a badger. The inept security forces letting it happen. The young Scottish reporter shot dead. A city in meltdown.

The News was now the news. A press conference where a twitchy-fingered security operative mistakenly shot a Scottish TV reporter live on air. A blonde, smiling TV reporter, a mother of three including twins with autism. As fuck-ups go this was the mother of all fuck-ups, no matter what language you reported it in.

'Any comment, sir?'

'Were you in the room when it happened?'

'What did you see?'

'Who was the man with the gun and how did he get that past security?'

Chilcoat ignored them all. The braying press. Hysterical hyperventilating over the biggest news story in the world that had just gotten bigger.

'Is it true that Prime Minister Crull is now back in London?'

'What happened to Dogovsky? Has he been arrested yet?'

The Times, The Telegraph, The Sun, The Guardian, The Herald, The Scotsman, The New York Times, The Washington Post, Le Monde. Battling for position with *BuzzFeed, TMZ, Mumsnet*. He walked past them all.

Clear of the building, his signal no longer jammed. A sudden influx of sounds. His phone ringing, his phone beeping, his phone vibrating. In his pocket, unanswered calls, unchecked voicemails and unread texts. He had no intention of speaking to anyone.

At the entrance to the walkway he paused to look back at the chaotic scene before joining the crowd heading over the expressway and towards the Exhibition Centre train station. His face reddening though it was barely ten degrees outside.

Chilcoat walked under the plastic roof in the cycle lane. His eyes straight ahead, ignoring all sounds around him. He strode confidently though occasionally had to stop as the crowd in front slowed. He ignored the steps down to the station and headed out into the small concourse. Turning a slight left, he walked past PC World and onto the main road.

The traffic was stationary. People were out of their cars, talking or staring at their phones. The constant whirring of a helicopter providing a war-like backdrop. He walked eastward, he needed to see the Great Lady. To seek her advice, to be with her, to be comforted by her. He would regroup and seek her counsel.

Things had not gone as he planned, but he could still turn this to his advantage. The protestors would be gathered up by the body collectors and sorted. Those whose genes made the grade would be shipped down to Grantham. A couple of months earlier than he had planned to get the live samples, but everything was speeding up now, it could be a good thing to accelerate the regeneration of the Great Lady.

He just needed to clear his head and get out of this fucked-up city. He'd feel so much better when he was back with her.

He had walked as far as the Mitchell Library when a man's voice called out.

'Terrible, isn't it?' Chilcoat glanced behind him. A black taxi parked, its yellow *for hire* sign still illuminated. Its driver, a chubby man with small, round glasses was leaning out of its window.

'Are you for hire?'

'Sure am. But you aren't going to get anywhere quick. Whole city is in gridlock. Be faster walking.' Chilcoat reached for the rear door handle. Smiling for the first time since firing the gun. The black door was painted with the Nobler Age logo. Close-up it looked more beautiful than ever.

'Where to, guvnor?' The driver's accent Essex rather than Glasgow.

'Grantham.'

'Is that a hotel?'

'No, it's a town.'

'Sorry?' The driver had turned to look at Chilcoat, the back hatch opened slightly so he could hear his reply more clearly.

'It's in England. Near Nottingham.'

'You're having me on, mate.' He had shut the hatch and had one hand on the driver's door. Chilcoat reached inside his briefcase. He pulled out a wad of fifty-pound notes. 'There's over a grand here, you can have the same again when we get there?'

'Sorry guvnor? Are you for real?'

Chilcoat sighed. 'Due to all the events of the last twenty-four hours, I am not where I need to be. Planes and trains are as they say fucked-up – and under such trying circumstances you are my best option.'

'Very good, sir, very good. Only I was going to finish my shift at noon, so if you don't mind, a quick call to my missus first. She'll be wondering where I've got to if I'm not back.'

Chilcoat waved his hand.

'Details, details, I don't need your details. £2000 to drive me to Grantham. And another £1000 for your return journey. Enough for your dear lady wife to have more than enough pleasure.' The driver switched on the ignition.

'Once we are out of Glasgow, we'll get moving fine, I'm sure. Best bet is probably heading for the Erskine Bridge and down the coast, avoid the city centre. I'll call the missus later rather than delay us now. Have you the postcode? For the satnav. Then we'll be on our way.'

'Details, I don't need details. Just drive. Just head south and I'll direct you when we get there.'

The driver was fiddling with buttons on his satnav.

'Grantham, NG31. That must be the one, near Nottingham. It's only 289 miles. That's really generous of you, sir.'

'Just drive. Once out of Glasgow we can stop somewhere en route for breakfast. And turn the radio off, will you, I have had enough news for one day.'

Chilcoat slumped back in his seat. His phone beeped twice and then started ringing. He would wait until the car was moving freely on the motorway before disposing of it.

SEVENTY-FOUR

Trapped

Amy has gone into the back room to put on the kettle. I can hear the water bubbling, beginning to boil. And then a deafening metallic rattle rocks its way through the shop. A metal bin has been pushed hard against the shop window, its shape obscuring much of the daylight. I am knocked sideways into shelving and lose my balance. The shop lights flicker off, on and then off again. I can see a mist, a white, smoke-like wraith seeping its way through the bottom of the door.

The lights stutter back on just as Amy emerges with a tray and starts to speak. Only it's not her voice I hear, but that of a bird. A voice not dissimilar to Raven's.

'What are you doing hiding here? Again? Are you really that afraid? Life is passing you by. Just get out there and get it over with.'

Amy places the tray down on top of a freezer and I pick up the cup nearest to me. Peppermint tea. It is too hot to drink.

'What are you doing? Just leaving your friends to die out on the street whilst you hang about drinking herbal tea?' Amy's starling voice is dismissive, angry.

I struggle to make sense of what I am hearing. She looks human, but sounds like a bird. Am I hallucinating? Am I concussed? Am I dreaming? Is Amy a mutant, just like Raven, Marek and Logan?

The white mist has faded. The shop smells of nutmeg and incense.

I repeat my introduction from earlier. 'I am a friend of Logan the Fox.'

'I knew that already, Marek told me.' Amy is now speaking in her human voice. 'He asked me to look out for you.' She leans forward; her demeanour is friendly, concerned.

'Marek? You know Marek? You know where he is?'

A flash of light. A squawk. A cry of affirmation. The woman in front of me is no longer human. She is a bird. A starling.

I sip at my tea, scrunch my eyes shut, then look again. Amy is still there. Still bird.

She flys up and lands gently on my shoulder. 'Don't worry, Blake, I'll explain everything later. You need to find Logan, get him back to the island. You were crazy to come into the city, you were so much safer on Bute.'

'Marek? You know Marek?'

'Everybody knows Marek now, Blake. He's been on TV.' Amy is smiling as she speaks. 'Only not many of us realise how powerful he really is.'

'Powerful…' I begin to feel weak, faint. My words trail off.

'You need to eat something Blake.' Amy's starling tone is now warm, reassuring.

I look at the shelf next to me and take hold of a pack of yoghurt-coated raisins.

I approach the till.

'How much are these?' I ask. Amy doesn't answer.

I leave two pound coins on the counter and look at the door. Outside is quiet again.

The bird is right. I should not be in here, hiding, and drinking herb tea. I should be on the street. Looking for Logan. Bringing him back to Bute, to be with Natalya, to be safe again. Be brave for once in your life, Blake Hardie. Take a risk. Get back out there.

I stride with a new determination to the door and stare at the metal panel that controls the shop security shutters. Turning the key anti-clockwise the shutter stutters downward with nowhere to go. I change direction and it moves slowly up.

'Not too far. I'll close it for you,' Amy calls out in a human voice. Looking over my shoulder, I see that she is no longer in her bird form.

Blake, just get out of here, I think, unable to comprehend what I'm experiencing.

I crouch down next to the door and Amy turns the key.

Drawing a deep breath, I roll out of the shop commando-style, colliding straight into a suited man running fast. The force of the impact sends him tumbling in an almost balletic fashion. I am winded, his foot had hit me hard above the navel. I count to three, hoping the pain will fade.

I hear a clunk of metal. The shop's shutter is closed. Amy's face is imprinted on the glass, mouthing to me in an exaggerated fashion so I can read her lips. 'Get... Logan... back... to... Bute.'

My adrenaline is kicking in. Standing up, I hear a voice shout, 'Sweet mother of Reynard.' The suited man too, is back on his feet. 'For fox sake watch where you are going.' He doesn't turn to face me, but brushes at his lower trouser leg and adjusts his shoelaces.

He starts to run, heading up Queen Street in the direction of the square. The back of his trousers are ripped. A good three or four-inch tear. Exposing a brilliant red flash of fur, of red fox fur, of Logan Fox fur.

A starling voice. A beak poking out of the shop's letter box. A small cylinder rolling towards me. 'Arnica,' squawks the voice. 'You'll both be needing it.'

I pick up the homeopathic remedy and put it in my pocket along with the yoghurt raisins. Logan is disappearing behind the line of empty police vans. I start running in the same direction.

SEVENTY-FIVE

The returning

Joan is in her kitchen, clearing up the last of her guests' breakfasts. She switches on the dishwasher and turns the radio off. There has been extended news coverage all morning. But it was getting repetitive. Nothing new or incisive being said. She would go online to see what was really happening, cleaning the bedrooms could wait.

There is a scratching and a muffled thump at her back door.

Joan's throat is dry, her fingers tingling. The kitchen oven clock flashes neon green: 09.58. Surely it was too soon for them to come looking? And why not just barge in, the door was unlocked, after all.

The scratching continues. Joan picks up a frying pan and holds it above her head. She peers through the window. She can't see anybody. Still though, an incessant scratching. She snatches open the door.

'Natalya!' The fox brushes past her in a red blur, running straight up the stairs. The frying pan falls with a clatter. Joan runs after Natalya, taking the stairs two at a time.

The fox – Natalya – is pacing on the small landing outside the attic bedroom, waiting for Joan to catch up. The door is locked and the key downstairs. Joan runs back down, grabbing the keys from the hedgehog-shaped hook. By the time she reaches the landing for the second time she is out of breath.

She fumbles with the keys whilst the fox continues her pacing. Then when the door opens Natalya leaps onto the double bed, grabs the TV remote from the table in her mouth and drops it at Joan's feet. Joan hits the on button and sits down next to the fox, stroking the back of her neck gently. BBC1. The clock on-screen hitting 10.00 hours.

I run towards the square, past the posh arts and crafts shop, past Royal Exchange Square where hordes of people hold smartphones in front of their faces. Recording, streaming, Snapchatting, Instagramming – doing everything except actually seeing what was happening.

Past Pret A Manger where two men wearing green balaclavas are loading sandwiches into a bin liner. Past the pub on the corner whose name keeps changing, whose window was cracked in a neat diagonal line. Finally I reach the square.

The Heras fence enclosures which had kettled in the protestors have been toppled. A crowd of people half standing, half squatting, their hands over their eyes.

Phuud… Phuud… Phuud.

Gas. Three cannisters. My eyes begin streaming.

Phuud… Phuud… Phuud.

Three more. The mist brings me to my knees. I am struggling to breathe. My chest tightens with both pain and panic.

The sky is darkening. I can no longer see.

The taxi is moving faster now. They are just six miles from Glasgow, but the motorway is clearing. Chilcoat lowers his window. Not fully, just a few inches. A blast of air and the smell of diesel. He pulls out his phone and holds it in the gap, his hand cooling and vibrating. And he lets it slip. Not dropped, not thrown, he just lets it slip. Pressing the button, the window clicks itself shut.

He allows himself a quick glimpse through the rear mirror. Two lorries, both emblazoned with the Nobler Age logo, are behind, but from his angle he couldn't know for sure if they had crushed the phone under their wheels.

Chilcoat leans forward, watching the dashboard: seventy-five, seventy-six, seventy-seven kilometres per hour. In his mind he is doing sums. Five, maybe six hours until he would be with her again.

SEVENTY-SIX

Red Square

Kneeling down. Scratching at my face. Some vision begins to return. There are bodies lying everywhere. Blood on the tarmac. The square's perimeter is surrounded by police in full riot gear.

My lips are burning. My skin itching. There is a constant ringing in my ears. A crazy buzzing. My balance is all wrong, it makes standing up impossible. I am struggling for breath. Crippled by the pain in my chest, I can't move.

The body collectors are spreading out now. Picking up the protestors who lay strewn across the square. Those doing the carrying wear sterile white suits and masks. People being packed into vans. The blacked-out windows. That logo, the Nobler Age Foods logo emblazoning their bonnets and doors.

Where are they taking them?

The sirens are getting louder.

In front of the City Chambers, the large screen is crackling with pixelated static.

I lie on my back now. Counting out loud to calm my breathing.

The footsteps and dragging sounds. They are getting closer. Less than a minute perhaps until they reach me, cart me off with the rest.

'Bringing the situation back under control.'

The voice, booming out over George Square belongs to Farringdon Crull. The new prime minister. From my prostrate position on the tarmac, his face appears upside down on the screen.

'The intruder at the press conference has been detained.'

It takes a few seconds for me to realise the significance of what Crull has just said.

Marek. They have got Marek.

SEVENTY-SEVEN

The body collectors

A fox lying on a woman's lap.

A man in a taxi laughing out loud.

Another group being carried away.

There are only a few metres of tarmac between me and them now. No more bodies, it would be me next.

'*Stand up.*' Amy's voice. Amy's starling voice. I can hear, but not see her. She is neither there as human or bird. Yet she is right there beside me, imploring me to get up.

I struggle to my knees, pushing hard with my wrists, but I am still not able to stand. There is a sharp stabbing in my chest. I cry out with despair. 'Is THIS what it feels like to die?'

'*No.*' Amy's voice again. '*You have a job to do. Get Logan back to the island. You are both more important than you realise in all this.*'

I sense a hand. A female hand, reaching over to me. Pulling at my arm. Tugging me upright. I feel lighter, smaller, yet less afraid.

'Come here.' Amy is calling me. She stands ten yards in front of me. Dressed in black. Black, green and purple. I cannot make out her face though. She is silhouetted.

I am on my knees, crawling. Panting with the exertion. Rubbing at my eyes, desperate to stop the burning. My vision clears for a few seconds. I see the body collectors closing the door of a van and walking back onto the square. Their masks anonymous, terrifying. Bloodstains on their white overalls. They are coming towards me.

Amy is fading from view. My eyes have closed shut. It is too painful to keep them open.

But I can hear the sound of birds calling. A twisted chorus of clacks and whistles. Starlings. I can hear starlings.

I crawl; inching, edging. My legs half-paralysed, but I can drag my torso. I develop a rhythm; like a caterpillar I shuffle forward.

My hand hits something metal. A phone, a Nokia. Old-fashioned, un-smart.

I don't know where the number comes from, but somehow it is in my head.

I press the digits. The body collectors have passed me and gone further south. Are they sweeping up the last remnants of the protest camp before coming back for me?

I hit the green call button.

I never expected *him* to answer.

'It's not over.' His voice. Marek's voice. And then the line goes dead.

In the attic room at the bed and breakfast, Joan is doing her best to comfort Natalya. Holding her, stroking her fur. Whispering words of reassurance.

Joan has not yet seen Logan. Perhaps, she tells Natalya, he isn't in the square. Perhaps he is safe. But Joan takes no solace in words she knows to be false. It is a slaughterhouse. An abattoir. The whole square is littered with corpses.

'*It's not over.*' A starling repeating Marek's words. Mimicking his nasal tone. A lone bird is circling above me.

'Amy, is that you?'

No answer.

I begin sobbing; a mix of snot and blood dribble from my nostrils.

And then, the human Amy is standing in front of me again. Tall. Defiant. Summoning me.

I am on my feet now. Walking towards her. And then I hesitate.

Is she death? Is she what death looks like?

'*Blake... Blake Hardie... come to me now.*'

I look ahead of me. Where Amy was standing there is now emptiness.

And then. The air fills with a high-pitched scream. Female, loud, terrifying. It echoes for an instant and then silence. A muffled, cloying silence.

I look around. At the corpses, the twisted shapes and broken shadows. Searching for him, for Logan. For his familiar tone of red. For his joy of life. For his optimism. For his hope. For his love. For his wit, his spirit, his goddam beautiful spirit.

'LOGAN FOX, WHERE ARE YOU?'

The sound of a phone ringing. I didn't realise I still had it in my hand. I answer it on the fourth ring. It is Marek.

'Tell Logan that Natalya is safe, that she is with Joan. And that she is carrying his daughter.'

'Marek? Where are you?'

He ignores my question.

'And Blake. I am sorry that we could not save you.'

'Marek! Marek!'

He is gone. Again.

The taxi has pulled into the service station. Chilcoat and Norman the driver, stretching their limbs. Not talking. One thinking about his wife who would not see him until late that night and how he could finally pay off their credit card with this one trip. The other thinking of the woman whose embrace he craved more than ever.

They fly in unison. A dancing, fast-moving cloud. A torrent of feather and hope. Each molecule within them a vibration. Each vibration a force. Each force a bird. Each bird an individual soul. Each soul a part of a bigger whole. A shared memory. A collective vision.

The murmuration.

A swirling mass of bodies. The energy throbbing. Humming, vibrating, pulling. Sheer magnetism holding their shape. Sheer willpower driving them forward.

Raven flies at the head. The lead starling, setting the pace, choosing the direction. The rest follow, flying in perfect synchronicity. Breathing as one. Moving as one. Being as one.

Raven concentrates hard. Banishing her human emotions. Banishing her fears, her doubts. Trying to connect back to her true starling self. The bird before the lab. The bird before the fire. The ancient bird within.

Time was so precious. They had to save Blake and Logan. Stop them being taken away in the Nobler Age vans. She didn't understand why they were so important. She just knew that they were.

The murmuration.

A swarm of thousands and thousands of birds. Enough to change the patterns of energy. A chance to distract the body collectors, a last chance to get Blake and Logan out alive.

Using the magnetic waves of the murmuration to stay afloat, inside a bubble of fear and flight, she can still see him. The face in the torchlight. The one that was driving her forward. Marek's face. The badger's face.

Defiance. She flew in defiance. Not as a solitary bird, not as a lonely human, but as a spirit of rebellion. She had escaped from the lab. Marek, Logan, Walinska too. They were disruptors, they were rogue agents, they were the enemy within. And now for the first time she was channelling Marek's power, rather than running away from it.

The air was changing. She was circling rather than moving forward. The pace of the flock slowed with her. She was at the centre now and not the head. The centre of a shape that sucked in and then blew out. A giant inhale. A giant exhale. A huge wave of shadow within her soul.

They had arrived. George Square. They had to be quick. There was not much time left.

'Open your eyes.' Amy's voice once more. Human this time.

She sounds defiant, brave. Unlike Marek she has *not* given up on us.

Perhaps she is life, not death after all.

Marek believes that I am about to die. That nothing more can be done to save me or Logan. That we are both finished.

Why then did he phone? Why give me that flutter of hope?

A daughter. Natalya is pregnant. That's why she decided to stay behind. Logan must be told. I am Marek's messenger. I have to tell him. He must have hope. I must have hope too.

I need to avoid the body collectors long enough to tell Logan that Natalya is safe. That he is going to be a father. That all of this has not been in vain.

I've moved less than ten yards since Marek rang. The body collectors are still to the south of me.

What is in their vans? What is in their Nobler Age vans? I can sense needles. I can smell meat. I know that to be taken inside is the end, but I don't know why and for what reason they are killing so many people with their toxic gas.

I feel nausea, a desire to retch. I trip and half-stumble over a body on the ground I had not seen. I look at it through eyes that are still watering.

A crumpled heap. Limbs twisted. A torn suit. A bright red patch of fur.

Logan. It is Logan.

The light is changing.

I look up and see a cloak of black. Thousands upon thousands of birds. Swirling into shape. Filling the whole sky. Black and white.

The shape is static now. Becoming clearer.

It is… two eyes… a snout… the familiar stripe… it is…it is… Marek's badger face.

SEVENTY-EIGHT

The murmuration

Natalya is shaking. Her body convulses. A lover grieving for her soulmate. She knows that Logan is gone. That there is no hope he will survive. Nothing Joan can do or say will bring her any comfort now.

Chilcoat orders scrambled eggs on toast and a pot of tea. Norman orders a bacon roll and a cappuccino. They are an unlikely pair, but nobody notices. Everybody's eyes are on the TV screen.

I lift his head. It lies limply in my hands.

But he is breathing. I can see his chest rise up, fall down, rise up, fall down.

The air is changing. The screen is changing. It is pixelating once more. I no longer feel alone.

Somewhere in another time and place, Walinska the weasel is sitting at the edge of a brook, looking at her reflection. She stares into the water and sees my death. And she screams.

I am in George Square in Glasgow. It is maybe an hour since I stepped off the train from Wemyss Bay. Yet I cannot be certain it is the same day. There is a smell of flesh burning. There is a smell of *flesh burning*.

Natalya is circling the room. Joan has turned off the TV. They are no longer watching. They cannot bear to see Logan die.

Chilcoat's scrambled eggs are microwaved and taste of rubber. Norman's bacon roll tastes very little of pig.

Walinska sits at the edge of the water and looks again at her reflection. She sees a shape, a great moving shadow. A force of life echoes in the whirl of water, giving her hope.

Marek is running. He is in his human form. He is running until he can breathe no more. He has reached a bridge. There are police to his left. There are police to his right. There are police behind him. In front of him is only water.

Chilcoat is smiling. He is talking to Norman of the Great Lady. She would not have allowed things to get in such a mess. Chilcoat watches Norman eating his bacon sandwich. He wonders if it tastes of salt and blood.

Logan is breathing.

Marek is jumping.

Raven is circling.

Natalya cries out loud.

I am cradling Logan, holding him, hugging him, whispering to him the last words he will hear.

'Logan. Marek rang me just now. He says that Natalya loves you. And I have to tell you that she is safe. That she is still with Joan. And that she is carrying your child. You are going to be a dad, Logan. You and Natalya are going to have a baby daughter.'

Logan's eyes have opened. He is smiling.

'Water. Something to drink. Mouth tastes of blood. Water.'

'I don't have any water.'

He closes his eyes. 'Water. I need water.'

His smile has faded, and he is silent once more. I remember about the yoghurt raisins and take them out of my pocket to offer him some, but the packet splits and the raisins tumble to the tarmac.

The light is changing again.

A speck.

Joan yelps as the television turns itself on.

'Logan, come on, don't die. I can't do this without you.'

I see nothing in his eyes.

The light above the square is different now.

'*It is not over,*' a thousand starling voices call as one.

The murmuration is closer to the ground than it was before. Everybody is seeing it now. The giant badger head. Everybody has stopped to watch.

The pixelated screen cracks into life.

Joan sits back down with Natalya. Watching the screen. Waiting.

One speck is joined by another and another.

The weasel stares into the brook and sees a shadow dancing. *A shadow dancing.*

I look up and see the starlings flying with great beauty.
I see them flying as one cell.
In a moving mountain of life.
I see love in their movement.
I see the divine in their coming together.
I see the beast within me taking shape.
I see hope and I see defiance.
And I see Amy. Flying alongside her daughter, Raven, reunited at last.
Raven is not flying alone. I am not alone. Amy, she is a part of her. Amy, she is life, not death.
Logan's head is on my lap. His eyes are closed. His breathing is laboured.

Chilcoat sips at the lukewarm tea that he has poured from the cheap, metallic teapot. He thinks of the Great Lady. The sheer enormity of what he has achieved. The sheer delightful horror of what is yet to come.

And the sky is dark now. A giant shadow. A shape moving west to east. Swaying across the whole square. Logan's eyes open. He looks at me. He looks straight through me.

Chilcoat is heading back to the taxi. He pulls open the door.

Looking for a moment at the emblem. His emblem. Her emblem. The sign.

The return of a nobler age.

When he got to Grantham there would be so much to tell her, so much to do to get things back on track.

'How much longer, Norman?' he asks.

'We're about a third of the way there.'

'Drive carefully,' Chilcoat says.

Norman turns the ignition key and the engine starts.

I can hear footsteps. The body collectors are approaching us. I rest my head in the nape of Logan's neck. His fur is soft, not yet cold.

The square has fallen into darkness. Every speck of air is filling with a dancing, swirling force of life. And a voice is carried on its magnetic waves.

Natalya is calling to Logan. She is calling him home. If he is to perish, she wants him to die with her.

Logan is looking at the sky. The murmuration. The starlings. Raven's return.

The air is dark with their mass. The air is filled with the sound of their wings flapping in unison. One giant force. One giant lung. One giant spark.

I am looking at the screen. The giant TV screen.

Lying on my back, everything turned upside down.

And Logan is pointing, not at the sky, not at the starlings, but at the men. The four men, wearing white suits. Wearing masks. Standing right next to us.

I am staring at the screen. The pixelated screen taking shape. It is not a human face.

A voice. Not a human voice.

'It's not over.' Marek in his badger form. Speaking to the nation.

Logan is sitting up. Looking at the men in the masks. The one closest to us is holding a gun. And Logan is reaching out towards him.

Gunfire. Two explosions of sound.

Deafening.

I can no longer feel my legs.

I turn my head to the right. I watch Logan being carried away. His body limp. A trail of red on the tarmac.

Natalya feels a kick inside. A pain is cutting and tearing its way through her skull, down her neck and into her chest. She has lost him. She *has* lost him. This is the moment she knew would come.

A thousand birds descending. A thousand birds landing.

The body collectors are carrying Logan to the van. The Nobler Age Van. They are placing him inside. And they are closing the door.

I am engulfed by the starlings. They land on me one after another. Covering my arms, my legs, my chest, my body. They cover my head.

I see Raven amongst them, and Amy too. They tell me to stay quiet, to hold my breath.

I want to shout out for Logan. I want to run after him. To bang on the door of the van and drag him out. But all I do is lie still. Invisible to the world under a cloud of feather and beak.

The body collectors who took Logan away come back for me, stop for a moment, then move away. They see only the birds. They can see *only* the birds.

I cannot see. But I can hear. A familiar voice. Filling the square.

He is on the screen. Being broadcast not just in George Square, but live across the globe. And he is talking to a world that will never again be the same.

'My name is Marek Dogovsky and I am part human, part badger.

I am an escapee from a genetic laboratory.

I am not alone. We are not alone. There are more of us than you think.

We will not be defeated.

We will resist.'

SEVENTY-NINE

The end of the beginning

The starling is a small bird. Many people would consider it a drab bird. But catch their feathers in the right light and you will be surprised. At the greens, the purples and the flashes of mother of pearl. Shining with a luminescence that belies a reputation for being a dull bird.

The starling is a sociable bird. They dance across the sky at dusk. Forming shapes, forming patterns, forming waves. The murmuration, a swirling mass of bodies moving as one.

The starling is a wise bird, a special bird. Their call is like no other. There is a reason for that. They can hear voices. All sorts of voices. Both real and imaginary. Both past and present.

There are birds that don't fly in formation, that can form different patterns.

Sunday 23rd June 2013. The day after they told us that Logan Fox had died.

A starling, reunited with her roost, hears a voice she had not expected to hear. And the voice said just one word: 'Water.'

Acknowledgements

I first thought about writing a novel after the disappointing outcome of the Scottish independence referendum of 2014. Prior to this I had dabbled in performance poetry and stand-up comedy. Over the years I'd grown frustrated at how much effort was involved in writing material that would be performed just once or twice. I wanted the challenge of writing a longer piece, something that would live on the page, rather than disappear into the ether.

The origins of this book come from a sketch that I wrote in 2013 for an evening class in stand-up comedy. This saw me combine the impacts of austerity, the badger cull and the imaginary death of George Osborne. With humans failing so miserably to stand up to the Tories, it was left to the beasts to resist.

In November 2015 I attended a course in Comic Novel Writing, tutored by Helen Lederer and Ian Macpherson at the magical Moniack Mhor (Scotland's creative writing centre). It was here that the ideas for *Banquet of the Beasts* began to emerge and I replaced Osborne with Margaret Thatcher; she is, after all, much more of a timeless baddie. From 2016-18 I went back for a further two courses and a writing retreat. This novel would not have happened without the impetus and ideas that came from those happy times at Moniack.

Another huge shout-out goes to that very funny and lovely woman, Viv Gee. She tutored me on my original stand-up comedy course and gave me really helpful feedback on an early draft.

Next up, take a bow my old friend and best man, John Richardson. In 2019 he brought his inner pedant and hatred of Margaret Thatcher to the fore with a detailed line-by-line edit of the near-finished manuscript. Great job, John and with hindsight I'm sorry that I gave Lynton Chilcoat the same birthday as yours. It was a coincidence, honest.

And well done, Ian Skewis, a man tasked with proof-editing my novel, which I thought was finished, but then he told me it wasn't. Your patient and professional attention to detail and friendly feedback made me totally rewrite the ending of the book and it is a much better work for your editing and proofing skills.

To the beautiful island of Bute, and to the birds and beasts that are my friends and constant companions – I salute you all! A special mention going to the starlings, badgers, weasels and foxes. For many years you've lived in my head, and it's great to see you at last on the page.

And finally to Maggie. Your comments, ideas, feedback and thoughts are a constant encouragement to me. Without you I would be lost and this novel would not exist. You remain my biggest love and inspiration.

 Matador